QUEEN

of the

WILD
RANGE

tales from adia
BOOK TWO

QUEEN
of the
WILD
RANGE

MAGGIE PLATT

Ambassador International
GREENVILLE, SOUTH CAROLINA & BELFAST, NORTHERN IRELAND

www.ambassador-international.com

Queen of the Wild Range

Tales from Adia, Book Two

© 2022 by Maggie Platt

Hardcover ISBN: 978-1-64960-447-7
Paperback ISBN: 978-1-64960-304-3
eISBN: 978-1-64960-326-5
Library of Congress Control Number: 2022938706

This is a work of fiction. Names, characters, and incidents are all products of the author's imagination or are used for fictional purposes. Any resemblance to actual events or persons, living or dead, is entirely coincidental. Any mentioned brand names, places, and trademarks remain the property of their respective owners, bear no association with the author or the publisher, and are used for fictional purposes only.

Cover Design by Hannah Linder Designs
Interior Typesetting by Dentelle Design
Author Photo by Hannah Lockhart Photography
Edited by Katie Cruice Smith

AMBASSADOR INTERNATIONAL
Emerald House
411 University Ridge, Suite B14
Greenville, SC 29601, USA
www.ambassador-international.com

AMBASSADOR BOOKS
The Mount
2 Woodstock Link
Belfast, BT6 8DD, Northern Ireland, UK
www.ambassadormedia.co.uk

The colophon is a trademark of Ambassador, a Christian publishing company.

For Maddie, Morgan, and A.J.—Your Auntie M loves you more than you know.

CHAPTER 1

Torches hissed and sputtered in the damp air as King Damien walked the long stone corridor between dungeon cells. Traitors and criminals cowered in corners behind rusted bars, illuminated by the flickering light. He considered each prisoner in turn, but none so far would do. Too strong. Too valuable. Too sneaky.

Near the end of the corridor, he came to a frail old woman, mumbling to herself and picking at her fingers. She kept her eyes trained on the floor, and her shoulders curled inward when the king moved closer.

She was perfect.

"Sweet lady, what is your name?"

She fell silent and looked up through stringy, lavender hair.

"I need a favor, my dear. You're going to come with me. But first I would like to know your name."

"Is-Is-Ismene, sir. My name's Ismene. Don't s'pose I'd be much help."

"Come, anyway." He did his best to smile, but her foul stench and uneducated tongue were hard to bear.

The big, rusty key screeched as it turned. Ismene held the bars to pull herself off the ground on wobbly knees. She joined the king, looking back at her cell several times. Guards shut the door behind her and followed the king and his prisoner up the stairs and out of the palace.

Out in the crisp night air, a golden litter waited with enough room to comfortably seat two. "In you go," Damien said, holding out his hand to help Ismene inside. She looked from his hand to his face several times before he realized she did not know what to do. "Hold my hand for balance and step inside. You're quite safe."

Once situated, eight guards lifted the litter by its poles and carried it across the courtyard, past the opulent homes of the most elite families. Passing under a stone arch, they traveled through the streets. Ismene never took her face from the window, her eyes wide and shining, reflecting the candlelight pouring from each home.

With each passing block, the homes, shops, and taverns grew shabbier. Still, Ismene did not look away. Damien briefly wondered how long she had been inside the dungeon with no view of the outside world, but he did not care enough to ask.

They reached the Bottom Rung, the poorest neighborhood in the kingdom. It was also the lowest in elevation, making it the closest zone to the mines, farms, and hard labor.

They stopped and disembarked at the shimmering curtain of light that extended all the way around the mountain. It was taller than any of their buildings, and it seemed to be made of light, like the little rainbows that danced on walls when light hit a diamond. When his guards tried to cross through this curtain of light, they were blocked by something invisible that they described as cold, hard glass.

Damien clenched his jaw as he surveyed the barrier that mocked him and his powerlessness. He dare not touch it. He didn't want anyone to witness his failure.

He had a theory about the properties of the wall, and he had brought Ismene there to test it. According to the guards who had witnessed Adwin's death, this curtain had sprung out of Adwin when those fools tried to kill him. It was Adwin's very own life force, hemming Damien inside this kingdom-turned-prison. The man's body might have disappeared, but that was likely temporary. He knew Adwin too well to believe he was really gone. Adwin had left his spirit surrounding the mountain, and that just might be as bad as having him there in the flesh.

He noticed pain in his jaw and willed his muscles to unclench, rolling his neck without taking his eyes from the curtain.

What was Adwin's plan? What was the purpose of this wall? To keep Damien's forces inside? To protect innocent, little Adia from his invasions? Perhaps. More likely, it was to buy time so that Damien's grandchildren could assemble their army and return, fulfilling the dreaded prophecy on his throne room walls.

He gritted his teeth again. His people were disappearing in droves. Empty homes. Deserted businesses. He suspected they had found a way through the curtain, just as Eryx had. Was this Adwin's doing? Where was he taking them? He clenched his fists so tightly that the seams of his gloves nearly ripped. Before long, his enemy would have plenty of these peasants to form an army. He had to do something to stop them, but first, he must understand the properties of the wall.

"Ismene, show us your hands."

She did as she was told. Damien scowled at the brown heart that curved across her scarred and wrinkled palm.

"Very good. Now, walk through the light."

She looked between him and the wall several times.

He nodded and repeated, "Walk through the light."

Ismene swallowed hard, and her mouth twitched. She took slow, hesitant steps toward the curtain with her arms out in front of her.

Her fingers pierced the light, and she looked back at him with wide eyes. She took another step, and the curtain was at her elbows. A few more steps, and she was on the other side of the barrier, looking at him through the shimmering waves.

"Just what I thought," King Damien said, shaking his head and clicking his tongue. "My own invention. My own creation. I should have known Adwin would use those hearts against me. You can come back now, Ismene."

Damien was inside the litter before he realized Ismene had not followed him. She stood on the other side of the curtain, staring at him, her mouth moving like she wanted to say something, but no words came out.

"Come now, Ismene. It is time to go back."

She backed up two steps.

"Come back this instant, Ismene," Damien commanded, stepping out of the litter.

She hobbled into the darkness, looking over her shoulder every few steps. The guards tried to follow but hit the curtain with a loud thud. No matter how hard they shoved their shoulders into the barrier, it held firm. One used both hands to slam a sword into the curtain, and it clattered to the ground as the guard yelped.

Damien pursed his lips and drew in a deep breath. "No matter," he said, willing his tone to be calm. "It's why I chose a weak prisoner for this experiment. She has no value here or anywhere else."

He returned to the litter and rubbed his temples. He must come up with a plan to stop the hearts from escaping. They were too important to his kingdom. Too important to his system. Without them, the city's trade would grind to a halt. There wouldn't be enough workers, servants, or soldiers.

He looked out the little window at the houses along the street, but he hardly saw them. He had too many goals, too many objectives, vying for his attention. He must keep the hearts on the mountain to keep the great system working. He must recruit new members of the Council of Masters, which had been so recently decimated. He must find his grandchildren and stop them from fulfilling the prophecy of his kingdom's demise. And he must stop Adwin from winning. That would always be the chief objective.

When they reached the palace, Damien hurried to his library. He spread a large map across his enormous table in the center of the room, smoothing it with his hands. Mount Damien took up the center, and sloping lands spread out to the edges in blotches of greens and browns. Adia lay to the west. Most of the other territories were unexplored and nameless.

He traced Adwin's barrier, the curtain that separated his city from the rest of the world, with his finger. He felt so powerless and so trapped, but he knew the secret now. It was that heart that would get people through—the heart emblazoned on so many palms, the heart he himself had invented as a young apprentice to Adwin.

Another barrier existed but did not appear on the map. Since the beginning of his reign, a thin layer of cloud had swirled around the mountain, keeping Adia and the surrounding lands out of view. That cloud was another of his own inventions, created with the powers Adwin soon after took away from him. Damien didn't want his people to see their options for life outside of his city. He needed them to stay on the mountain, playing their part in his grand machine.

He believed that if he could just keep his people within the confines of the city, he could mold them into just what he wanted and needed: a people devoted to him and his power. They were all born with a natural pull toward the former ways of King Adwin, but all they needed was time with good teachers to break them of that habit.

Now he faced a new difficulty. This shimmering curtain lay inside the city, above the cloud. The cloud kept his people from seeing a different way of life. Now, no matter where someone went in the city, the wall of light rose above the buildings, beckoning his people toward questions with dangerous answers. "Where did this curtain come from? Is it true it sprang from King Adwin himself? Is there something better on the other side?"

The solution was obvious to him. A third ring must be constructed within the city. A wall of stone, rather than wisps of cloud or waves of light. Cold rock and mortar would hold his people inside, giving him time to change their hearts and pledge their fealty to King Damien alone. It would also stop his grandchildren and their prophesied armies from entering his kingdom. Yes, a new, glorious, terrifying wall was just the thing.

A tap on the door and the squeak of hinges made him look up. One of his most prized weapons stepped inside his sanctuary. Her yellow eyes were dull and rimmed in red. Her usual dark makeup—usually so perfect—was a tad smudged.

Rhaxma took a seat in a cushioned chair by the fire and stared at the flames. She didn't turn at the sound of Damien's approach, so he took his time filling two glass goblets with dark red wine. She only glanced toward him when he held the drink in front of her.

He sat in the opposite chair, crossed his leg, and swirled the liquid around his glass. "I could ask how you're feeling. I could let you fall apart and cry over your beloved brother. But you're stronger than that. You aren't a weepy damsel needing a grandfatherly pat on the head. You are brilliant, fierce, and cunning. And I need you."

She wiped her cheeks with her gloved fingers, but there were still black tears pooling along her eyelids. She took a long gulp of wine before looking at the king.

He continued. "I know you hate Calix. I don't blame you, after what happened. But can you put that aside? Can you keep your control and composure? Can you remain on the Council of Masters?"

"You would remove me from the council?"

Damien took another sip. "I don't see any other way if you can't get along."

"Remove *him*. He killed my brother. He should be hanging in the courtyard by now."

"Now, now. We can't cast blame. You know I have listened to all witnesses and ruled Leeto's death a terrible accident."

Rhaxma's lip curled, and she turned back toward the fire.

"My dear Rhaxma, you are showing me that you are not cut out for this work anymore. Must I replace you, along with the others?"

"What happens if I leave the council?"

"I see only two options, really," the king drawled. "You could leave your home on the courtyard to make room for a new Master of Perfection, or you could go to the dungeon with the others who displease me."

"Leave the courtyard? What about my family? My grandfather is your closest friend. My father is practically your son. You wouldn't do that to us."

"Wouldn't I? Have you ever seen me give up easily when there is something I want?"

"And what exactly do you want from me?"

"I want you to wield your influence and help me win this war with Adwin. I want you to put this unfortunate incident behind you and remain my Master of Perfection."

"Unfortunate incident?" Rhaxma's laugh was quiet, high-pitched, unhinged.

King Damien set down his goblet. Her behavior was concerning but not shocking. Grief, where there had been real love, was a mighty, unpredictable force. "Can you do this? Can you hold yourself together and work with Calix and the rest of the council?"

Rhaxma traced the rim of her goblet with her gloved finger, leaving a red stain on the silver fabric. "Yes," she whispered.

Another knock on the door told him that the rest of the remaining council had arrived. He stood, walked to the table and map, and called for the weapons. They joined him at the table.

There should have been seven, but betrayals had whittled the group to four. In private, he had flipped tables, shattered priceless vases, and thrown ink wells at the walls. In the presence of his young weapons, he had to keep his composure if he wanted to overcome so much death and treason. He would have to let the rage boil and sputter but not overflow. He closed his eyes for just a moment and willed his temper back into its cage. Control. Power. Wisdom. He must draw on these great virtues in this time of terrible uncertainty.

He placed four gray tokens on the map, right over the heart of the kingdom. Each had a symbol drawn on it, mirroring the symbols displayed on their backs.

First, a crown for Calix, Master of Adoration. Fury still burned in his eyes—or was that humiliation? To bring an Adian to the mountain, ignorant that she was an heir to His Majesty, that she had already been marked by a competitor—that was enough to make anyone feel like a fool. But to lose her back to Adwin? Calix would never forgive himself.

Second, chains for Megara, Master of Wisdom. She was even thinner than usual, looking so brittle and boney that he wouldn't be surprised if her joints failed and she crumbled to the floor. Her cheeks were hollow, and she looked more like a skeleton every day.

Third, a diamond for BiBi, Master of Prosperity. With her round face and dimples when she smiled, she looked angelic and sweet but so very sad. She was not tough like the others, and all of the recent events had been difficult for her. Damien liked that about her. It was useful. Of all the people in the room, she was the one the fools in Adia would trust. He just had to find a way to get her there, now that the curtain hemmed them in.

Fourth, a set of scales for Rhaxma, his grief-stricken Master of Perfection. She stood at one end of the table, directly across from Calix. Her gaze was locked on him with a dullness that was perhaps more terrifying than if her hatred was raving and out of control.

Calix did not look Rhaxma's way. He was focused on his king. Such a good boy.

Damien produced three more gray tokens. Rose. Flames. Snake. Rhaxma choked on a whimper, and he saw that her tears had spilled over. "It is time to replace our fallen member and the others who have betrayed us. But we will get to that in due time.

"Here *you* are," Damien said, motioning to the first four tokens with their symbols. "And here *they* are." He pulled four trinkets from his pocket. "Tovi is likely in Adia." He placed a gold brooch shaped like a flower in the green area to the west. The stem was inlaid with emeralds, and the bloom was made of light blue stones. He placed the other three items on the edge of the map: a thick copper ring with a dark ruby embedded in it, a little girl's golden locket with tiny amethysts around the edge, and a large, dark sapphire without a setting. He moved the sapphire to the north of the mountain. "The last we knew, Tali was in the caves to the north. Jairus can't be far. We do not know if Lena lives." He touched the ring and locket as he spoke of them, but he didn't move them onto the map.

He traced the thin line once more with his quill. "This curtain holds us in. It is an evil barrier, a wall that keeps us from food, water, and victory. It is Adwin's very own life, laying siege to those loyal to me while allowing the weakest to flee from their responsibilities and work."

The four weapons leaned toward him and the map, listening intently. Good. He needed their full attention.

"It holds *us* in," he said. "But not everyone. And I know how to get through."

"Your Majesty," Calix said, eyes wide. "What is the secret?"

He kept his voice nonchalant. "My own invention, actually. My great enemy, Adwin, has turned it against me. The foul heart that hides beneath so many gloves allows a person through the barrier. We must stop the flow of deserters. We shall build a wall."

The room was quiet except for the dull roar and occasional crack from the fire in the hearth. Damien had expected excited gasps or at least a few nods of approval. Instead, their faces were mostly blank, with a few incredulous eyebrows raised.

"A wall, Your Majesty?" BiBi asked. "Isn't there already a wall?"

Damien pointed to the thin line on the map. "Not the curtain. Not the shimmering waves of dark magic. I want a real wall. Stone and metal and mortar that will keep our people in and our enemies out." He used his finger to draw another ring on the map, just inside the other.

"I have assignments for each of you, and our success depends on your dedication to these tasks. I want you to work together toward our overall goals, but each of you will take point on one of the projects.

"Megara, you will take charge of the defense. Set up patrols along the curtain. No one gets in or out. You must stop the flow of desertion. Those trying to escape go to the dungeon. Anyone trying to enter should be brought straight to me."

She nodded.

"Calix, you will organize a census and assign duties. We need to know which laborers have a heart and which do not. We'll send those with hearts through the curtain and below the cloud to mine, hunt, cart water, and tend the fields—under careful supervision, of course. Those without a heart will work here in the city, join Megara's defense, or build the wall. Start with the Bottom Rung. There should be plenty for our purposes among the most expendable of our people."

"Couldn't we just outlaw gloves?" Megara asked. "It would be easier to identify—"

"No, no, no, dear girl," he interrupted firmly. He had been prepared for that argument, and he knew he must squash it. "That would cause panic, chaos, mayhem. Better to surprise the Bottom Rung with hand checks and leave everyone else alone."

She nodded, but her frown told him that she wasn't convinced.

"BiBi, you will study the mural. I have not let new eyes examine the old prophecies in quite some time, and I think you are the person to bring me fresh insight. You will look for any clue, any sign, of Adwin's next move or how he is leading so many to escape. We must stop him."

She swallowed. "Yes, Your Majesty."

"Rhaxma, you will find a discreet way to search among the elite for a few with hearts who are still loyal to me. I need a few I trust to supervise the groups that will travel through the curtain to work. This will be tricky, but I think you are up for it. They must still have the heart yet remain loyal to me."

She nodded. He noted the sweat on her brow. She was nervous about this task. He couldn't decide if this was good or bad.

"All of you will bring candidate names to me for our three open council seats. We need a new Master of Pleasure, Master of Power, and Master of Control. I want the names delivered to me by tomorrow evening for my consideration."

There was a chorus of assent.

"Good. Now go get some sleep. We need to be rested and ready to take on what tomorrow brings."

CHAPTER 2

In the rocky crags and scraggly pine forest east of Mount Damien, Jairus stared at the smoking ash that had once been a small fire. He had left to search for food in the woods, and he expected the flames to be burning when he returned. That fire had taken great effort to build, and he blinked away the sting of tears now that it was gone. He could hear his grandfather's voice so clearly in his mind, mocking his failure. He was no good at any of this, and he knew it. Pampered all of his royal life, how was he supposed to survive in the wilderness? How was he supposed to care for Xanthe when he couldn't even keep a fire going?

He turned his back on the ashes and stepped inside the mouth of the cave. It was gray and dark, but at least it was dry. The ground was hard and uneven, and every footfall and flint strike echoed against the walls. Xanthe lay on a pile of leaves, the best bedding Jairus could find. She twitched and twisted, groaning and calling out words and phrases that made no sense. Her silk gown, torn and stained, looked ridiculous in their rustic surroundings, and her hair was matted with sweat and dirt. A rumpled traveling cloak was her only blanket.

He had thought the escape from the dungeon would be easy. A servant in the palace—one of his father's valets and a member of the Hidden Heart—had come to him and claimed that Silas had sent him. He urged Jairus to leave immediately, before things got worse. He explained that the heart in Jairus' hand would provide safe passage through the curtain that surrounded the city.

"What about Xanthe?"

The valet looked pained. "Silas said you would ask that. You are supposed to leave her. Silas will get her out at the right time. Trust him."

Jairus hardly heard him. He grabbed keys from a drawer in his grandfather's desk and paid the dungeon guards to take a break. The key screeched in the rusty lock, waking Xanthe. Her look of confusion lasted only a moment before her eyes found his face. The rest of the prisoners looked on with interest but said nothing. She threw her cloak around her shoulders and stepped out of the cell.

He knew right away that something was wrong. Xanthe wailed in agony, and he had to cover her mouth with his hands to stifle the sound. She jerked and clawed at her back, her pain written in the deep creases on her usually smooth forehead. Gray tears streamed down her cheeks, and her whole body arched and spasmed relentlessly.

Not knowing what else to do, Jairus removed one of his gloves and gagged her, wrapping the cloak tighter around her flailing arms and carrying her out of the dungeon. The valet was at the top of the stairs, mouth in a straight line and brow furrowed. They locked eyes, and Jairus knew what the valet was thinking: he was supposed to leave Xanthe behind.

But the valet didn't say a word. He motioned for Jairus to follow him.

It took all of his concentration to keep her quiet as he followed the valet into the underground hallways of the palace, meant for servants to move room to room without interrupting the royals. They passed crates and cobwebs and old brooms, and mice scurried into hiding at the sound of their approach. They reached the far end of a dark corridor. The valet felt along the side of a torch bracket and pulled out a thin metal rod, which he inserted into a hole in the floor that Jairus never would have noticed.

"Go," the valet said, motioning to the trap door that swung open. "It will take you to the orchards on the east slopes of the mountain. Don't stop there. Take her as far into the woods as you can manage."

"And after that? Do we just stay in the forest forever?"

"Help will come," the valet promised. "It always does."

The further they moved through the tunnel and away from the dungeon, the more Xanthe relaxed. She still trembled and mumbled incoherently on their journey, but she didn't fight Jairus' hold. When they approached the shimmering curtain that blocked forward passage through the tunnel, Jairus stepped straight through the light. There was no resistance at all, just the sensation of a warm breeze.

The tunnel ended with steep wooden stairs leading up toward a door at the top. He climbed the stairs and pushed it open, stepping into a dark shed lit only by moonbeams through one small window. The shed was full of baskets, crates, shovels, and burlap sacks. The other side of the secret door had shelves attached to it. When it clicked shut behind him, there was no sign that it was a door at all.

He rested Xanthe against some crates and gave himself a short break. He didn't know how he could keep going. Xanthe was small, but he doubted his strength would last as he climbed down a mountain. He wasn't exactly used to this type of travel.

His eyes fell on a wheelbarrow, and his body relaxed with relief. It wasn't glamorous, but it would have to do.

It was a slow journey. The wheelbarrow was rickety and didn't like to turn. The straight rows of the orchard were easy to traverse, but the path through the forest on the other side was not. By the time Jairus spotted the cave that had become their home, Xanthe was asleep, her face against the side of the dirty wheelbarrow. He looked at her for a long time, his eyes not moving from her quiet beauty. What a shock to go from the glitter of the palace to the mud of the wilderness in just one evening.

He gathered the leaves for her bed and fumbled over sticks and kindling. He had watched a thousand fires built in the palace hearths, but it was harder than he had imagined to strike the flint just right and convince the flames to grow.

Then, the long wait for morning began. He couldn't sleep and had nothing to do but stare at the orange glow and listen to Xanthe's groans.

What had happened to Xanthe? He hadn't expected this complication. The plan was to escape the mountain and survive together, as a team. They would learn to live a peaceful, independent life, away from the horrors of his grandfather's kingdom. They had imagined a little stone cottage somewhere in the forest where no one would ever find them. They would raise vegetables and flowers and babies in peace. It was all they needed.

Now, after finding nothing but a few berries and mushrooms, he realized he had been a fool. He had a little bit of bread in his pack, but it was quickly becoming hard and stale. He frequently had to leave Xanthe to go to a nearby creek to fill the two cups and one small pot he had packed. The water was full of dirt and he didn't know what else.

Why had this seemed like such a good plan? Surely, they would die out here—hungry, thirsty, and cold.

Outside of the cave, he sat down with his back to the rock wall. He popped a few berries in his mouth and leaned his head back. He breathed deeply, wishing for a sign or some sort of aid, but he knew there was no help to be had. The valet was wrong. They were on their own.

The sound of a twig snapping made him sit up straight and grab hold of his dagger. He hadn't seen another human since leaving the mountain, but his grandfather's army could be looking for him by now. Or was it a beast lurking in the shadows?

Jairus jumped to his feet, pointing his blade toward the trees. "Who's there? Show yourself," he called, sounding much braver than he felt.

The thick underbrush parted, and a man walked into the clearing. His hair was two-toned, maroon on one side and dark brown on the other. A shock of recognition zinged through Jairus. Those were his own colors, from long ago when he was just a boy. The only other place he had seen those colors was on a fabled man in the prophetic mural of the palace. He was in nearly every scene. Adwin.

"Who are you, and why are you here?" Jairus asked, the hand holding the dagger shaking.

"I'm here to help," the stranger said, taking a step forward.

"Stop where you are," Jairus commanded. "Don't move. Who are you?"

The stranger obeyed, stopping just at the tree line. The quick burst of shock that Jairus first experienced had settled in his chest, making his heart race and his lungs struggle for breath. His pulse throbbed in his ears.

"My name is Silas," he said. The moment the name was out of his mouth, a heart-stopping scream blasted from inside the cave.

Jairus ran to Xanthe. She had been moaning and speaking gibberish since they had left the mountain, but she hadn't screamed like this, not even in the dungeon. She was sweating heavily, all of it tinted black.

As Jairus knelt beside her, frantically looking for some way to help, he heard footsteps at the mouth of the cave. Jairus spun around on his knees, touching Silas' chest with the point of his knife. Xanthe's screams became shorter and more piercing, echoing off the walls of the cave in a terrible, overwhelming rhythm.

"I can help her," Silas said.

Another of Xanthe's screams tore through the air, and Jairus turned his face toward her without moving the knife away from Silas' chest. She had curled into a ball and rocked and trembled as she screamed. She seemed to get worse as Silas came closer.

Jairus got to his feet and walked toward Silas, knife out. Silas took several steps backward out of the cave. "Stay away from us," Jairus said. "Can't you see you're hurting her?"

There was sadness in the set of Silas' jaw and the brief twitch in his eye.

"Call for me if you change your mind. I'll come back when you're ready." Silas paused for a moment, and then he walked into the woods, the brush rustling once more as Jairus lost sight of him.

Xanthe moaned nonsensical words and twisted on the ground. She sounded like she was having a conversation in another language with someone only she could see. Then, the most horrible scream yet tore from her wide-open mouth. It was shrill, like her very vocal cords must have shredded with the effort.

"Silas! Silas! Come back! Silas!" Her voice echoed through the cave and down the hillside.

Silas burst back through the leaves at a run. Jairus put up a modest defense with his dagger, which Silas brushed aside.

Silas wasted no time. He dropped to his knees and placed one hand on Xanthe's wet hair and the other on her shaking arm. She stilled at once.

Jairus' heart thudded, and he couldn't take his eyes from the miracle. One touch from this stranger, and Xanthe was at peace. Could the stories of the great Adwin be true? Were Silas and King Adwin one and the same? He shook his head.

Her eyes fluttered open. "Don't leave me."

Silas' hand rested on Xanthe's hair, his thumb stroking her forehead. "Never."

"Get . . . get it out. Get it out of me," she whispered, her voice hoarse and weary.

Silas wiped black sweat from her brow and stayed close to her. "You aren't strong enough yet," he said.

She barely smiled. "But you are."

CHAPTER 3

Mallets pounding wooden pegs into boards and tree trunks woke Tovi out of a deep sleep. She frowned before opening her eyes. She turned over, burrowing beneath her pillow to block out the noise and the light. Her movements made her body ache all over, and the pain brought the events of the past few days racing through her mind. A dungeon cell. A knife. Running for her life. Silas losing his.

She could see the swords slicing through his body. She could feel the pain from her own wounds and see the red, pinched faces of the guards. She was right back in that moment, devastated by his death, giving in to the darkness and pain.

Another crash of the hammer brought her back home, and she sat straight up in bed. She looked around her room, calmed by the sight of vines in the windows and willow leaves beyond.

Home. She was home. She was weak, but recovering.

And Silas was very much alive. He was probably up in his studio, paint speckled on his skin. She took a deep breath and stretched, and the muscles of her legs cried out for a good run. She wanted to feel the wind in her hair and the earth beneath her feet. She wanted to breathe and feel life in her lungs. She hadn't run to the Ridge since before her dark adventure on the mountain. It was time to return to her paths. Her lips curled into a sleepy smile at the thought.

She left the treetop cottage as quietly as she could. She didn't want to disturb Ganya so early in the morning, although the pounding nearby had probably done the job already. Regardless, she wanted to run, and she didn't want anyone to stop her, even if she knew she should rest her exhausted body another day.

As soon as she stepped outside, motion in a nearby tree caught her eye. The pounding came from a brand-new platform taking shape, perched in a tree just two trunks over.

Eryx's hulking silhouette was dark against the rising sun as he bent over his work. Tovi's cousin, Gil, and his wife, Diza, were showing Eryx how to secure the boards properly.

Eryx paused with the mallet in midair and looked up at Tovi. Gil and Diza looked, too. Eryx turned to fumble with his toolbox, and Tovi took that as her cue to leave. Eryx hadn't said a single word to her since their arrival in Adia, and she accepted his coldness as an invitation to stay far away. She waved at Gil and Diza before moving along.

She climbed gingerly down a weathered rope ladder, each knot and foothold so familiar that she didn't need to look. She landed with a little squish in the mud at the bottom. The waters were certainly rising.

She took off at a slow trot. Her knees and lungs begged her to stop, and she could feel her pulse in the scar on her hand where Damien had tried to cut away the brown heart. Her ribs protested with each deep inhale.

She only stopped when the world tilted sideways and she thought she would tip over. When the dizzy spell dissipated, she pushed on, this time walking. She didn't mind the slow pace. She looked at the trees and the grass and the sparkling bits of escaped sunshine with a new gratitude. What had she been thinking, leaving this place?

When she came to the spot where the trees parted and opened to the ridge and the view of Mount Damien, she paused. A rock-like feeling plummeted into her stomach. It was just a mountain. She never had to go above the cloud again. So why did she feel such fear?

She took a seat with her mud-splattered legs over the edge, and she wasn't surprised when Silas sauntered through the leaves and sat beside her. They both looked out into the distance. The cloud that concealed the city on the mountain floated in slow circles. She pictured the cobblestone streets and the tall, stone buildings with their iron balconies. She thought about the swinging green sign in the Bottom Rung and the dazzling window displays in the Halo.

She shook her head and looked around her. This rock ledge, the trees, the flowers growing all around—these were her reality. She closed her eyes, breathed deeply, and smiled.

"You weren't ready to run," Silas said.

"I figured that out about two paces in." Tovi leaned back on her elbows, squinting toward the sun. "You know, I thought Tali would be home if I ever made it back to Adia. In all of my daydreams of coming home, he was always here."

"I have work for him to do."

"When will you have work for me? I'm ready to do whatever you say. I'll do anything to fight back, to outsmart Damien. I'm ready."

Silas considered her for a long moment, his expression indecipherable. "Just like you weren't ready to run, you aren't ready for the type of tasks that you are imagining. Grand adventures, exploration, and even some battles are in your future. But not yet."

"When?" she prodded.

"That is up to you and how willing you are to learn. And between you and me, you've never made the learning process easy on yourself."

She scowled. "So, what do I need to learn? What do I need to do?"

Silas hopped to his feet and held a hand out to help Tovi. "Come with me." They walked a few minutes into the woods and came out in a clearing familiar to Tovi. A huge tree covered in vines and yellow flowers stood in the middle, and butterflies glided around it. Tovi thought about the last time she was here, sitting in the tree with Calix before she knew who he really was. The hot, uncomfortable feeling of shame rose in her throat, nearly choking her, and she couldn't look Silas in the eye.

Silas put his arm around her. "That is a topic for another day. I brought you here to see these." He turned her around. There on the edge of the clearing was a cascading strawberry bush, so thick that the vines created a wall. There were many bright red berries and a few that were unripe and whitish green. The rest of the vines were covered in delicate, pink flowers with fluffy, yellow centers. Each petal was so intricate, dark pink in the center and lightening to almost white on the edges. She brushed her fingers across a few before plucking a ripe berry and biting off the end.

Silas touched one of the pink blossoms. "There are several things this flower needs before it becomes a berry. Sun, water, nourishment, time. You cannot rush the ripening. You are like these flowers, Tovi. You are beautiful and bright, but you aren't ready. You're not who you are meant to be. You need to grow, weather some storms, and draw strength from my words. And mostly, you need time. Time to heal and think and flourish."

Tovi flicked one of the white berries. "Otherwise, I'll be good for nothing, like a berry picked before it is ripe."

"You're getting it." Silas grinned. "We're going to work on it, little by little. Every day. We have to take each of those lessons you learned on the mountain and do what we can to undo them."

"And then you'll send me?"

"Yes."

"Why do I feel like I am ready now? I want to go. I want to do something. Anything."

"What is it that you think you are ready to do?"

She scowled. "I've already told you. Fight back. Beat Damien."

"What if that's not my intention for you right now?"

The words were deflating.

"You are eager, and you want to get to work. But you must wait for your own sake and for others. You have to learn to do what I say, even when you don't like it. I promise, it's always better that way. Right now, I do not need you to outwit Damien. I don't need you to strategize, plot, or plan. I don't need you to fight. I want you to stay, learn, be still."

Tovi's lip curled like she had smelled something terrible. "Stay? Be still?"

"And learn. That may be the most important part."

She picked an unripe berry and threw it as far as she could into the trees with a growl.

With a half-smile, half-grimace, Silas said, "Whether or not it is easy is up to you. I don't regret giving you a mind of your own, but it does cause some . . . difficulties. But when you're ready, when you've grown into more of who I made you to be, it will be a little easier to do what I say without argument."

"More of who you made me to be?" She held a fistful of her hair for him to see. "I have your colors now. You took my marks. What else has to change?"

"Your colors and marks are a good start, but there is much to do on the inside."

"When will I be ready? And how will I know?"

"You will know you are ready when I send you. As for timing, my best guess is that you will be ready by Low Tidings. Until then, I want you to stay put."

"*Low Tidings?*" she cried, hands on her hips. Low Tidings was a holiday celebrated up in the trees. Every few years, floodwaters would rise, and water would rush over the edge of the ridge, isolating Adia from all the lands to the east until the river calmed. It could be weeks or months before the waters receded and she heard the cries of "Low Tidings!" shouted from each treehouse. Must she wait that long to join her brother? Must she wait that long to take part in Silas' grand plan?

"Please, Silas. Please give me something to do. And if not, please bring Tali home before the flood. I beg you."

Silas put an arm around Tovi's shoulder and drew her closer into his side. "I'll see what I can do."

CHAPTER 4

Eryx ran his hand over the boards that would eventually be his kitchen wall. Evening was fading, and only a faint light reached through the canopy. He had to stop for the night.

He sat back on his heels, proud of the progress he, Gil, and Diza made that day. The platform was complete, and they had framed a few walls. He had been sleeping in Silas' extra room, which was fine by him. But now that he had built this platform with his own two hands, he seriously considered sleeping on the hard floor that night.

He looked up when he heard footsteps. Ganya stood with a basket over one arm. "Won't you join us for dinner?" she asked. "You've been working hard all day, and you skipped lunch."

"No, thank you, ma'am," he said, fumbling with his mallet. Her kindness made him uncomfortable. "I'll find dinner on my own."

"No neighbor of mine will ever starve to death," she said firmly, putting the basket down. "You can't say no forever. I'll be here when you give in. And bring the basket back to me tomorrow." She went home.

His stomach growled as he eyed the basket.

"I need to talk to you," Silas called from his neighboring home. Eryx looked up to where the voice came from, and he saw Silas slip back inside his studio.

Eryx tossed a few scattered tools into Gil's tool box and grabbed Ganya's basket. When he entered the studio, Silas was painting. His brush hovered over the form of an animal, and his head was tilted to one side. The walls were nearly covered with scenes and colors and shapes, and there were tall piles of canvases in the corners. Splatters of paint covered every surface; and there were countless little glass jars of paint, water, and brushes.

"What do you want?" Eryx asked. He sat down at Silas' table and unpacked the basket.

"I have a big job for you." Silas put his brush down and sat on a stool, spinning so that he faced Eryx. "Ah, Ganya's turkey pie," he said. "You're a lucky man."

Eryx put a bite in his mouth. He had to agree.

Silas grabbed a fork from his kitchen and helped himself to the crusty, tasty morsels on the other side of the tin. "You're going to bring Tali home. And I'm going to hold the waters so you make it home before the flood."

Eryx looked directly at Silas as he chewed. There were several moments of silence as a war raged within Eryx. He had been walking the tricky line of avoiding Tovi while living next door. He had refused Ganya's offers of meals on the porch. He walked the other direction when he saw her coming. He even averted his eyes when she looked toward his growing house. It was necessary. Being near her was pure misery. Her flower-picking, sunset-watching sweetness stood completely counter to his temper bent on destruction. He must stay away for her sake. And his own.

Yet Silas was giving him the chance to make Tovi happier than she had ever been. He could saunter back into Adia with Tali, making her wish come true. She would throw her arms around him and—

He stabbed the pie with his fork much harder than necessary. "Where is he?"

"You'll follow the river southeast to the sea. He is there, a short way from where the river meets the ocean. You'll have to travel east along the shore to get to their cove, but it isn't far. You'll find two huts on the sand. They will be expecting you."

"They?"

"Yes, Tali, Thomae, and Lena."

Eryx leaned forward and stared at Silas. The candle in the lantern flickered several times, and the only sounds came from the frogs and crickets outside.

"Thomae and Lena are alive?" Eryx asked.

"Yes."

"And Tali is with them?"

"Yes."

"Why not bring them back yourself?"

"I have my reasons."

"Why do they need someone? Just give them directions to follow the river upstream."

"I need to send Lena and Thomae somewhere else, and I don't want Tali traveling alone. There are too many people looking for him."

"Even with the curtain?" he asked through a mouthful.

"Yes."

"Then why not send Tovi? She wants to go."

"She isn't ready. And I don't want her to be alone on the way there for the same reasons."

Eryx looked away. "I can't do it."

"I'll be the judge of that."

"So, I have to?"

"You never have to. But I want you to, and that should be enough."

Eryx let his gaze wander over the paintings that covered the walls of the treehouse. Most meant nothing to him, filled with people he didn't know and places he had never been.

"Is that him?" he asked, nodding to a scene of a man with navy blue hair. He was standing on a platform near the top of a tree taller than all the others in the surrounding forest.

Silas nodded. Eryx took another bite.

"I want you to go," Silas said.

"Why me?"

"How about this: I promise to tell you when you get back."

Eryx studied the painted walls a little while longer and finished the pie before asking, "When do I leave?"

"In a couple of days. I'll help you gather what you need."

"Does Tovi know Tali will be back?"

"No, and it's important that you don't tell her either. It will be a chance for her to learn what can happen when she asks for something and waits patiently for the answer."

"Patiently?" Eryx asked, one eyebrow cocked. He snorted and took another bite of Ganya's pie. "I can't wait to see that."

CHAPTER 5

Lyra bumped and crashed around the kitchen of the Hidden Heart's headquarters, flustered and excited over Silas' return. She grabbed a fluffy loaf of bread and added it to the collection of treats balanced precariously in her arms. As she reached for a jar of jam, several apples toppled from her pile and rolled across the floor. "For goodness' sake," she muttered, leaving the apples. Retrieving them would risk the rest of her stash.

The Hidden Heart, known among its members as the HH, was a safe haven for the kingdom's underground resistance. Most members were poor, living in the lowest rungs of the city; but there were a few, like Thad Pyralis, who came from the most powerful families on the mountain.

They shared a central belief: the great Adwin remained the true king, and their sole life purpose was to fight against Damien's evil regime.

Using her foot to open the kitchen door, Lyra climbed several flights of stairs and entered the candle-lit gathering, dumping the food in the middle of the crowd. Everyone was speaking all at once, telling Silas the news of the mountain.

Lyra whistled loudly. When all eyes were on her and mouths were closed (most of them chewing the food they had grabbed from the pile), she said, "Give the poor man some space and peace. He came here for a reason. Let's hear it."

Just then, her husband, Hesper, came down from an upper floor with Thad Pyralis right behind him. They had been watching the streets from a balcony near the roof. "Yes, let's hear it," Hesper said, embracing Silas in a bear hug and thumping him several times on the back.

When Silas turned to the gathering, his face was both warm and grave. "I'm afraid I have come to ask all of you to be very brave. I knew this day would eventually come, and it is here. Very soon, it will seem like everything good is gone, replaced with danger and heartache. I need you to hold on through all of it because I'm taking you somewhere so much better."

The silence in the room was strained.

Silas continued, "A few of you will take the children and the elders north to the desert. You've been preparing those tunnels for years, and it's time to use them. It's not safe here for anyone the king deems 'unuseful,' and everyone knows how much he underestimates the wisdom of the old and young."

"We'll be separated? From our children?" one man asked.

"Can't we go with them?" a woman cried.

Silas put his hand on the woman's shoulder. "I need the rest of you to be found."

A cold chill ran through Lyra. "Found?"

He nodded somberly. "Yes. Found. The masters will come and take a census. They will register every heart, looking for those who can pass through the curtain. They will send some to do labor below the clouds and force others into military service. Don't resist them when they come to register and recruit. Don't hide. I need you within the ranks."

Lyra looked to Hesper. He looked back with a reassuring smile. "You can count on us, Silas," he said.

Others stomped their feet and added, "Here, here!" to the growing sounds of courage. Even the man who had questioned the separation from his children had a new determination in the set of his jaw.

This is what they were made for, what they had prepared for. They could be brave even when they were scared.

"Yes, I am absolutely sure I can count on you," Silas said. "And there's something else, and it isn't small." The crowd hushed. "You've done a wonderful job getting hearts off the mountain. It's driving Damien mad. But our strategy must change. Damien is sending an army to defend the curtain, and you mustn't be discovered leading people to escape. I need you too badly for you to end up in the dungeons. I still want you to look for them, to give them hope and encouragement. Bring them here to headquarters every new moon, and I will send an old friend to usher them through the tunnels and into the desert. Do you understand?"

"An old friend? Who?" Lyra asked.

Silas smiled. "You'll see. Do you understand the task? Bring hearts to headquarters only on the nights when the moon is completely dark. Understood?"

They nodded.

"The city in the desert will grow quickly. There is already a large camp of refugees. Voskos, you will lead a council of the elders, keeping order. I'm depending on you."

The old barkeep nodded, holding his head regally high. "It will be my honor."

"Take everything you can through the tunnels," Silas said. "Take multiple trips if you need to. There will be carts waiting at the end with creatures to pull you and your supplies to the oasis in the desert. You'll find anything else you could need once you are there."

"Be found. Join Damien's ranks. Look for hearts and bring them here on the nights of the new moon," Thad said. "I think we can do that."

"That's the simplified version, yes." Silas laughed. "But I have something else for you. I must speak to you privately. Magan and Rhea, you come, too."

Lyra wondered what it could mean. She watched Thad and Silas climb up the stairs, and the two girls who worked in the palace laundry followed eagerly behind them.

Lyra took a deep breath and looked around the room. "All right, you heard the man. Let's get a move on. Pack what your children may need and get it to the tunnels. It's going to be a busy night."

Her own children were already asleep in their beds as she scurried around tossing clothes, blankets, and a few odds and ends in the one trunk they owned. Hesper sat at his desk scribbling furiously with a quill and waving the papers to help them dry. When Lyra started to close the lid of the trunk, he stopped her.

He folded the letter and wrote the names of their three children on the outside, placing it in the trunk. "Just in case," he said quietly.

Lyra wrapped her arms around his waist and leaned her head on his chest. "We can't think like that, sweetheart. All will be well." The tremor in her voice betrayed her.

Hesper rubbed her back and rested his chin on the top of her head. "We have to be prepared for anything. But you're right. No matter what, all will be well."

"Do you think it's the end?"

"Of what, dear?"

"Of Damien. Of the kingdom. Is Silas finally coming to defeat him?"

"It certainly sounds that way."

CHAPTER 6

Tovi leaned against the doorframe and watched Silas mix white into his brown paint, swirling it around the palette and creating a lighter hue. He bent close to his work, a painting of a four-legged creature taking shape on his wall. He used the light brown to add a long tail and a stripe of hair that traveled down its neck.

"What is it?" she asked, not bothering to say hello. Outside, the crickets chirped in the darkening night.

He did not look up, but he smiled a bit at the sound of her voice. "I'm calling it a 'horse.' It will be bigger than the deer you sometimes see. It can quickly carry heavy loads for great distances. And it will be a loyal companion, mostly sweet-tempered."

After messing with the mane a little longer, he dropped the brush in a jar of water and wiped his hands on his shirt. "Let's get out of here."

They walked along branches, saying hello to others as they passed. The entire valley of Adia was tucking in after a busy day. Windows glowed with candlelight, and fireflies blinked as they flew past families on porches.

There was no doubt now that the waters were rising. The river was already overtaking the shoreline, inch by inch. The people of Adia had much to do to prepare, and most tasks centered on hunting and gathering enough rations to keep the village fed for however long the flood lasted. But the warm evenings were still for gathering over supper and sitting in rocking chairs.

They would be able to reach apples, peaches, pears, and nuts no matter how high the waters came. They could always find eggs, birds, and squirrels. But they had learned from mistakes during past floods that they quickly tired of eating the same foods for weeks at a time. It was wise to bring in berries, vegetables, herbs, wheat, and anything they could find. They hunted deer, hogs, and turkeys before they could scurry to higher altitudes, prepping the animals to provide meat, hides, and bones for all sorts of uses. Nothing went to waste. It was a whole community affair. Even the very young and the very old stayed busy with preparations.

Tovi had lived through several floods, and she had to admit that they were exciting. Maybe nostalgic was a better word for it. The floods came around once every few years, and the people of Adia had traditions that must be observed. Of course, there was the preparation—almost a game to them—as the ground became squishy and the river swelled. Then there were the weeks of entrapment in the trees. New routes had to be made to get from one place to another, and they had to find new vines or a ladder or a rope to help them on their way. The elders gathered the young around them to tell stories of Adwin, floods, and provision. The sound of the water rushing just below their village was soothing, even as the river itself looked angry and frothy. There was always a day of gift-giving (gifts made while they were trapped above the water) on Low Tidings, the day the water began to recede. Many months later, there was the Feast of Promise as soon as the ground recovered and produced its vegetation once more.

The excitement and joy over the coming flood were contagious, but Tovi was shadowed with worry. She couldn't stop thinking about Tali. The flood would separate them for many more months. He couldn't come home even if he tried. And what if he was caught up in the flood? She doubted anyone could survive the raging flow.

Silas led them past Main Street and the treehouses on the other side of town. They climbed a bit higher, finding a cedar tree taller than most of the others. They sat on a thick limb, above the rest of the canopy but still fifty feet from the crown. The fragrant needles were silver under the moon, and the light from the village made the whole forest glow.

Tovi's lip trembled. "Thank you for bringing me home, Silas."

"Eryx brought you home."

"You know what I mean."

"Yes, I know what you mean. And I think it's time for you to tell me more about what happened up there," he said, nodding toward the mountains in the distance.

Tovi looked away. She had been dreading this.

Silas scooted a little closer. "I know everything that happened, but I want to hear it in your words. It'll be good for you. It'll be good for us."

She nodded, blinking back the feeling that she needed to cry. "How? Where do I start?" If this was part of being ready and would lead to her reunion with Tali, then she must get it over with.

Silas took her hand in his and flipped it so her palm faced up. The brown outline of a heart was there, and so were the scars from Damien's knife when he had tried to cut it away. "Start from the moment you met Calix, and I want you to end with this. Damien tried to cut your heart away because you wouldn't let go of me. I know talking about the other stuff will be really tough, but remember that by the end, you were brave and loyal to me. I couldn't ask for anything more."

She didn't want to talk about her failures and the ways she had changed on the mountain. She didn't want to talk about all the lies she fell for and her moments of darkness. But here he was, holding her hand and pointing out that there was a painful but good ending.

The words came slowly at first, and she halted and paused as she tried to find just the right way to say things. But as the moon crept higher in the sky, she relaxed. It was just her friend Silas listening to her tale. She was home. She was safe. And telling the story felt good somehow.

She spoke of breakfast lessons and time with the masters. Fights, ball gowns, wine, and dark intrigue. She looked at her hands whenever Calix came into the story, but her eyes did not fill with tears until she mentioned learning the truth about her father and grandfather. Her voice cracked, and she wiped her cheeks with her sleeve.

"I dreamed of something so different. Parents who loved me and missed me. I had made up so many different stories to explain why I couldn't be with them. I was wrong. My father let them kill my mother, and that's what he intended for Tali and me, too. How . . . how do I move on from that? How can it be so different from what I always imagined?"

Silas' eyes moved over her face, and his brow creased with his concentration. "There is still much more of your story for you to discover. I want you to be further along in your time with me before you learn everything. I want your heart to be filled with peace before you hear the full truth. Only then will you be able to take it all in without it crushing you. But for now, I will give you this: your mother loves you deeply."

"Present tense," she whispered, shaking her head. She squeezed her eyes tightly, and tears dripped from beneath the lids. "You shouldn't use present tense."

"I meant what I said."

"My mother is dead."

"You were supposed to be executed, too."

Tovi opened her eyes and stared at Silas as her mind pieced together what Silas was saying. "Is . . . is she alive?"

"Yes."

Her heart beat wildly in her chest and thumped in her ears. Hope that she didn't want to feel coursed through every nerve, and goose bumps rose on her arms. "Will I get to see her someday?"

Silas squeezed her hand. "Yes."

Tovi couldn't hold it in any longer. She wrapped her arms around Silas and cried into his shoulder as the stars twinkled above.

When she was done, Silas pulled out a white handkerchief. "I need to show you something," he said.

She flinched as he used the cloth to wipe away her tears. When he held it up for her to see, the once snow-white cloth was blotched with dark gray stains.

"I saw that on the mountain," she said, reaching out to touch the cloth. "Black in the blood. Black in the sweat and tears. What does it mean?"

"You know all about Damien's marks. It has to do with them. Anytime you learn those lessons on the mountain and put them into practice, you are filled with a little more of the sludge that plagues the mountain. It's on the inside where you can't see it at first, and it works its way into every part of you until you are full of it. It takes over your tears, your heart, your mind. Everything."

"But you took my marks. You said they were gone."

"That's true. They're gone forever. But the sludge is still there until you learn new ways and unlearn the old."

"How do I do it? How do I get rid of it, unlearn it?" Tovi asked.

"You spend time with me. And as you spend time with me, we will do this," he said, pulling a small, folded knife out of his pocket and flipping it open. He took hold of her hand again, and he touched the point of the knife to one of the scars.

Tovi jerked her hand away, memories of Damien's knife too fresh in her mind.

Silas put the blade down. "Maybe you aren't ready yet. That's okay. You have to trust me with the knife before we can open your scars and remove the darkness."

"And you probably won't send me to find Tali and defeat Damien until the sludge is gone. Am I right?" she asked.

Silas grinned. "Something like that."

Tovi gritted her teeth and put out her hand.

Silas put his blade to the scar and carefully sliced it open. It hurt, but not as badly as she had expected. A few drops of red blood rose to the surface.

A small curl of black seeped into the red blood, and her vision went white with blinding pain. As she screamed and tried to push Silas away, he took hold of her hand and wiped away the tainted blood. The pain stopped, leaving her shaken and weak.

Struggling for breath, she asked, "What was that?"

He held out his hand, smudged with her blood, for her to see. There was just the tiniest swirl of black sludge that had oozed out of her scar.

"That's it?"

He nodded, and she took a deep, ragged breath.

"How many times do we have to do that?"

"That depends on how much is in there and how willing you are to spend time with me and do what I say. It's going to be painful, but it gets a little easier as we go. The pain will lessen as you get rid of it. It will even feel good after a while."

Feel good? Tovi doubted that very much. She leaned her head against Silas' shoulder. "I don't think I can do any more today," she said.

Silas leaned his head on top of hers, resting his cheek on her hair. "You'll get there eventually. I'm not worried. Do you remember what I told you to do?

"Stay. Learn. Be still."

She felt his nod against her hair.

They sat in silence for a long time, listening to the rustling leaves and the hooting owls. Tovi's mind spun with thoughts of the black sludge, the coming flood, and, most of all, Tali.

"Silas, please . . . please bring him home. We've all been through so much. If I have to stay and be still, please bring him home to be with Ganya and me during the flood. It will be months and months longer before we see him if he isn't home before the water rises."

Silas sighed deeply. "Last time you asked, I said I would see what I could do."

"Please, Silas. *Please.*"

CHAPTER 7

King Damien sat in his library, his glasses slipping down his nose as he scoured the list of possible council replacements. Prince Ajax slumped in the chair opposite him, staring glumly at the fire, only looking up occasionally at the portrait of a young, yellow-haired girl above the mantel.

Damien tossed half of the papers in the fire and stood to refill his glass.

"Anyone promising?" Ajax asked.

"Perhaps. Myron, the fighter, has been on my short list for years. I just don't know if I prefer him as a Master of Control or Power. He could do well at either. Calix has nominated his friend Bronte as the new Master of Pleasure. I recall being impressed by the young man. There is some potential there."

Damien took a sip from his glass and pondered his son. So alike him in looks, but so different at his core. He shared none of Damien's ambitions and spent most days wandering the palace under a melancholy cloud.

He had been a sweet, little boy, maybe a tad too sensitive. One of Damien's greatest regrets was not putting more effort into the boy's development. Instead, he had left Ajax in the hands of his mother, a team of tutors, and the masters who frequented the palace. As a boy, Ajax loved to read and ask questions. Damien had seen much promise in him, even if he wasn't as hungry and driven as others vying for positions of power in his court.

Ajax made steady progress in his training as heir to the mountain until the fateful day when Damien agreed to a marriage match for his son. The daughter of a courtyard family, Thomae Admetus was elegant, educated, and the perfect specimen to serve as future queen.

She changed him. Some would say for the better. Damien disagreed. The couple was quick to laugh and spent more time traveling than helping him run his kingdom. Ajax came alive in those early days of their marriage, and Damien felt a rift opening between him and his son.

The first baby came. Little Lena. Damien glanced up at the portrait above the fire. When he had held that baby for the first time, Damien felt filled with whatever it was that made Ajax's face shine so brightly. The whole family doted on that little girl. Her perfection nearly took Damien's breath away.

Next came baby Jairus, and Damien grew nervous. The colors of the conquerors in the mural. Lena and Jairus matched them perfectly. How could it be? Could the sweetness of these babes hide his future demise within them?

He watched Ajax teach his children to walk on the carpeted corridors of the palace. He watched Ajax and Thomae play with them outside, kissing their soft little foreheads as they carried them back inside. He watched the way Ajax kept a tender arm around his wife at parties, smiling at her with adoration in his eyes.

Thomae's belly swelled for the third time, and Damien waited for the night of the birth, sensing that the future of his kingdom rested on the colors of this child. He could not let Thomae conceive a fourth if it appeared the third was also one of the four conquerors in the prophecy. He dreaded the idea of sending Thomae to her death, but what other choice could there be if the fateful colors appeared?

He paced outside Thomae's chambers as she groaned. A baby's cry filled the air, followed by muffled voices. Thomae wailed, and Damien worried that something was wrong. He wondered if Thomae would die in childbirth, solving his problem for him.

The baby was still crying, and then something odd happened. It sounded like an echo—or like two babies crying at the same time.

The door opened, and little Lena slipped out, her eyes wide and shining, her grin reaching ear to ear.

"Grandpapa!" she squealed.

"What were you doing in there, young lady? You are supposed to be in bed."

"I wanted to see the baby. And guess what," she whispered like a great conspirator, her yellow curls falling in her eyes.

"What, my darling?"

She held up two pudgy little fingers. "There are two of them. A boy *and* a girl."

The prophecy flashed before Damien's eyes, and his mind moved swiftly and methodically. He gave orders he never dreamed he would utter, and he had closed himself in his library so that he wouldn't hear their cries.

After that night, Ajax was an empty shell. He did his best to parent his only remaining child, Prince Jairus, but his mind was always somewhere else. It was months before he agreed to stand in the same room as his father. It was years before he actually spoke to him. Now, two decades later, they had a peaceful coexistence, but nothing more.

There were times when Damien wondered what would have happened if he had never sent those execution orders.

Now that he knew the children were likely all alive, he wondered if Thomae was out there, too. There was only one way they all could have escaped. He was certain of it. Adwin had interfered.

Damien looked again at his son. What a terrible existence to love and lose as they both had. If only little Lena hadn't slipped into that chamber. She wouldn't have known there were twins, and she could have been spared. She could have grown up and filled the palace with some of the laughter and warmth and comfort that had been missing.

It was no wonder that Ajax was a pathetic excuse for an heir and future king. Lost in his grief for his wife and children, he likely would never recover. Damien had spent much of his time over the years seeking a way to replace him, to find someone who could shoulder the burden of running the kingdom. If he could find just the right future king, he could send Ajax to a merciful death or, perhaps, exile. He had hoped it would be Jairus, but his grandson had never shown any hunger either. And now Jairus was gone. It would hurt Damien's pride for someone other than his blood to be on the throne, but he would rather give his crown to a like-minded protege than a lackluster descendent. He could not let his decades of planning and power be undone. It must go on.

A loud knock on the door interrupted Damien's musings.

"Enter," he commanded, setting his glass on the mantel.

Dungeon guards pulled two trembling servants into the room. "These two tried to force their way into the dungeon just now. We caught 'em and made 'em show us their hands. They got the heart, Your Majesty."

Damien stood and approached the girls. "Names?"

When they didn't answer, one of the guards shook the girl closest to the king.

"M-Magan."

"Rhea," said the other.

"And what type of work do you do here in my home?"

The one called Rhea met his eye and flinched. "Laundry, Your Majesty."

"And what business did you have in the dungeon?"

"We took a wrong turn."

"A wrong turn. How unfortunate."

"We didn't mean any harm."

Damien's mind spun. What could these girls be up to? Prisoners had been disappearing out from under the noses of the guards. First Tovi and then Xanthe. There had been others, but they were less important. He couldn't remember the other escapees' names or even how many there had been. Surely, these pathetic, little things couldn't be responsible. Or could they? What else might they be doing in the bowels of his castle?

"Tell me what you were really doing."

"Nothing, sir. Honest. Just taking a walk, and—"

"Since you tried so hard to visit the dungeon, I think a few nights behind bars might teach you to stop snooping where you're unwelcome."

"Please, sir, please don't send us there."

"Your other option is death. Which do you choose? The sword or the dungeon?"

Magan whimpered. Rhea answered, "The dungeon, Your Majesty. I'm so sorry that we caused trouble. It won't happen again."

The guards took them away, and Damien returned to his notes regarding potential council members.

"Let's ask Bronte to come for lunch later this week. I like what I'm hearing about him," Damien said.

"I'll see to it," Ajax said.

"Good, good. And what of these?" He handed the rest of the stack to his son. "What do you think of our other options?"

Ajax leafed through the pages. "I'd say Myron for power. What about this one for control?"

Damien took a sheet from him and glanced over it. Kalonice, daughter of a courtyard family, achieved master status soon after her twentieth birthday. The notes submitted by Calix mentioned that Kalonice was particularly talented in negotiating property and business deals.

"And if Calix suggested her, you know she must be good," Ajax said. "He wouldn't want to disappoint you."

"True," Damien mused. He put Kalonice's description on top of the others.

The Council of Masters had been one of his best ideas, or so he had thought. Bringing together the best of the young, ambitious masters to do his bidding, he would be able to sort out who could be his future heir. He had hoped that Xanthe would rise to the top. Once she married Jairus, his blood would return to the throne in the next generation. How deflating to discover her loyalties were never as they had seemed.

The group had worked. He had been comfortable with those seven. Now, searching to replace three of them, he felt a bit uneasy. How to combine the old and new? Would they work together or against each other? He must pick just the right candidates to bring the group back to its vision and goals. Outwardly, to support him and his reign on the mountain. Secretly, to find the next king or queen of the mountain.

One of the dungeon guards returned, red-faced and out of breath.

"Empty, Your Majesty."

"Excuse me?"

"It's empty." He gulped in the air and wiped his brow.

"What is empty?"

"The dungeon. Every cell."

Damien could feel his pulse hammering through his veins as he marched through the halls, his servants curtsying and trembling as he passed. He descended the stone steps into the torchlit underbelly of the castle. Every cell door was closed and locked, but not a single prisoner was there, except the two girls held in the grip of one of the guards.

"When were they last seen?" Damien demanded.

"Just before we brought these girls to you. When we caught them down here, wandering where they shouldn't be, the cells were full, sir."

Damien glanced at the girls and caught the tiniest flicker of a look pass between them. His vision darkened. "Who sent you?" he asked, taking two long strides toward them.

They tried to back away, but the guards held them tight. He reached for their throats.

"WHO SENT YOU?" Black spit sprayed across their faces. One of them whimpered, but neither answered. Damien roared, drew a sword from one of his guards' sheathes, and split both of their stomachs open with one terrible blow. The girls toppled into one another, clutching their wounds with shaking hands as red seeped through them.

Damien turned to the guards who had collected behind him. "Leave. Find the prisoners. Find them all. *Now*."

The guards ran to do his bidding, and it was just in the nick of time. As the guards clambered up the stairs, Damien eyed the bleeding girls. Their eyes were closed, and the red stains crept across their gray dresses and pooled around them.

A shimmering light came over them. Damien watched them closely, knowing what would come next. Their fear relaxed into peaceful smiles just before they faded and disappeared completely.

He knew not where they went, but he had his suspicions. He had seen it before, whenever he had killed a follower of Adwin. These disappearing acts kept him from one of his deepest desires: rooting out all citizens who had the heart in their palms. It would be so much easier if he could set up heart checks and put every traitor to the sword. But the disappearances . . . They would lead to questions about the hearts and Adwin. It was too dangerous. Better to keep them inside his city until they had learned their lessons, earned their marks, and turned their loyalty to him alone.

He rolled his neck. He must do a better job controlling himself. Fits of rage against little girls would do him no good. He walked back to his library, taking deep breaths.

He pulled out a little drawer in his desk and removed one sheet of paper from a pile of sketches. It was a drawing of his defensive wall, his own barrier that he had dreamed of and designed. It would be made of stone and tower fifty feet high and ten feet wide. There were guard towers, arched gates, and multiple layers of chains and locking mechanisms.

It was time to start building. Long ago, before Adwin stole his powers back from him, Damien could have created this wall in the time it took to paint a picture. But here he was, hands tied, having to work at a human pace. He gritted his teeth. Even if it was slow work, he would beat Adwin. He would not let him steal even one more person from his kingdom. Not through the wall and not through death. He must trap them inside and keep them alive until every single one of them had clean, heartless hands.

CHAPTER 8

Rhaxma brushed her long, orange hair, letting it drape over her silk robe. The yellow eyes in her gilded mirror were tired. Joyless. The open window let in the cool night breeze, and she breathed deeply.

She replayed happy memories from when her family had been complete. Loud family dinners on the patio, childhood games in the palace gardens, the lavish parties thrown when Leeto and Rhaxma became masters. She and her brothers used to build forts in the parlor. The boys were soldiers, and she was always the princess they saved from monsters.

She didn't see a princess in the mirror, and no one was coming to save her from the monster within—the growing, clawing, raging beast that consumed her, little by little. Soon, there would be nothing left.

They would never be the same without Leeto. *She* would never be the same. Tears welled, and she didn't bother to stop them. They were constant these days, never leaving her for long. But it wasn't just sadness. She felt split in two and shoved back into one beast that couldn't decide if it was heartbroken or vengeful. The ups and downs of rage and grief were utterly exhausting. She folded her arms on the vanity and buried her face in them. She let the sobs roll, one after the other. This wasn't how life was supposed to be. This wasn't what any of them wanted. And no amount of power or control could bring him back.

She knew what he would want her to do. He would want her to keep going, to keep pressing on for control of the mountain. He would want her to be conniving and merciless, just like him, for the sake of their family's fortune and destiny. He would want a Pyralis on the throne.

She raised her head and stared at her reflection. She could see the monster in the dullness of her puffy eyes and her colorless, flat lips that used to know how to smile.

A tap on her window startled her. "Let me in, Rhax."

She breathed heavily, still looking into the mirror. She would know that voice anywhere, and it stoked the fire in the belly of the beast. Her lips curled back in an ugly snarl.

She stood and wrapped her robe more tightly around her. Leaning out her open window, she looked Calix in the eye and said, "Leave before I scream."

"Come on, Rhax," he said. "We need to talk."

"How dare you come to this house? My brother's body is still downstairs. One scream and my father will come. He's been looking for an excuse to cut your heart out."

Calix's jaw clenched. "I'm sorry. I know it's not enough, but it's all I have. His Majesty commanded that we work together. So, here I am, humbling myself before you, asking how we can make it work."

She shook her head and gave a cold laugh. "Do you remember the last time we were alone on this balcony?"

His frown deepened.

"You were breaking my young heart. What a little fool I was, thinking I could never hate you more than I did then."

"That was a long time ago. We need to talk about now."

Rhaxma crossed her arms. "All right, let's talk about now. You found a way to make me hate you more than I did at sixteen. I loathe you and want you dead."

"This isn't helping anything."

"You wouldn't come here unless you were desperate. Tell me what has you so bothered, and maybe I won't scream for Father."

"I'm warning you, Rha—"

"You're warning me?" His condescending tone pushed the monster over the edge. She left the window and threw open the door to her balcony. It crashed into the stone wall, and several panes of glass shattered. Calix jumped back to avoid the shards, and Rhaxma used his imbalance to shove him backward. He toppled over the arm of a patio sofa. She knelt on his chest, her knees digging into his collar bone.

"I'm warning *you,* Calix," she said, running a gloved fingernail across his neck. "Come here again, and I'll slit your throat."

CHAPTER 9

Tovi watched the sun rise through the willow leaves, casting an orange glow all around her as she sipped some tea. She looked at her palm, and her eyes traced the heart outline and the scar that Silas had reopened. What a strange thing, to be glad that she was still marked by one of Damien's creations. All those years ago, he had intended the heart to identify all who belonged to Adwin. It was still doing its job, despite Damien's change in loyalties.

Just as she took the last drink of tea, leaving nothing but a few stray bits at the bottom of her cup, she heard voices and the clank of tools pulled from their boxes. She breathed deeply. Another day of pounding began.

Tovi set down her mug and wandered toward the construction site. She was still a few yards away when Gil's voice carried over the distance. "And you've never been there before?" he asked. There was a loud thud as he dropped a heavy board. "It's not a long journey, but I'm sure it's a challenge if you've never done it. And then the caves are even further."

Tovi stopped where she was and listened intently. "Silas told me the way," Eryx's voice responded, followed by the slamming of a mallet into a peg. "They need to keep him safe from good, old Grandpa. I'm only a glorified bodyguard."

Tovi's heart raced. Tali. Tali was in the caves. She knew the northern caves and was sure she could get there on her own. She and Tali had explored them over and over again. She crept closer to the conversation.

"I just don't get it," Eryx said. "Why did he tell me to build this house if I'm just going to leave as soon as it is finished?"

Gil considered this for a moment as he sized up a couple of boards. "I don't always understand what Silas tells me to do, but it always makes sense in hindsight."

"Like this porch," Eryx said, ignoring Gil's comment. "I told him I don't need a porch. I told him I don't need the big kitchen or the bedrooms or any of it. I was fine sleeping in his extra room, and if I really need a place of my own, I am fine with a single room that can be used for it all. He told me I should build all of this whether I see the purpose or not."

"Maybe you won't be living alone forever," Gil said.

Eryx didn't respond but pounded the next peg a little harder than necessary.

Just then, Silas came out of his house and spotted Tovi watching the men build. "Good morning," he called. Tovi could feel heat rising in her cheeks as Gil and Eryx looked her way.

"Send me," Tovi said, snatching a vine ladder and climbing toward Silas. "Send me to the caves. I want to find Tali. I want to fight."

"Tovi, that's not—"

"Please, Silas. I'm ready," she begged, grabbing hold of Silas' arm. He pulled her onto the limb where he stood. Gil started to say something, but Silas held up a hand to quiet him.

"Tovi, listen to me. You're still recovering. Your job is to stay. Remember? What were your three instructions?"

"I'm strong. I've recovered. Why does Eryx get to go? He was a *master* on the mountain. Doesn't he have to get rid of the darkness first? Doesn't he have to have his scars opened? Why does he get to go, and I don't? Why does he get to see Tali before I do? Why does he get a mission? Send me, Silas. I swear to you that I'm ready."

Silas put one hand on each of her shoulders. "No."

She shrugged out from under his touch. "That's all you have to say? No? You know how badly I want this. How could you send *him* and leave me here? I beg you, Silas, send me."

A little louder but still gentle, he said, "No, you're not ready."

Tovi growled and turned her back on Silas, descending quickly to the forest floor. She fumed all the way to the ridge, kicking at the soggy ground, gratified by the splashing mud. Her mind raced with her options. She could leave and find the caves by herself, but hadn't she decided to be loyal to Adwin? To Silas? She kicked harder at the ground and screamed angry words.

She wiped sweat from her brow, and what she saw nearly stopped her heart. Her sweat was black. Her conversation with Silas from the previous night screamed back into her mind.

She took deep breaths and looked at the green valley below. *Be still.* Somehow, when she was sitting at the ridge looking at the magnificent world that Silas had created, reality was easier to bear. Her sweat and tears were proof of how unready she was for anything more than to stay, learn, and be still. She ran her fingers through her hair and kicked the ground once more, this time with less violence.

She turned around and walked back toward the village, and Silas met her halfway. She stopped when she saw him and looked at the ground.

"This part isn't easy," he said softly. "But it gets better."

She nodded and let him hold her. His shirt was soft below her cheek and smelled like the woods. It absorbed her embarrassed tears.

"I thought it would be easy once I found Adwin," she cried. "I thought everything would make sense. But somehow, it's harder."

He rubbed her back. "It won't always be this hard."

A scorching pain burned her hand.

"Look," he said, turning her palm toward the sun. He wiped away the sludge that was bubbling up out of her scar. "Every drop brings you a little closer."

She turned away from him and wept.

"Talk to me, Tovi. This is a good thing. What's wrong?"

"There is so much left, and it hurts so much."

He held her a while longer and walked her home, kissing her forehead and sending her inside to rest.

When she got to her room, fresh tears fell from her eyes. Sitting on her windowsill in a glass jar was a bouquet of little, pink, strawberry flowers. A note sat beside it in Silas' perfect handwriting.

Proof that the "unready" season can be beautiful.

Stay. Learn. Be Still.

She picked one from the jar and twirled it between her fingers, thinking about how far she had to go. She doubted this season could really be beautiful, but she supposed she would have to wait to find out.

Later that afternoon, Tovi dumped an armful of carrots into a barrel on the porch. Ganya hummed to herself in the kitchen, and the ever-present sound of hammering pounded in the distance. Tovi closed her eyes and sighed, wishing for some peace and quiet so that she could think.

She wanted to be alone. That ruled out the ridge because Silas would probably follow her there. She didn't want to go in the house because Ganya would want to talk to her. The whole village was bustling with activity, and it felt like there was no escape.

Then the perfect place popped into her mind, and she left without saying goodbye to Ganya. Her special little hideaway in the woods was a little bit of a distance, but it was worth it on a frustrating day like today.

She had discovered this magical spot with Silas and Tali when they were young. Four trees grew over a stream, their limbs interlocking and making a giant, bottomless nest with water running beneath.

The stream was very high, flooding well past its banks. The water moved swiftly, and she didn't dare try to swim. Instead, she grabbed hold of one of the trees and climbed up and over the water, shimmying along the leaning trunk toward the place where all four trees met.

With one leg already over the top branch of the enclosure and her arms poised to pull herself inside, she spotted him. She let out a shriek and slid sideways, barely keeping hold.

"It's just me," Eryx said, rising from his seat on a lower branch. He glanced at Tovi but looked away quickly. "Sorry if I startled you."

"How do you know about this place?"

"Silas sent me here."

"For what?"

"For some peace and quiet. And you're going to fall," he said. He climbed up and gave her a hand, keeping his eyes mostly averted.

Once Tovi was seated on a sturdy limb, Eryx began to climb out. "Where are you going?" she asked.

He paused, one hand reaching up for his next hold. "I'm going to leave you in peace. You must have come out here for a reason."

"You were here for a reason, too. You said Silas sent you."

"I can come back another time."

"Oh, just stay," Tovi said, throwing a piece of bark at the water. "You were here first, and I don't want to be the reason you disobey Silas."

Eryx did not look at her as he considered this and quietly sat down well away from Tovi.

There was a horrible, long silence with just the splashing of the stream against the trees. Tovi's mind wandered to her new information about Tali. He was in the caves. Eryx knew exactly where and was going to find him. And here she was, in this space with Eryx, the man who was getting to do what she so longed to do.

She studied him. He was leaning back against the wall of the enclosure, his arms crossed in front of his chest. He looked different in the soft fabric of the tunic Ganya had made for him—so different from the stiff, white shirts he wore on the mountain. Tovi noticed that his hair was just barely growing in. Light brown with golden flecks, just like Silas. Just like her.

An idea formed so suddenly that it took her by surprise. She didn't know if she could pull it off, but she was going to try. She pulled up her memories of the people on the mountain and how they always knew how to get what they wanted. She bit her lip and looked over Eryx. She had to try.

She took her time climbing to a branch closer to Eryx, and he watched her with his eyebrows slightly scrunched. When she was settled so that their knees almost touched, she said, "That's better. It will be easier to talk like this." She smiled, hoping she sounded casual. He frowned.

"When do you leave to find Tali?" she asked.

"You know I can't tell you anything."

"Of course. I don't want you telling me anything Silas wouldn't *want* you to tell me," she said. "I'm just curious when he'll be back. I miss him."

"That . . . that must be hard," Eryx said. He shifted uncomfortably.

Tovi blinked and looked at Eryx, making her eyes as big as she could. She leaned forward, and he jerked back when their knees touched. "I'm so glad that you're going to find him. I know he'll be safe with you, and that's all that matters to me." She leaned in further, trying her best to remember everything Calix had said and done to woo her. She smiled softly, not breaking eye contact, except for a quick glance down at his mouth. "You're so strong and so brave and—" Tovi stopped short when, instead of kissing her, Eryx leaned further away, his brow pinched in horror.

"What is wrong with you?" she cried, punching him in the shoulder. It was rock hard, and she cringed and shook her hand.

"What is wrong with *me*?" he bellowed back. He grabbed a lock of her hair and held it for her to see. Dark blue. Tovi looked up at the short bristles on Eryx's head. They had darkened. His eyes were back to brown with a little purple star.

She opened her mouth to say something, but no words came. She pulled her hair into her fist and brought it before her eyes. Every last strand was dark blue, a badge declaring her weakness and shame. She had chosen Tali over Silas in the deepest places in her heart. She had been willing to do whatever it took to get what she wanted, even if it meant hurting Eryx. She knew her cheeks were bright red, and there was a large lump in her throat. She dropped her hair and looked at Eryx, who was climbing out of the enclosure.

"Stop. Wait, please," Tovi called. "I'm sorry. I didn't know colors could change back so easily."

He stopped, straddling one of the uppermost limbs. He stared at her with a mean glare and raked his fingers forcefully across his skull. "Do you really think I'm angry about your colors? Can you not see that it's deeper than that?"

She bit her lip and could feel tears welling just below her eyelids.

He went on, "You're using me. You don't care about anyone but yourself and sometimes Tali. But even your longing for Tali is selfish. It's not about his happiness or what Silas wants for him. It's all about you. You see me as someone you can use to get what you want. Maybe you do belong on Mount Damien."

"I'm so sorry," Tovi said weakly, meaning it. "I'll never do it again."

"Tell me this. What did you hope would happen?"

She put her face in her hands, unsure if she would ever be able to look at him again. "I thought I could get you to tell me when you're leaving, and then I could follow."

Eryx shook his head and left without another look or another word.

CHAPTER 10

Hesper pulled the pot of oatmeal away from the fire with a long, metal hook, letting it cool on the kitchen hearth. Lyra sliced an apple, arranging a few pieces on each of their plates. The house was too quiet without the children, and Hesper said a silent prayer that they had safely arrived at the oasis.

They hadn't slept at all the night before. Magan and Rhea had not returned from their mission to the palace, and they feared the risky mission had ended with their capture. But Silas was supposed to rescue them from the dungeon if that happened. What had kept them?

A loud knock made Hesper and Lyra jump. When Hesper opened the door, a young soldier dressed in the gray uniform of the royal army barged inside. "I come in the name of His Majesty, King Damien. Every person over fifteen years of age must exit the building immediately for registration. Are there others in the household?"

Hesper nodded. "We have tenants on every floor."

The soldier went up the stairs, commanding everyone to leave their rooms at once. Members of the Hidden Heart paraded down the stairs a few minutes later, tucking in shirts and smoothing their hair. Hesper counted them as they came. The soldier found them all.

"All right, everyone outside," he said. "Line up with the others and follow instructions."

When Hesper stepped into the morning light, he took in the chaos and crowds. People streamed out of buildings, some yelling at the soldiers or carrying crying children. Everyone looked confused, scared, or angry. If it wasn't for Silas' warnings, he would have felt all three.

He followed the gaze of several onlookers, who pointed into the sky. He reached for Lyra, hoping she wouldn't see.

"No!" she whimpered, her hand over her mouth.

Towering above the crowd were two long poles with a banner stretched between. The banner read, "Traitor's Warning." Below the words were two palace servant dresses, soaked in crimson blood and slashed through the middle. The names Magan and Rhea were painted below the dresses. A heart like the one in their palms took up the rest of the banner.

Some of the HH couldn't look away. Some couldn't stand to look at all. They moved through the crowd, their knees weak and hearts broken. Such brave girls. They had been so excited for their mission.

"We knew it could come to that," Hesper whispered. "They are on their great adventure now."

Lyra was crying too hard to respond.

The soldiers prodded them into a long line that was forming in the street. After inching forward for several minutes, Hesper could hear what was happening in the front. A soldier looked into each person's glove and sent them to specific tables. Those with hearts went to Calix or BiBi, and those without went to Megara or Rhaxma.

Zephne was the first of the HH to reach the front of the line. The soldier peeked into her glove and said, "Heart-free. Please go this way." He pointed to Megara.

"But, sir—"

"I said, go that way," he snarled, glaring at Zephne.

With a whimper, she did as she was told, followed by several others in the HH who certainly had hearts in their palms. Hesper was dumbfounded. Why was the soldier sending them to the heart-free tables? Shouldn't they go to Calix to be registered for his heart army? Hadn't Silas *wanted* them to be found?

He craned his neck to see what happened at Megara's table. She double checked the hands and spoke to each person, but he couldn't hear what she was saying. Hadn't she noticed Zephne's heart? How could she have missed it?

The soldier sent Lyra to Rhaxma, and Hesper's heart thudded harder. He prayed she would be all right.

Then it was Hesper's turn. The soldier looked in his glove, glanced toward the long lines, and then pointed to Calix. "You've got a heart. Go see Master Calix."

When Hesper reached the front of the new line, Calix glanced up and appraised Hesper's frame and stature before turning back to his ledger.

"Name?"

"Hesper Avel."

"Age?"

"Thirty-seven."

"Occupation?"

"Hunter."

Calix looked up and peered closely at Hesper. "In the king's employ?"

"Yes, sir. Since I was ten. And my father hunted for His Majesty before me."

Calix made some notes in his book. "Report to the courtyard at sunrise tomorrow. Bring your bow." He handed Hesper a small rectangular card that said, "Heart Labor" in large letters on the front. Calix had added Hesper's name and status as a hunter/archer to the back. "Keep this registration on your person at all times. Show it to any soldier who asks."

"Yes, sir."

Hesper pushed his way through the crowd. The sun was getting hotter, and the stench in the street was unbearable. As soon as he stepped in his own home, he breathed deeply, relaxing the muscles he hadn't realized were so tense.

Lyra had waited for him in the entry, and they held each other for a moment before going up the stairs. Everyone was back, comparing the papers they had received and crying as they spoke of Magan and Rhea.

"Look what she gave me," Lyra said. She held up her registration card, which said, "Heart-free."

"She made a mistake?" Hesper wondered aloud.

"I don't think so," Lyra said. "All of us who went through the heart-free line got the same thing." Several others held theirs up. "They told each of us to report to the Jolly Barrel tonight after dark for a special mission and to not ask any questions or tell anyone. She said she had taken down our names and would come find us if we don't show up. What could this mean?" Lyra asked. "And why the Jolly Barrel?"

Hesper shook his head. "I don't know, but Silas wanted us to be found. I suppose we'll find out what 'found' means tonight."

Until these past few weeks, the Jolly Barrel had been a lively pub right next door to HH headquarters. It was the favorite social scene for the Bottom Rung, with music and ale flowing every night. The owner was their friend and HH member Voskos, whom Silas had sent to the desert to lead the efforts there. When he had owned the Jolly Barrel, he served his patrons below and housed many of the HH above.

Just a few weeks earlier, Silas had arrived with a warning. Damien's weapons would visit the Jolly Barrel in the coming days, and it must be empty when the time came. Voskos had argued bitterly with Silas, but he had given up in the end. His tenants moved over to HH headquarters, and they packed his food stores into crates, hauling them to the tunnels to be stored underground. Only days after this was complete, Silas had returned to tell them to send the children and elders to the desert, taking the food crates with them.

Now, Hesper understood. The elders and children would need those provisions in the desert. He shook his head in utter amazement. Silas always thought of everything. He had arranged all the details well in advance to keep Voskos and the HH safe from the raids on the Jolly Barrel, prepare their provisions, and then send them to the desert before the heart checks. He thought about old Voskos and hoped he and the children were safely at the oasis, eating their fill of pub food cooked over a fire. Magan and Rhea would never make it there, and his heart twisted painfully. He reminded himself that their adventure with Silas was far better than the desert oasis. But even that thought did not cure his ache.

He walked to the window and looked out at the deserted Jolly Barrel. There was movement inside, and he was fairly certain he saw long, thick, orange hair pass by an upstairs window. "They are up to something," he said.

Lyra joined him, putting her arm around his waist and looking out. "I'm frightened."

He pulled her closer. "Silas told us to be found. The safest place for you is wherever Silas wants you to be."

CHAPTER 11

"I have to leave," Eryx said, bursting into Silas' treehouse. "Right now. I can't stay."

Silas dropped his brush into a cup of water and wiped his hands on his linen pants, leaving a blue streak. "What's on your mind?"

"It's Tovi. It's too much. She's trying . . . She's . . . She's doing what they taught her up on the mountain." He paused, even though he had so much more to say.

"So, you want to leave? What about the task I asked you to complete?"

"That's what I mean," Eryx said, sitting at Silas' table. "I need to go now. Don't make me wait any longer. Let me go now. I . . . I don't think I can take any more of it. Not . . . not with how I'm trying to live now." How humiliating to have to say it out loud. "She'll try to follow me if I wait any longer. I should leave now when she isn't expecting it. That will keep her safe."

Eryx was doing his best to start a new life. That first day, when he had refused to leave the porch outside of Tovi's window, Silas had sat with him, waiting for Tovi to stir. He had told him what life could look like and what it would take. Harnessing his anger, finding the right outlets to turn it into something positive. Digging deep to heal the places where it lived. No more instant gratification. No more fighting. No more living for Tovi Tivka. He would have to put Silas in the center of his life.

And it wasn't going to happen with her making eyes at him and trying to get what she wanted.

Silas' face split into a wide grin.

"What?" Eryx asked, a wave of frustration tempting him to lash out at his friend. It took concentration to remain calm. He had so far to go.

Silas sat across from Eryx, still smiling with a twinkle in his eye. "I'm so proud of you. You have come so much further than you think—and in such a short amount of time."

"Proud? Proud that I can't be near a woman without wanting to go back on everything I've promised you? Proud that I need to leave early just to escape what she's trying to do to me?"

"Very. Very proud of those things. Proud that you understand what I am asking of you as you change your life and proud that you are making choices that respect my wishes."

"And what about her?"

Silas' smile faded into a thin line. "That's between Tovi and me."

"So, can I leave now?" Eryx asked.

"Yes. Do you remember everything I told you?"

"Follow the river to the sea. Bring Tali back. Easy enough."

A few minutes later, Eryx was on his way. Silas tried to give him a new creature called a horse, but Eryx refused. He didn't like the idea of riding. He would travel by foot, and Silas estimated it would take him a few days depending on how hard he pushed himself. Eryx told himself he would make it in under two just to prove he could.

He made it to the ridge and turned south. Silas had told him there was a way down the face of the cliff, but he would have to travel along it for a while to get there. Then he would move east to reconnect with the river a little way downstream.

It was very silent, and his mind wandered. What would his parents think of him now, wandering in the wilderness on the orders of Adwin? They would probably be proud.

He didn't let himself think of them too often. His parents. His kid brother, Prax, who did anything he told him to. His baby sister, Eleni, who called them, "Wyx and Wax." He swallowed hard and pushed through the undergrowth, but the memories would not go away.

***

His parents worked hard, but it didn't matter. His father toiled in the mines, and his mother made candles in their kitchen. She often strapped Baby Eleni to her back and walked through the Bottom Rung hoping someone would buy her candles each day. Whether or not they did determined how much was on the table that night. His father's wages went to their landlord.

He was just a teenager, yet he had made a name for himself with his fighting, bringing gold home to his family whenever he won. Gold meant there was always food in the pantry, wood for the fire, and even a bottle of wine on very special occasions.

The king himself chose Eryx for a showcase. Rising stars would fight the old favorites, and Eryx knew this was his chance for glory.

On the night before the fight, there was a knock on the door. His aunt and uncle, infamous for making money off the courtyard fights, entered. Eryx's mother handed Eleni to Prax and shooed them from the room.

"I need you to understand something about this fight," his uncle said. "This isn't like your fights here in the Bottom Rung. The courtyard crowd expects a certain level of entertainment. You'll each take some swings. He'll let you connect a few times; you let him connect a few times. Nobody wins quickly. It wouldn't be good for business."

His aunt beamed at him. "The drama is important. You're up against a veteran. The crowd loves him. We decided you'll get the first few hits, but then when it looks like he's down and out, he will win. Got it?"

Eryx stared at his aunt.

"Kid, you hear us?" his uncle asked.

"You want me to throw the fight?"

"Yeah, if that's what you want to call it."

"No," Eryx said. "I'm a good fighter. I can win."

"Yeah, we know that. That's why we're telling you to lose."

"No, I won't do it."

"Eryx . . . " his mom said, halfway between a whisper and a sigh.

"No, I'm not throwing the fight. It will ruin my career."

"Career?" His aunt laughed. "You won't have a career if you don't do what we tell you. We'll make sure you're never chosen for another fight as long as you live. Got it?"

After they left, Eryx looked to his father. "What should I do?"

"I'm embarrassed to call them family. I think the whole idea reeks. But, son, I'm afraid. They have powerful friends. Maybe you should do what they say, just this once. And if you do, maybe they'll set it up for you to win in the future."

After a sleepless night of thinking through his options, Eryx entered the ring, prepared to follow his father's advice. He and the star veteran were evenly matched, and it was a good fight. He tried his best to follow his aunt's script, but his frustration grew. He knew he could beat that man. With every missed opportunity, his rage at his circumstances grew. He hated faking weakness. Then, when Eryx saw his opportunity for a knockout, his instincts prevailed, and he took it, defeating the old favorite in front of a packed courtyard. The crowd went wild. A woman jumped into the ring just to kiss him. He was handed bags of gold and was ushered away to a party in one of the fine homes along the courtyard. He even met King Damien himself.

He woke the next morning in the glitzy house, his head pounding from too much wine. He shuffled home, the sunlight making the headache worse.

When he reached the Bottom Rung, the first thing he saw was the smoking, charred pile of rubble where his apartment should have been. The whole building and part of the one next door had burned all night.

All of his neighbors had made it out, but there was no sign of his parents, Prax, or Eleni. One of his neighbors approached him and grasped his shoulder. "I'm so sorry."

He led Eryx closer to the building. "There's nothing left. We know your family was home last night. When we tried to put the fire out, there was a chain and lock on your door. Someone did this on purpose."

The next minutes, hours, and days were the worst of Eryx's life. They buried four mostly empty boxes, bought with his winnings from the fight. He had shoveled a bit of the ashes from the building into the coffins, hoping that a little of them was in there.

His aunt and uncle had the nerve to show up at the funeral. "I swear we didn't do it," his uncle said. "I would never, not to my brother. We couldn't do anything about it. They were mad. They lost a lot of money."

Eryx became an overnight sensation. His story spread. Not only had he beaten a champion, but he had also been orphaned the very same night. The fans gobbled it up. When the king heard the story, Eryx was invited to stay at the palace until a suitable home could be found. He quickly become one of the most famous men on the mountain, the favorite of every crowd. Within a few years, he was unbeatable and extremely wealthy, and he had learned the painful lesson that no amount of money could make up for what he had caused.

***

Lost in these memories, Eryx made his way down the ridge where it became less steep, just as Silas had instructed. He hadn't thought about that fight or that morning in a long time. He hadn't thought about Prax and Eleni or his mom and dad.

He reached the valley floor and marched due east. Another uninvited memory forced itself upon him. Several years after the fight, he had invited his aunt and uncle for dinner in his new home on the courtyard.

"I'm glad we can put the past behind us and be family. We're all we've got," his uncle had said.

He had intended to take his revenge that night, but he couldn't do it. The next day, he had hired others to take care of them and their business associates, and he had paid extra to ensure they were all burned alive.

Eryx shook his head, desperate to put the past back where it belonged. "Forgive me, Silas," he said, feeling foolish but needing to say it out loud. "Forgive me." Silas knew all about it and still said he loved him. He would never understand how that man worked.

He marched on toward the sea, holding tight to a different memory. On that first day in Adia, sitting on the porch outside of Tovi's window, Silas had told him why they had never found the bodies. He wept in Silas' arms until he fell asleep against the porch railing, utterly exhausted from his travels carrying Tovi and this new, wonderful information.

He smiled and breathed in the air of the wilderness. He would see his family again someday when it was time for his great adventure.

CHAPTER 12

Tovi sat on her bed and watched the willow leaves sway outside her window in the afternoon light. Her absent-minded fingers played with her blue hair, and she thought about the lesson of the strawberry flowers. It seemed like every recent experience was more proof she was unready. Why was it so hard to let go of the things she had learned on the mountain? Why was it so easy to forget Silas and try to do things her own way? Her three instructions sounded so easy. Stay, learn, be still. So why were they so hard? She fell back against her pillow with a loud, "Hmph."

She knew exactly why. She was made for action, not waiting. She wanted to make a difference, do *something*. The waiting was excruciating. "I'm not ready. I'm not ready. I'm not ready," she repeated to herself, staring at the ceiling. "Be still, be still, be still."

After a tap on the door, Ganya stuck her head inside. "Stop sulking and come have a cup of tea with me."

Tovi rolled onto her elbow to look at Ganya. "I'm not sulking."

Ganya raised an unconvinced eyebrow. "Come out here, anyway."

Before long, they had steaming cups in hand, and they took their seats on the porch. Ganya hummed a little to herself as she rocked. Without looking at Tovi, she asked, "So what's on your mind? Why have you been so moody today?"

Tovi sipped her tea, closed her eyes, and sighed. She rocked back and forth several times before taking a deep breath and opening her eyes again. "I did something terrible," she said.

"Ah, well. We all do something terrible from time to time," Ganya said.

Tovi looked at Ganya and watched her rock back and forth. That was it? No reprimand? No disappointment? No anger? Ganya's eyes were soft, and her smile was peaceful.

"You don't understand. It was really terrible," Tovi insisted.

"Do you want to tell me what happened?"

Tovi could feel her cheeks flush. "Not particularly."

Ganya tilted her head and seemed to consider the situation. "Have you made amends for it?"

"Amends?"

"Have you made it right?"

"How would I do that?"

"That's hard for me to say when I don't know what happened."

Tovi pursed her lips. "It's embarrassing. I'm so jealous, and I know I shouldn't be. I'm jealous of Tali being out there, going on adventures for Silas. I'm jealous of Eryx getting to go find him. I just want to be out there, too. I want to be with Tali."

Ganya nodded. "That's understandable, sweetheart."

"That's not the really terrible part. I overheard Eryx and Gil, and that's how I found out Eryx is going after Tali. So, I tried to . . . trick Eryx into giving me more information."

Ganya seemed unperturbed as she rocked and sipped her tea. "And how did you trick him?"

Tovi shifted in her seat and leaned her head back against the rocking chair. She heard Ganya giggle, and she whipped her face toward the older woman. "What is funny?"

Ganya set her cup down on a little table between them. "Let's skip to the part where I tell you how to make amends. Is that all right with you?"

Tovi nodded, relieved that she didn't have to talk about her failed attempts to woo Eryx. She wondered if her humiliation would ever fade.

Ganya said, "First, you should name what you did and why it wasn't right. You accept that you can't go back and change it but that you can be better moving forward. Then, you think of anyone who may have been hurt by what you did. And don't forget to put Silas on that list. You find ways to apologize and make it up to them. If there is a lie that should be corrected, you tell the truth. If there is a deed left undone, you get up and do it. If there is a deed that shouldn't have been done, you talk to Silas about how to undo it or at least how to pick up the pieces of what is left. So, let's start from the beginning. Do you know why what you did wasn't right?"

"I learned some things on the mountain, some ways to make people do what I want. I tried to use those . . . skills . . . against Eryx." She looked down at her cup so she wouldn't have to see Ganya's face and any judgment that might be there.

"Mmm," Ganya mused. "I can see how it could be difficult to forget those lessons. I'm glad you know there is a better way. How do you want to do things differently in the future?"

"I don't know. Not like that."

Ganya laughed again. "Well, it's a start. We'll have to work on that. Now, who is on your list? Who did you hurt?"

"Eryx. And probably Silas."

"And it sounds like it was a deed that needs undoing. Is that right?"

"Yes. I better start with Silas. I have no idea how to make any of it right." She had made such a mess of things.

She and Ganya rose to go their separate ways, but Tovi paused. "Ganya?"

Ganya stopped and turned. "Yes, sweetheart?"

"You make it sound so simple."

She tucked a piece of hair behind Tovi's ear. "Yes and no, dear. Very simple in theory and thought. Very difficult for our stubborn and wayward hearts to get it right. But it gets easier with experience."

Ganya patted her cheek and headed toward the muddy ground to search for more provisions. They could sense the flood drawing very near in the smell of the air and stillness of the trees. Tovi's mind turned to Tali and her fears that he would not be home before the flood. She took a deep breath and reminded herself to focus on her tasks. Stay, learn, be still.

Tovi made the short climb up to Silas' house, but he was not there. There was a loud bang next door, and she nearly jumped out of her skin. Walking toward Eryx's platform, there was another loud bang.

"Hey, Tovi," Gil greeted, slamming his mallet into a peg. A wall was taking shape, resting on its side. "Want to help?"

"Where's Eryx?"

He paused and eyed his cousin with sympathy in the tilt of his head.

She hated that look. She could feel her anger rising, and she tried to swallow it back. "Don't be condescending. Just tell me where he is."

Gil's brow furrowed. "When was I condescending?"

"Where is he?"

"You are impossible. He left earlier than planned because he was worried you would try to follow. It was for your own good."

Tovi's heart beat loudly in her ears, and her vision turned gray. "For my own good?" she hissed.

"Yes, for your own good," Gil answered, matching her stance. "And calm down. He's already gone. You can't do anything about it."

"Oh, yes, I can." Tovi stormed back to her willow tree and stuffed clothing and supplies into her worn-out bag that she always strapped to her back when she went on explorations with Tali.

How dare Silas try to hide this from her? How dare he send Eryx right away just to thwart her attempts to follow? She hadn't even had a chance to talk it over with him, to give him more reasons why she should be allowed to go. Tali was her brother—her twin—for goodness' sake. She should be allowed to go to him, to find him, to bring him home.

A tiny voice, which grew quieter with each word, spoke in the back of her mind.

This is unwise, Tovi. Your anger is blinding you. You know you can trust me. It's for your own good. Stay in Adia. Be still. You're not ready yet.

She shook her head, descended to the swampy ground, and marched toward the ridge. She would travel northeast, the quickest route to the caves without skirting too close to the dangerous mountain. She was good at living off the land, having had so much practice on her adventures with Avi and Tali. Besides, Eryx couldn't be too far ahead of her. She could surely catch up.

She made it to the ridge, her mind still calculating and scheming. With the mountain in sight in the distance, she plowed forward northeast along a curve of the ridge. She knew just where to find the switchbacks that would take her to the valley floor, and she marched down them, cursing Silas at each turn. She would show him.

Usually dusty, Tovi noticed the winding path down the side of the ridge was muddy. She knew the entire ridge would be dangerous in a matter of days, and she wouldn't have been able to look for Tali. When the flood waters rose in Adia, the ridge would become a massive waterfall, and everything in the water's path would be swept over the edge. Then the lower valley would flood, and the waters would race to the distant sea.

When the flood took control of Adia, she would have been trapped inside, with Tali trapped somewhere outside. Her anger toward Silas boiled further.

The voice in her mind pleaded with her. *Turn around. You are not helping. You're going the wrong way. I heard your plea, and I sent Eryx to get Tali. Turn around and trust that I will get them home safely.*

She trudged on, too stubborn to listen. She reached the valley floor just as the sky turned pink above her. It cast an ominous glow in the woods, and she looked for someplace that could shelter her for the night.

As the forest darkened, she tripped on a root and jumped at the rustling sound of animals. She had traveled this route many times with Tali, but never alone. They had always stopped at dusk to eat and make camp. Traveling alone through the trees in the dark was new to Tovi. She stumbled again.

"Go home, Tovi," a voice commanded. This time, the voice wasn't in her mind. It was real, and she frantically swung her head in all directions, looking for Silas. Finally, she spotted him, directly in front of her, but far enough away that he was mostly concealed by the fading gray twilight.

Silas took a step forward, and she could see him just barely better than before. It reminded her of the time in the dungeons on Mount Damien when she waited for him to inch closer to her, slowly approaching along the long aisle of dungeon cells. But this time, she was angry. This time, she wasn't reaching desperately for him. This time, she wanted nothing to do with this man who held back everything she wanted.

He said it again. "Go home."

"What if I don't?" she asked, placing her fists on her hips.

"You'll make a mess of things. You'll get lost. You'll get hurt."

"I'm going to find my brother."

"You're going the wrong way. Go home." Silas remained calm and steady, taking more steps and closing the gap between them.

"Wrong way? Don't lie to me. I heard everything. You're just as bad as Leeto, lying to get me to do what you want."

"That is not what I'm doing, and that is not how I work. I am telling you that you are going the wrong way and should go home. I'll lead you so you can find your way in the dark." His tone was firm, verging on angry.

"I can find my way just fine by myself. I heard them. Tali is in the caves. Don't try to tell me he's not. I don't believe you, Silas. I won't fall for it just so you can make me go back home. And how dare you lie to me!"

Silas was now close enough to touch, but she didn't reach out. He stopped just in front of her, staring into her face, unblinking and unreadable.

Flames erupted all around them. She heard the roar, felt the heat, and saw them reflected in his eyes before she turned to look. The fire licked at the limbs of the trees, encircling Tovi and Silas in a cage of red light. She swung her glance back to Silas. "I'm not afraid of your tricks."

Silas ignored her declaration. "You have a choice to make. You could go home that way." The flames opened to reveal a tunnel of fire that led back toward the switchbacks. The fire raced up both sides of the path, making a violent, burning zig zag up the side of the ridge. "Or, you can move along this way." His face turned toward the south, where the inferno opened to form another path, a flaming tunnel for as far as she could see.

Her desired path to the caves northeast of their location remained blocked by a wall of flame. "And what if I don't want to go in either of your directions?"

"Then you have two more choices. You can stay here forever, never moving forward, and wasting away. Or you can choose your own direction and walk through the fire."

Tovi's eyebrows flew up in surprise. "That's an option?"

"That's always an option, but it will hurt, and you will never be the same."

"They are real flames?"

He nodded.

"But I am free to walk through them?"

"If you want to get burned and open yourself up to the pain and danger of not trusting me, then yes, you are free to walk through them. But I hope you won't."

Tovi considered her options. She looked at the flames blocking her from the northern caves. She looked at the path leading home. Then, she looked at the tunnel going south. "Where does that one go?"

"Somewhere safe."

"Where?"

"You'll find out when you get there."

Without any more thought, she turned her back on him and walked with long, confident strides down the mysterious, fire-lined southern path. She refused to satisfy him and go home. She wanted to go north to the caves, but she was too afraid to walk through the flames. She figured she could walk the southern route until she reached Silas' so-called "safe destination," and then she could get out of the flames and travel north to find Tali.

It was eerie inside the walls of flame, and the air was hot and thick. Sweat poured down her forehead, and when she wiped it away, she noticed it was tinged with black. She walked for hours, wishing she had packed water. Her eyes stung; her lungs ached; and there was no end in sight. She cringed when she thought about the zig zag leading home. If she had followed Silas, she would be in her bed by now.

When she was so exhausted that she couldn't take another step, she sat on the hot, hard ground, halfway between the flaming walls. The air was slightly less hot and smoky. She breathed deeply and coughed hard. Using her bag as a pillow, she stretched out, lay her head down, and fell into an uneasy sleep.

CHAPTER 13

Calix put down his quill and stretched his weary fingers. He scrunched his nose. The Bottom Rung's stench had surely made its way into the fibers of his clothing. He would need to burn them when they were done with this census. How anyone could live here all the time was beyond his imagination. Even when his family had been poor before his father died, they still lived a few streets up with the other army families.

He had started the previous day proud of the system he had devised, but now he was worried. The sun was setting on this second day of the census. The crowd was gone, and there had been far fewer hearts than he had suspected for this disgusting little corner of the kingdom. They had processed thousands of people. Calix looked over the ledger: eighty-seven hearts. He had expected nearly ten times that many.

"Let's go home," Megara suggested.

He ignored her, looking over the ledger again, obsessing over the number. Eighty-seven. Even if the pace picked up in the next neighborhood, he wasn't confident there would be enough to man the farms below the cloud, mine stone to build an enormous wall, and search for the missing heirs. He sat back, sighed, and pinched the bridge of his nose. His Majesty would not be pleased.

"How many heart-frees?" he asked, looking up at Megara for the first time.

She shrugged. "More than we expected. There are plenty for wall construction. More than enough for palace and house servants, guards, and the like."

Calix looked closer at the list, particularly at the ages. Seventy-nine. Fifteen. Seventeen. Sixty-two. Something wasn't right. He looked at Megara. "There's hardly anyone between twenty and sixty years old." He looked again. Scattered through the entries were a small handful of men and women in their prime, just about a dozen of them. The rest were teenagers or elders.

She ran her finger down his list. "That's odd. Do you think someone tipped them off?" she asked. "Maybe they're hiding."

He sat back. "Maybe. But how could they have known? And why wouldn't their children be in hiding with them?" He raked his fingers through his hair. A face popped into his mind, and it suddenly seemed clear. "Rhaxma." He crumpled a scrap of paper in his fist. "Rhaxma," he repeated. How had he been such a fool? How had he missed it? He didn't know exactly what she'd done or how she had done it, but he did know one thing. "She got to them first."

He stood so suddenly his chair fell backward, and he stormed toward the curtain where BiBi and Rhaxma examined the shimmering waves.

"What have you done?" he growled.

Rhaxma smiled, but it was cold and didn't reach her eyes. "Whatever do you mean?"

"You tipped them off. The hearts. They knew about the census and hid."

"Why would I do that?"

"I don't know how or why, but I know it's you."

She peered at him, and her ugly smile broadened. "Which has you more terrified? Failing His Majesty or losing to me?"

"Rhax—"

"Don't 'Rhax' me. We aren't children anymore. We aren't lovers. We aren't friends."

"I *will* tell His Majesty that you are working against us."

"I've obeyed his orders not to kill you. Isn't that enough?"

Calix glared at her.

She went on, her cold, yellow eyes glaring straight into his. "My task is finding elite citizens to turn into commanders on the other side of the curtain. Why would I tip off the riff raff from the Bottom Rung and then turn over my powerful friends? Go take a nap. You're not thinking straight."

He wanted to claw that pretty face off, to cause her so much pain she would beg for mercy. He lunged, and she ducked just in time. He hit the barrier hard. It was cold as ice and rock-solid.

He reached for her again and grabbed hold of her throat. She spluttered and pried at his hand while BiBi pleaded for him to stop.

"That wasn't nice, Rhax," he said through gritted teeth. "Say you're sorry." He squeezed tighter.

"Let her go," BiBi demanded, rushing forward and tugging at her brother's arm. With his free hand, he shoved her away.

BiBi stumbled violently, falling head first and trying to catch herself with her outstretched arms. She fell through the curtain of light and hit the cobblestones on the other side. Calix released his grip on Rhaxma and stared silently at his sister. Rhaxma gulped for air and rubbed her neck, never taking her round eyes from BiBi.

"How? How?" BiBi stammered. She struggled to stand, her legs and shoes caught in her dress. When she managed to get to her feet, she passed back through the curtain. "How did that happen?" she cried.

"Come with me," Calix said, grabbing her arm. His fingers dug into her skin.

"You're hurting me." BiBi tried to swat him away, but he didn't let go.

He shoved her into a waiting litter and yelled for the servants to take them to the palace.

"How?" she asked weakly, color rising up her throat. "How did I get through?"

"Think. What makes you different?"

"I don't know," she whimpered.

"Try harder. Do you understand how valuable you will be to His Majesty? Of course, you don't." He growled and looked out the small window, barely seeing the nicer homes passing by.

When they arrived at the palace, a butler escorted them straight to the king's library.

"She got through, Your Majesty. Only moments ago," Calix said. "BiBi went through the curtain."

Rhaxma and Megara barged in right on their heels. King Damien ignored them, focusing his attention on Calix's little sister. "How did this happen? How did you get through, my dear?"

She trembled and wouldn't look the king in the eye. "I don't know, Your Majesty. I just fell through. I didn't do anything to make it happen."

The king's gaze moved over each of them, one by one, and the rest of his face stayed completely still. His eyes lingered on BiBi the longest.

Damien's voice was cold and quiet when he finally spoke. "Bibianna, take off your gloves."

She gaped at the king and whimpered, "I—Your Majesty, I—I'm sure you don't need to look—"

"It is time for you to be honest with me. Take off your gloves."

BiBi looked to Calix with wide, tear-filled eyes, as if he would save her. He would do nothing of the sort. "Do as he says, BiBi. Now."

How long had she been hiding it? He would have turned her in long ago if he had known.

BiBi's hands shook so much that she struggled to remove her gloves. Tears flowed freely, and she was sniffling and pathetic. Would His Majesty throw her in the dungeon for this? That's where Xanthe had gone. What would become of his sister? He swallowed back some rising bile. There had been a heart in his own home.

Holding her gloves in her right hand, BiBi turned her other hand face up. She looked at the ground as the others were exposed to the heart in her left palm.

Calix looked away, catching Rhaxma's eye. She was pale and looked like she might faint. Megara snickered.

His Majesty's face remained unmoved, not registering any emotion. He rose from his desk and approached the sobbing and miserable BiBi. He put one finger below her chin and raised her face up so that she could meet his eye. "It's all right, dear girl. You will be quite useful."

She shuddered and gasped, falling into the king's grandfatherly embrace. He patted her hair. "Now, now. You have nothing to fear. I know you have tried to be loyal to me. It is not your fault. After all, I made those hearts. Perhaps it is my fault for making them so stubborn. Now, pull yourself together. I know exactly what needs to be done." He moved back around his desk and sat down, putting on his glasses and considering several documents and maps before continuing.

She sniffled, but she had mostly pulled herself together. Calix couldn't look at her, despite the king's attitude. He couldn't believe his own sister, of all people, could have that disgusting mark. And now, even worse, it seemed His Majesty was honoring her with a lofty task. He burned with jealousy.

"Megara, Rhaxma, and Calix, you may go," King Damien said.

Calix's heart pounded, and he wanted to argue. He looked from his king to his sister and back again. Holding back words that he knew would be foolish, he took a deep breath and exited the room with a straight back and clenched teeth. He went straight home, fuming.

He sat near his fireplace in a tall wingback chair, staring into a large goblet of wine. Servants came in and out of the room, stoking the fire, refilling his glass, and asking if there was anything they could do for him. He silently sent them away with a wave of his hand. Over an hour later, the door opened.

"That took quite some time," he said nastily and with a slight slur. BiBi just looked at him. "Come on," he jeered. "Tell me everything. What's His Majesty asking you to do?"

"I can't tell you."

"Liar! He wouldn't tell you something that he wouldn't tell me." He rose and stumbled a bit, walking toward her and sloshing wine over the side of his cup. "I'm his most loyal servant. What could he ask of you that has to be kept secret from me?" He jabbed his chest so hard with his cup that its contents spilled down his white shirt.

"Go to bed."

Enraged, he threw the cup to the ground, letting it clatter toward the fireplace. He took hold of his sister, backing her against a wall. "Tell me. Now!"

He was just about to shake her harder when he saw her eyes dart to a place just behind him. Then, with a splitting pain in the back of his head, all went black.

CHAPTER 14

BiBi's mind was empty with shock, but she let her unexpected protectors lead her out of the house, leaving Calix unconscious on the floor near the hearth. The women had firm grips on her arms, Megara on the left and Rhaxma on the right.

They marched her through the city streets, all the way to the same neighborhood in the Bottom Rung where they had taken names just a few hours before. Their destination was an empty pub on a dirty corner. Rhaxma unlocked a side door and pushed her inside. Megara bolted the door behind them.

Upstairs, there was a mostly-empty room. Two chairs sat in the middle, and Rhaxma pulled up a third. "Sit," she said.

BiBi obeyed. Her chair faced the other two, and Rhaxma and Megara looked terrifying and elegant compared to their ramshackle surroundings.

"Can we trust you?" Rhaxma asked.

"With what?"

Rhaxma laughed, and it was too high-pitched. "With what, she asks." She looked at Megara. "Do you think we can trust her?"

"Probably not," Megara replied, her eyes boring into BiBi's.

"Oh, I don't know. I think I'm convinced after watching Calix nearly kill her."

BiBi didn't understand anything that was happening.

Rhaxma crossed her arms and cocked her head to the side, studying BiBi. "After His Majesty gave us our new orders, Megara and I had a little chat. These tasks we've been given . . . Well, they do nothing for us. King Damien will use our efforts to protect the future of his kingdom and dynasty. We decided it was time for us to work together to get what *we* want instead. We are smart and powerful. Why would we devote ourselves to His Majesty's plans instead of our own?"

"What do you want from me?" BiBi asked.

"Excellent question," Rhaxma said with a clap of her hands. "And it brings us to our reason for leaving you out of our plans until tonight. We are going to take this kingdom for ourselves, and we're going to destroy Damien and Calix. We thought you might be too close to Calix, but now I think you'll be perfect for what we need. We want you to join us."

"You want me to help you destroy my brother?"

Megara smirked. "Wasn't he strangling you just now when we came to get you?"

BiBi stayed quiet.

"You have two choices," Rhaxma said. "You can join us, or we can kill you."

BiBi gasped. "You wouldn't."

"We most certainly would. We shared our treason with you. You're either in, or you're dead."

BiBi looked between the two. Their faces were fierce, and she knew they meant it. "Then I'm in."

"Excellent," Rhaxma said. "Can't you picture it? When we've succeeded, we'll be the Three Queens. All the power in the world will be ours. But first, we need to know what Damien told you after he dismissed us tonight."

"I'm not supposed to say."

Rhaxma raised an eyebrow. "Three Queens, BiBi. This alliance comes before anything Damien demanded of you. Three Queens. Say it."

"Say what?"

"Three Queens," Rhaxma said coldly. "Say it. Promise it."

"Three Queens," BiBi said, taking a deep breath.

"What did he say? What did Damien order you to do?" Megara asked.

She hesitated a moment longer and looked up into Rhaxma's yellow eyes. "He is sending me to Adia. I'm supposed to leave as soon as I'm packed."

"To find Tovi?"

"No, to steal paint."

Megara and Rhaxma looked at one another, eyebrows drawn in.

"Paint? You're sure?" Rhaxma asked.

"Yes. I'm supposed to steal paint from a man named Silas."

"Why?"

"He didn't say."

"It has to be important, or he wouldn't send her," Megara said, as if BiBi wasn't sitting right there.

"You'll bring that paint and any information about Tovi straight to us, understood? If you find out why the paint is important, that information comes to us, too."

BiBi shook her head. "Damien will kill me if I don't take it to him."

"We'll keep you hidden and safe. Don't you worry about that. You *will* bring the paint to us."

"You're forgetting something, Rhax," Megara said. "Don't you remember how BiBi behaved during the game, when we were supposed to be marking Adians?"

"What do you mean?" Rhaxma asked.

Megara turned to BiBi. "You liked it there. You didn't even try to mark them. You wanted to stay and live in the trees, didn't you?"

BiBi sat very still. How had Megara read her thoughts so clearly?

"She won't stay there," Rhaxma said.

"How do you know?" Megara asked.

"Because this time, she'll know that our army is coming for her if she fails. They'll find her, Tovi, and the paint, and then they'll burn the forest to the ground." She paused for a moment before flashing a chilling smile. "Three Queens."

CHAPTER 15

Water, Silas. Please. Some water, Tovi begged in her mind.

She didn't know how much longer she could make it. Her muscles ached. Her throat was so dry that it was painful to swallow, and sweat stung her eyes. She had no water, no food, and nothing to protect her from the heat radiating from all sides.

With no idea how long this flaming tunnel stretched ahead of her, fear was taking over. When she had set out from Adia, bent on defying Silas and finding her brother, not a single thought of her own death had entered her mind. Now, wasting away on this path, dark thoughts circled. She never realized that heat and exhaustion would be such a terrible way to die.

Water, Silas. Wherever you are, please help me, she thought. She would have cried it out loud, but her mouth was too dry. She had considered turning back, but she worried she wouldn't make it that far in the inferno. Her only hope was that the end of the tunnel was near and she would exit into this safe place Silas promised was waiting.

And then she heard it, even though she couldn't see it—water running over rocks with a musical tinkle. With her last remaining strength, she forged ahead, praying it was near and not blocked by the flames.

Then she caught sight of it. The river. Her river. The river that wound its way through Adia and veered southeast to the sea. Her fiery path crossed directly over it at an intersection of fire and water. She yelped and rushed forward as quickly as her fatigued legs and lungs could take her. It took longer than she thought, and she stumbled a few times. But she was energized and knew nothing could stop her from reaching the life-saving river.

She didn't stop at the edge. Instead, she toppled straight into the shallows of a small pool blocked by large rocks. The river was high, and the waters raged, but this cove was calm by comparison. It swirled a bit, but it was gentle and refreshing. After drinking and bathing and sitting on a submerged rock, letting the water soothe her, she looked around. The fire tunnel still blocked her from seeing most of her surroundings, but there was a clear path of rocks she could jump between in order to get across to the other side. *Silas must have put them there for me.* She took another drink.

She contemplated staying there in the beautiful, cold water. Would Silas let her starve to death, or would he come to get her? Her other option was to keep going. She eyed the tunnel. No matter how hard she squinted, she couldn't see the end. It was just more flames. Would she reach the destination in hours? Or would it be days? Would there be more water along the way? Anything to eat?

She looked at the water again, and she squinted and tilted her head. Where the flames crossed the water, they seemed to dance on the surface. She took a deep breath and dove beneath. All was dark. She swam toward Silas' boundary. The water in the river was moving very fast, so she stayed close to the rocks that blocked her little pool. She could see the flames above her. With one arm looped around a rock, she reached out the other hand.

It didn't hurt. She wasn't burned. The flames were only above the water, and there was no barrier beneath. She surfaced, gulped in some air, and thought fast. She had been moving northeast when Silas stopped her. The tunnel of fire had brought her south. The river flowed mostly southeast. To swim below the flames and head back toward Adia, she would have to go against the rushing current. That would be difficult in normal times. With the flood waters rising, it would be impossible.

Her other option was to go with the current, just until she was on the other side of the flames. It would carry her away from Adia; but at least she would live, and she would be out of the fire. Then, she could move straight north, carefully skirting the mountain on her way to the caves and her brother. She would get relief from the flames, and she could search for food and a place to rest.

Hoping her calculations were correct, she took another deep breath and dove below the water. Holding fast to the rocks along the edge, she inched along. Flood water pulled at her legs, and her arms were losing the little strength they had left. But she was determined. The fire wall was not thick, and soon, she was emerging on the other side.

Pulling herself onto the bank, she laughed in relief and looked around. It was a peaceful spot, if she could ignore the inferno stretching in a straight line behind her. With her back to the flames, the river continued downstream to her right. Forest stretched ahead of her. Through the canopy, she saw glimpses of the distant mountain towering above her.

The rocks beneath her feet rattled, and a few fell into the river. She spun around to look upstream, but she couldn't see anything through the flames. Was the roaring of the fire growing louder, or was that a different sound? She looked all around, but she couldn't find any answers.

She saw it only seconds before she was engulfed, and she froze in wide-eyed terror. A wall of flood water taller than the flames slammed into her body and took her with it. She tumbled in the water, her body twisting this way and that at the mercy of the flood. Her first panicked thought was that she may be torn in half.

She was pummeled by other objects that had been swept away, but there was no telling what they were. Something smacked hard against her shins. Her lungs burned, and she didn't know which way was up. For the second time that day, she was sure she would die.

She was at the mercy of the water and took gasping breaths each time her face found the surface. She wasn't sure how long she'd be swept downstream in the roaring, chaotic current. She was too terrified to think of anything but groping for air.

As the water carried her swiftly toward the sea, it grabbed trees and rocks and anything else in its way. Her body was bumped and bruised as she hit against the debris. She was powerless to protect herself. There were times she couldn't tell if she was alive or drowning.

She surfaced once more, and in that split second, she saw another face do the same, just a few feet away. She wasn't alone.

She was tossed under again, and she kept her eyes tightly shut against the dirty water. Something rock-like hit her in the side and then again on the shoulder. Suddenly, she was bombarded all around her, and she realized she was tangled in something. Most of it felt too soft to be a tree and too thick to be the smaller branches of the canopy. Then, something distinctly foot-like kicked at her stomach. She reached out and grabbed a fistful of what must be clothing.

She surfaced. So did he. She recognized his scarred face instantly. They had just enough time for one deep breath before they both disappeared beneath the water again.

They tumbled some more, caught in the same current. She felt her knee ram into his nose, and his elbow found her temple, making her see pops of color against her closed eyelids. She wondered how much longer they could go on like this. After everything she'd been through in the past few weeks, she was going to die with this man she hardly knew, in this river far from home.

The next time she surfaced, Eryx's face was bloody. His mouth was open, and his eyes were closed. Had her knee done that to him? They sank back below the water. She blindly grabbed for him, and her hands found his shirt. As they flipped and tossed in the water, she refused to let go. She walked her hands up to his throat and then his chin. She forced his mouth shut, unsure if this would help. Their legs hit against each other, and the water tried to pull them apart. New purpose gave her strength, and she clung to Eryx.

They were both tossed up above the surface again. She took a giant breath and then another. When they plunged below again, she held his face firmly with both hands and forced her breath through his mouth. She then clamped his mouth shut.

Help me, Silas! she screamed in her mind. *Please!*

Instead of miraculous help, she felt the weight of Eryx's body dragging them deeper. Her lungs felt ready to burst, but all other feelings and awareness were growing dim. She had reached the end. *I'm sorry, Silas. I'm so sorry* were the words repeating over and over again in her fading consciousness. *I'm sorry. I'm sorry, Silas.* Then, only darkness.

CHAPTER 16

Water rushed below the treehouses, and Adians gathered on porches and along bridges. There was always a sense of wonder on the first day of the flood.

Ganya stood beside her friend Leora and watched as a little boy shrieked and clapped his hands. "Look at the water, Mama! Look at it!" Several teenagers sat on one of the bridges, their legs dangling over as they watched and pointed.

The water was far enough below that only an occasional spray reached the village. It was moving very fast, and the water had turned brown from all of the dirt it picked up. It looked like frothy, bubbling mud.

"It came quicker than we expected," Leora observed.

"Yes, but we're ready," Ganya said, her usual cheer dimmed.

Leora put an arm around Ganya. "You're worrying about Tovi."

Ganya nodded, thankful for a friend who understood. Tovi had not come home the night before, and she feared what this could mean. Was she out there somewhere in the flood?

Leora hadn't seen her little boy in thirty years. She didn't speak of it often (except to Silas), but Ganya knew he weighed heavily on dear Leora's heart. So, when Ganya worried over Tali being gone for weeks at a time or Tovi being gone for less than a day, she remembered that Leora had made it thirty years. It gave her a little bit of peace.

A strange murmur went through the crowd, and both Ganya and Leora looked up. Leaves and branches obscured whatever it was that had people craning their necks and whispering to one another.

With a swish of leaves, Silas raced through the crowd, running full speed along a branch, pushing vines out of his way and upsetting the festive environment. "Ganya! Leora!" he called. "Grab some blankets!"

It took a moment to take in the shift of the atmosphere. When her mind caught up with what she was seeing, Ganya rushed inside, Leora at her heels. She threw open a trunk and tossed a blanket to Leora. She grabbed another, and they ran back outside.

Silas was perched precariously above the water, swinging with one arm anchored in a rope ladder, the other reaching for what looked to be a bundle of dark cloth that had washed against the trunk of Silas' tree. "What is he doing?" Leora asked. Silas' mouth was moving, as if he was talking to the bundle, but they couldn't hear his voice over the roar of the water.

Then, the bundle moved. First a hand shot out, and then a round, pale face looked up. The girl squinted as water sprayed in her eyes, and she nodded at Silas. They climbed ever so slowly up the rope ladder. She slipped several times, sagging against the rope and clutching Silas' hand.

The gathering above held their collective breath. The youngsters had moved closer to the action, intrigued by the stranger. What had happened to this poor girl? Where did she come from? How had she survived the surging water?

When Silas and the girl reached the thick limb at the top of the ladder, Ganya and Leora rushed to them. They were soaked through, and the girl was trembling. Leora wrapped her in one of the blankets while Ganya offered hers to Silas.

"No, I'm fine," he said. "She could use that one, too."

Ganya draped the second blanket around the girl and gently combed the dark hair out of her face. "Can you stand up, dear? We'll get you dry and warmed up by my fire."

The girl looked at Silas, her eyes big in her pale face.

"It's safe, BiBi. Ganya will take good care of you. I will come see you when you're settled in."

She nodded. Her face turned toward the crowd, and her cheeks turned pink.

"Come this way. They're just curious is all. It's not every day that a stranger is rescued in front of their very eyes."

The poor dear. What a story she must have to tell, being swept up in the flood and finding herself clinging to that tree for dear life. She definitely wasn't from Adia. Ganya knew everyone who lived in the village, but she could not think of any settlements upriver. She ticked through the villages and towns she knew. Mount Damien to the east, a small handful in the northern desert, the marshlands directly south. But upriver to the northwest? She was very interested to hear this young one's tale.

"Come, come. Let's get you dry," Ganya said, leading her to the house in the willow.

The girl stopped just outside. "This . . . this is Tovi's house," she said.

Ganya's heart skipped a beat, and she peered closer at the girl. "How do you know my Tovi? And how do you know our house?"

She opened her mouth a few times like she was trying to say something but couldn't quite find the words.

"We'll get to that later," Ganya said, trying her best to comfort the girl with a smile and a grandmotherly arm around the shoulders. "Come inside. We'll find some dry clothes."

The girl fit well enough into one of Tovi's soft dresses. She kept running her hands over the blue-green fabric as she sat in one of the big comfy chairs. Ganya warmed some brothy soup and water for tea. "What is your name, child?"

"Bibianna. But most people call me BiBi."

"And how did you find yourself in your predicament today?"

Silas appeared in the doorway, wearing dry clothes. His hair still dripped a bit. "That story will have to wait for now," he said, taking the other big chair near the fire. "BiBi, I know why you are here, and I know who sent you."

Ganya did her best to stir the soup and act like nothing was amiss. Was she hearing correctly that this sweet girl was a villain of some sort? But why was Silas smiling at her with such comfort and understanding?

She took a peek at the girl, who was staring at Silas, her hands trembling in her lap and her bottom lip quivering.

"You don't need to be afraid of me," Silas continued. "Do you remember what I told you the last time you were here?"

"You said I could come back."

Silas nodded. "No matter your reasons, I am glad you are back. This is where you belong. There are many people trying to control you on the mountain now that they know about that heart. None of them are here. They cannot get to you, at least until this flood is over. I hope you will use this time to learn a thing or two before the water recedes. You will stay here with Ganya. She could use the company."

"Where is Tovi?" she asked shyly.

Silas glanced up and locked eyes with Ganya, and she did not like the look on his face.

CHAPTER 17

Tovi did not know how long had passed in the darkness, but her senses slowly reawakened. It was the strangest, most surreal dream. Strong hands tugged her through shallow water and across grainy, wet sand. It hurt, but not as much as the recent journey. She smelled salt water and seaweed and a hint of tropical sweetness.

She was pulled from wet sand onto dry, and it was warm and soothing on her cold back. Blurry, green trees swayed above her. The sun was so bright, she had to squint and turn away, and the movement made her head feel like it was cleaved in two. Through the commotion of legs and splashing water, she saw someone tugging Eryx onto the beach. His head rolled to the side.

Her eyes fluttered shut. She was so very tired. The sounds around her dimmed once more, and the roaring of the ocean waves hushed. She barely heard the two women tending to Eryx and forcing water out of his stomach and lungs. She wasn't disturbed by their chaos and yelling to one another, giving directions for saving his life. She hardly felt the rough, work-worn hands checking her pulse or the long hair tickle her face as someone listened for her breath.

"Go!" one of the women screamed. "You know the orders. You have to go!"

"Will she be okay?" a familiar voice screamed back. Tovi's heart jolted, but she was powerless to move or call out. She wanted so badly to see him, to speak to him. She strained to lift her eyelids. He gently smoothed her hair out of her face, even while his long, blue hair stuck in strands to his own.

"She'll be fine," the woman yelled. "I'll take care of her. Go! Now!"

Tovi felt him kiss her cheek, and she managed to barely keep her eyes open. He stood and got out of the way as another form hovered over her. A blurry face. Whitish green hair—or was that a cloud? A fragrance of fruit and flowers.

"My darling!" Her voice was as musical as the tide and as warm as the sun. Her hands were rough, too, and they cupped Tovi's face, the calloused thumbs rubbing her cheeks. "We will see each other soon. I promise." And then she was gone.

Unable to stay awake any longer, Tovi fell back into the darkness.

CHAPTER 18

Glasses clinked amidst the fake laughter and haughty stories told by all of those in attendance at Megara's posh party. There were shiny dresses, sparkling jewels, and the strong scent of too many different expensive colognes.

Megara stood at the top of the curved stairs, looking down on the gathering. No one seemed to notice that the hostess was not enjoying the night of revelry, and she didn't mind. The less they paid attention to her, the better for the task at hand.

Her eyes never stopped moving. They swept from the musicians in the corner to the waiters lifting their trays of delicate finger foods and sparkling wine glasses. Everyone seemed to be enjoying themselves, which was all part of the plan.

As she glanced once more around the room, one face was turned up toward her. Calix. He broke their eye contact and moved through the crowd, schmoozing and gladhanding. But there was no doubt that he was moving toward the stairs.

Megara stayed put. This was her party. She and Rhaxma had a plan, and she would not let Calix ruin it. It would be just like him to want some of the credit, to cause a scene if he wasn't getting enough attention. She glared down at him as he approached the foot of the stairs, willing him to stop and look up. He did not oblige.

All the way around the curve, he took his time. He lifted his glass several times in greeting to friends who called from below. She didn't take her eyes off him, wishing he wasn't so handsome.

There had been a time when Megara was pretty, like the other girls. She had even been told she was the prettiest by more than one lovesick boy. Yet Calix, who collected beautiful women, had never chosen her. It made her doubt every compliment she had ever received. Why had he never tried to collect her?

She remembered when he first turned his eyes on Rhaxma. They were teenagers, desperate to be adults, recreating the grown-up party scene. They had danced together all night at one of these pearl and crystal affairs, and that evening had launched months of an inseparable, obsessive love.

And every day Megara would see them, wondering why it wasn't her, wondering why she had never felt anything close to what looked to be such passionate love and deep happiness.

But their love had ended as suddenly as it had begun, and with the same intensity. There was screaming and throwing. Accusations and threats. Calix already had another girl on his arm, and it wasn't Megara.

She laughed to herself, standing on that balcony. She had been such a stupid, little girl. The world was so simple when the most important thing was love and attention from a boy.

When Calix reached the top of the stairs, he stood shoulder to shoulder with Megara, looking over the party. "It's a little obvious, don't you think?" he asked, eyeing the crowd from her vantage point.

"Obvious?" she asked.

"Gathering everyone who is anyone, giving us food and drink until we're drunk enough to reveal what is beneath our gloves? These glasses are far too small, by the way. You would have been more successful with something a bit bigger. I myself am enjoying your fine wine, as I have nothing to hide."

Megara smiled at him, and it was darkly genuine. "Nothing to hide. Wouldn't that be nice?"

"Have you seen BiBi?" Calix asked.

Megara made a show of glancing around the room below. "Perhaps you should go look for her."

"And miss whatever you have planned for this party?"

"What could I possibly have planned?"

Calix set his glass on the railing in front of him. "Something sinister, I'm sure. His Majesty wanted Rhaxma to find him a few high-ranking hearts. So, you're either joining forces with her or stabbing her in the back."

Megara smirked. "Would that scare you if I had a plan of my own?" She watched his face closely. His gaze followed Rhaxma's bouncing orange hair as she moved through the crowd. She always stood out among the grays and blacks of the elite.

Then, he focused on something else, and Megara turned to see what had grabbed his attention. A gentleman had swooned, caught in the arms of another party attendee.

There was a shriek from the other side of the room as a woman collapsed, followed by another. One by one, they all fell, glasses shattering as they hit the floor. Calix turned to look at Megara with a new respect dawning in his gaze. "What have you done?"

She took in his handsome face that had never shined toward her. He looked genuinely bewildered.

Calix tugged at his collar. "His Majesty said to be discreet."

She leaned close, kissed him on the cheek, and whispered, "Then I would stand further from the railing."

He stared at her. She could see the black veins in his eyes. He looked at his glass and back at her. He took a few steps away from the stairs to avoid the long fall down to the party below. As he was nearing the walls, his eyes rolled back in his head, and his knees hit the ground.

Megara laughed and patted him on the cheek. He was so pitiful.

She peeked inside his glove just to be sure. Heart-free, just as she suspected.

She looked at him just a moment longer and then walked down the stairs, taking in the full glory of their achieved plan. Bodies—still alive, but just barely—were draped everywhere, lying in their puddles of spilled wine. The servants stood around the perimeter, trembling hands covering their mouths or weeping with fear.

"Quickly," Rhaxma snapped. She was the only party guest still awake. "Check beneath their gloves. I need to know every person who has a heart. Then, take them home to their beds. And clean up the mess. Understood?"

The servants moved timidly through the crowd, calling for Megara or Rhaxma any time there was a heart. They kept a running list, shocked by some of the names. His Majesty would not like this.

"Over here, miss," one of the servants called. "This one has a heart."

Megara walked toward the voice, and she stopped short. Rhaxma looked up and gasped.

Thad Pyralis. Brother of Leeto and Rhaxma. The Pyralis family was second only to the royal family in power and prestige. They were practically royal themselves. And one of their own had the heart? Megara approached and took his hand in hers. Sure enough, there it was. The untidy brown heart marred his skin.

Megara clicked her tongue and dropped his hand. Whispering so the servants wouldn't hear, she asked, "Do we tell His Majesty, or do we keep him for ourselves?"

Rhaxma looked miserable, staring down at him like he had committed an unspeakable crime. "I can't believe I'm about to say this, but I think he may be more valuable in the palace. His Majesty will be convinced of my loyalty if I turn in my own brother." She touched his clammy face. "Oh, Thad. How could you?"

CHAPTER 19

Tovi's eyes were gritty as she tried to open them. Her nose and throat burned, and her tongue was miserably dry. Her mouth tasted like salt. She was in darkness, except for the dancing flickers of a fire shining through a low doorway.

The next thing she noticed was the scratchy mattress. It was made of something similar to straw. She moved slowly, grimacing but not allowing herself to cry out as she sat up and put her feet to the ground. Cool, velvety sand greeted her feet. She must have made it all the way to the sea. She tried to comb her fingers through her hair, but it was too knotted and tangled.

She stood for a while in the dark room, trying to think of what she should do. She had a vague recollection of the fire tunnel, the wall of water, Eryx bobbing in the flood, and being pulled ashore. She had been sure she heard Tali's voice. Or had that been a dream?

She heard something sizzle, and the smell of cooking fish filled the small space. Her stomach growled hopefully, and she edged closer to the fire-lit door. With the added light, she could see for the first time that she wore a dress that was not her own. It was similar in shape to those worn in Adia, but it was made of worn-out material that looked like it had once been a fancy pattern of blues and golds.

When she stepped out of the hut, she found a young woman close to her age tending the fire. Her hair was wild from the salt air and held back from her face with a band of patterned fabric.

"How are you feeling?" the stranger asked, slowly turning skewered fish over the flames.

Tovi didn't answer. She studied the woman, trying to take her in. She was nothing like anyone Tovi had ever seen before. She seemed untamed and far fiercer than any Adian. Her eyes were large in a thin face, and her cheekbones and jaw were strong and pronounced. There was something oddly familiar about her.

After several moments with no sound but the fire and the crashing waves, the woman looked up. She met Tovi's stare.

Tovi shifted her weight awkwardly. "What happened to the man who washed up with me?"

Her new companion jerked her head toward another hut. "He's still sleeping, but I think he's on the mend." She motioned to the sand across the fire. "Take a seat. You must be weak and hungry."

"Who are you?" Tovi asked as she sat down.

The woman was silent as she observed Tovi, the darkness and shadows hiding her features enough that Tovi could not tell what she might be thinking. Finally, she answered. "My name is Helena. You can call me Lena."

Tovi stared across the fire. "Then, you're my—"

"Sister, yes," Lena interrupted. "And you need to eat." She took a skewer off the rack and used a stick to slide its contents onto a plate. She handed the plate to Tovi.

She kept looking at this wild woman who shared her blood and the shape of her eyes. There was quite a bit of Tali in the set of her jaw and the shape of her nose. The sharp planes of Lena's face were more like her own. Her sister.

Tovi swallowed hard. Her throat constricted, and she felt tears just below the surface. She put the plate down, suddenly not hungry. She ran her hands and toes through the cool, silky sand and watched the waves roll in one after another.

"Where did Tali go?" she asked quietly. "I saw him, just for a moment, after he pulled me onto the beach."

"Ahh. I wish you hadn't seen that," Lena said, pulling her fish apart with her fingers.

"Why?"

"I've been warned about your temper and that you're impulsive and reckless. That you would do anything to follow him. I thought you were too out of it to recognize him. That would have been easier."

Tovi's anger prickled. "It was Silas, wasn't it? He told you to keep Tali from me."

"Yes, and for good reason," Lena answered, matching Tovi's surly tone.

"Good reason?" Tovi shot back.

Lena's face was fierce on its own, but she looked positively fearsome lit by the flames. "Your unwillingness to do as Silas says is becoming legendary. You have had countless hours with him right by your side, and yet you still can't manage to follow his orders, even when they are for your own good. You've been foolish, and I don't trust you to suddenly be wise. Frankly, I don't trust you at all. If I told you where Tali went, you'd leave here tonight, following his trail, no matter what Silas said. You've already ruined enough. Don't ruin more."

Tovi simmered and dug her toes further into the sand. Heat crept up her throat, and ashamed tears stung her eyes. She wasn't used to being spoken to this way. And the worst part was that she knew it was all true.

Quieter and softer than before, Lena said, "I'm sorry. I shouldn't let my anger get the best of me. I suppose I have a temper, too."

"Why are *you* angry?" Tovi asked. "I'm the one who was in the dungeon. I'm the one with scars from King Damien." She put up her hand to show Lena. "I'm the one who has been longing for my brother for months, only to find out Silas was sending someone else to get him."

Lena's glare was ice cold. "We need to get something straight, right now. You are not the only one who has had a hard life. You are not the only one who was torn from her family that night. You are not the only one who misses her brother. I have been missing Jairus for twenty years. You are not the only one who has been in danger. And I might add, most of us are in danger because we are obeying Silas and doing hard work for him. You have been in danger because you won't control yourself. It is your own fault. No one put you in this position but yourself. The sooner you end the self-pity, the better."

Tovi didn't know what to say. Eryx's words from the hideaway came back to her, shouting in her mind that she was selfish and thought of no one but herself. And here she was, doing it again. Her unworthiness felt heavy, and suddenly all she wanted was a cup of tea in the peace and comfort of Ganya's porch.

At Tovi's silence, Lena continued. "You are supposed to be safe in Adia. Tell me what happened."

Tovi swallowed. "I begged Silas to bring Tali back before the flood. Then I heard he was sending Eryx to the caves to find him. Eryx left early so that I couldn't follow, and I lost it. I followed anyway." Her explanation sounded childish and whiney in her own ears. She took a deep breath, trying to release the hot, prickling feel of humiliation. "I don't understand how Tali could be here when they said he was in the caves to the north."

"Caves to the north?" Lena asked, her brows creased. "What exactly did you hear?"

Tovi thought back. "It was something my cousin Gil said. He and Eryx were together, and I heard them talking about my brother being in the caves."

The skin around Lena's jaw shifted as she clenched her teeth. "Did they say anything else? Anything more specific?"

Tovi shook her head.

"You *are* a fool." Lena leaned forward, and the flames illuminated her face and danced in her purple eyes. "The northern caves aren't the only caves. And Tali isn't your only brother."

"What do you—"

Lena interrupted again. "If you had taken the time to ask questions and understand, we would both be with the brothers we miss. Tali was here, on this beach, not the caves to the north. Eryx was being sent here, to get Tali, to bring him back to you."

"Then why—"

"Jairus and Xanthe are sheltered in caves east of the mountain. Mother and I were supposed to go to them as soon as Eryx arrived to escort Tali home."

Tovi's head swirled. "So, when Silas stopped me from going north . . ."

"You were going the wrong direction," Lena finished sharply.

Tovi felt sick. She saw it all clearly, and she didn't like how she looked in her memory.

"You said Jairus is in the caves to the east. Is that where Mother and Tali have gone? To find Jairus?"

Lena looked across the flames that were slowly lowering toward the embers. "Mother and I were supposed to go to Jairus, but now I can't. I assume that is where they went, but it all happened so fast that I don't know for sure."

"Why didn't you go to Jairus if you wanted to so badly?"

"Do you really want to know?"

Tovi suddenly knew the answer. There had been a plan, and now it was ruined by her appearance at the sea. "But why couldn't you still go to Jairus?" she asked desperately, her lip trembling and her cheeks warm. "Tali could have stayed to take care of me."

Lena appraised Tovi over the fire. "I'll tell you, but it's going to hurt. Are you sure you want to know?"

Tovi nodded.

"Several weeks ago, Silas gave us very specific instructions. Mother and I were supposed to go find Jairus to care for him and Xanthe. However, Silas didn't want Tali to be alone in these dangerous times, just in case Damien sent someone after him. So, Silas told us he would send Eryx to escort Tali back to Adia when the timing was just right. He wanted Tali to remain with us as long as possible, but he wanted him to get back to Adia before the flood, per your request."

Tovi struggled to take in a breath. She replayed her pleas in her mind, how she had begged Silas for this very thing. He was doing what she had asked, and she had ruined it.

Lena went on, "But there was a second plan, a back-up plan. He warned us that you might not listen to him, and there might come a time when you appeared. He said that if that happened, I would have to stay behind, and Tali and Mother would have to flee. He said that no matter how badly you wanted to see Tali, getting your way after blatant disobedience would cause permanent damage.

"When you and the beat-up giant washed ashore, we had to act quickly. Unlike you, we do as Silas says. I had to stay behind to care for you and Eryx. Mother and Tali had to go to Jairus. And I don't think any of us are happy about it. I have been missing Jairus for twenty years, and I was so close to finally being with him. Tali couldn't wait to be with you and . . . What's her name? Ganya? Your refusal to do what Silas said hurt you, me, and everyone else."

Tovi couldn't take any more. The truth hurt so deeply that she feared she would be sick. She stood and walked toward the surf, hugging her arms close to her body in the chilly air. When her toes met the lapping water, she stopped and looked out at the dark sea and the twinkling stars above it. Thoughts of Silas, Tali, strawberries, flames, and water moved through her mind in a painful, chaotic dance.

Lena came to stand next to her. They stood this way for a long time, both deep in thought.

"Silas could have told me I heard it wrong. He could have told me that no one was in the caves to the north. Why didn't he stop me from messing all of this up?"

"I suppose it was a test," Lena responded, just loud enough for Tovi to hear her over the waves. "And I suppose you failed."

Somehow, Tovi couldn't be angry at the blunt response. The truth hurt, but it was still the truth.

They walked along the edge of the water in silence. The moon sparkled in a path that led out to sea, and their hair blew around them on the breeze. Tovi took a deep breath. It was peaceful here.

Lena looped her arm through Tovi's. Her sister. She was walking along the shore with her sister. She thought back to the morning, waking uneasily amid flames on an unknown path. She thought about her desperate need for water to soothe her aching throat. She thought about the flood that had led her to the sea—which led her to her sister.

Lena turned her head to peer at Tovi in the moonlight. "He misses you, too, you know. Tali. He told me. He misses you, too."

Tovi let the tears flow freely down her exhausted face. Lena just kept walking beside her. Neither spoke for the rest of the night. It was the most peace Tovi had felt in a very long time.

CHAPTER 20

Thad's head throbbed painfully, like his brain was repeatedly banging into his skull. He lifted an eyelid as best he could. Unfamiliar, blurred images surrounded him. Were those books? And a fire?

"I'm glad to see you are stirring," a familiar voice cooed from outside of his view.

Damien. He was with the king. This thought sobered him, and he tried to sit up.

"Careful, my boy. Move slowly. You're still recovering from last night. You must have had a very good time."

"How . . . How did I end up here?" he asked and cringed. Even moving his mouth hurt.

A glass clinked in front of him, followed by the sound of pouring water.

King Damien sat in a large cushioned chair a few feet from him. Rhaxma stood behind him. What was she doing here? "Drink up. The water will help."

Thad tried to remember the previous evening. A party at Megara's house. He had only had one glass. He was very careful about this. He always kept a glass in his hand to maintain his cover as a lazy, drunken son living off his family's wealth. But he only sipped, never letting himself drink to the point of dulling his senses. So, how had he become so ill? Something wasn't right.

The water glass was cold in his hand, and he took another drink. He paused with the glass to his lips when a very important detail filled his body with dread. His skin touched the cold glass. He was not wearing gloves.

King Damien gave a low laugh that was close to a growl. "We have something important to discuss, Thaddeus."

He felt sweat pop up on his forehead and lip. He didn't dare speak. He looked up. For the first time, he noticed Megara leering at him from the corner.

"How long have you been hiding that heart from me, young man?"

He swallowed and set the glass down, buying some time as his mind frantically searched for a plan. All was blank. He could not think of a story. He could not come up with a lie. All he had was a soft voice in the back of his head, reminding him to be found.

"All my life, Your Majesty."

Rhaxma looked at the floor, her cheeks red.

"What have you done to try to rid yourself of this abomination?"

"Many things when I was young. But I . . . well, I gave up trying after a while. It seemed best just to cover it with my glove and stop wasting my effort."

King Damien swirled a goblet of wine and studied Thad. The fireplace crackled, and Thad's headache pounded mercilessly.

"Are you loyal to me, Thaddeus?"

The magnitude and simplicity of the question sent chills through Thad's body. "I have been raised to revere no one but you. To honor and respect you before all others. It is the greatest pride of our family that you love us as your own."

Damien smiled and set down his glass. "I'm glad to hear the passion in your voice, my boy. You haven't lived up to your potential, you know. Others think you are a failure. Lazy, good for nothing. But I see potential. I alone believe in you, Thaddeus. If you trust me and do what I say, you could achieve great things. Do you promise to obey me?"

Thad's voice shook. "Yes, Your Majesty."

"Excellent," Damien said. "As soon as you are recovered, you will go below the cloud on a special errand. Are you well enough to stand and look at the map with me?"

Thad rose to his feet, a bit shaky but starting to feel better. He approached the giant table in the center of the library, where a map was unrolled. Rhaxma and Megara joined them at the table.

"This is Adia," Damien explained, gesturing to a green area of the map to the west of the mountain. He touched a dark sapphire that rested on the foothills to the north. "I want you to go north to look for Tali. You will select someone to go with you, someone who will help you navigate below the cloud and find what I am looking for. There are two treasures you are seeking. One of them is my grandson, Tali. The other is the regiment that I sent to look for Tali long before the curtain went up. I fear they are trapped below the cloud with no way to return or communicate. Once you find them, they are yours to command. They could assist you in your search for Tali. Tell these soldiers that the man who finds Tali will move his whole family into a home on the courtyard. Everyone in the regiment will receive an extra year's wage when the mission is accomplished."

Thad pretended to study the map, but his mind was whirling.

"Where was their last known location?" Rhaxma asked.

Damien picked up a blank, gray token from a pile near the map and used a quill to draw a shield on it. He placed the token north of the mountain, near the sapphire. "They were looking for Tali here, but that was quite some time ago. They could have moved on."

After a little more discussion, Thad was sent home to rest.

He took a deep breath, wishing this task had fallen to anyone but him.

CHAPTER 21

The seaside cove was even more beautiful in the daylight than it had been under the moon. Tovi sat at the edge of the beach, picking shells out of the sand and letting the waves wash past her ankles. She held half of a coconut filled with fresh water dipped from a rain barrel. She sipped the sweet water and listened to the sounds of the beach.

Lena came out of the other hut, yawning and stretching in the doorway. She called down to Tovi, "Can you come sit with him a bit? I'll make breakfast, but I don't want to leave him alone for too long. I think he's stirring, and someone should be in there when he wakes up."

Tovi got up and walked toward her.

"And if he tries to get up, don't let him," Lena added.

Tovi wasn't sure anyone could stop Eryx from doing exactly what he pleased, but she nodded and entered.

This second hut was made of greenish-yellow palm fronds. Lena had slept on the ground in a pile of blankets, just in case Eryx took a turn for the worse in the middle of the night. Tovi had slept next door in the older hut, which usually housed both Thomae and Lena. It felt strangely intrusive to sleep in her mother's bed.

Eryx lay on a low bed made of more palm fronds, covered to his bare chest by a thin blanket. His breathing was steady, and he occasionally twisted and turned as if he was trying to wake up.

Tovi looked around. This had been Tali's hut, but there were no personal belongings. He probably didn't have much since he had been living such a nomadic life. What little he had must have been thrown in a pack and taken with him when he ran.

She had been so close in so many ways. They had shared a few moments on this beach, even if she was too weak to interact. And if she had just stayed in Adia, he would have been home soon. She sat on the sand floor and rested her chin on her bent knees. She studied Eryx, noting traces of blood still on his face and neck. There were bruises under his eyes, and his nose looked more crooked than it used to be.

There were rags next to him that were already a bit bloodstained. Tovi dipped one in the last remaining water in her coconut shell and knelt beside him. As carefully as she could, she wiped the blood from below his chin and near his ears.

And that was when she saw it. A patch of green hair in an almost-perfect circle above his right ear. She ran her finger over it and some of the hair around it. In the dim light, she could not be sure, but she didn't think the rest of his hair was navy blue. She grabbed a lock of her own hair. Still blue. Eryx's hair had always mimicked hers. So, what were these new colors? She ran her hand over the short bristles again. Brown with that one green spot.

Then, she noticed his eyes were open. They were not the dark brown with a little purple star that she was accustomed to seeing in his face. They were light. Maybe green? She couldn't quite tell. And they had little speckles in them, almost like freckles.

"How many times will we have to nurse each other back to health?" Tovi asked with a forced laugh.

Eryx didn't smile.

"I suppose you want to know what happened and where we are," she continued, trying to fill the awkward silence.

"I already know," he said, his voice hoarse.

"How?"

"Silas," he rasped. "He came to me. Spoke to me. Can I have some water?"

"What do you mean, he came to you?"

"Water first. Please."

Tovi fumed as she walked out to the rain barrel and filled a new coconut shell. How dare Silas come to Eryx and not speak to her as well? When she re-entered the hut, Eryx was sitting up, his back to the wall.

"Silas came to you?" she repeated, handing him the coconut.

He drank deeply and nodded. "It was like a dream. I don't know how else to describe it. He told me what happened, what you had done. And he told me what I need to do next."

"Which is?"

He didn't answer and kept his eyes averted.

Tovi went a different direction. "Your hair and eyes. They are different."

"We talked about that, too," Eryx said, a lightness in his face that Tovi had never seen. "He's been after me for a while. Nearly dying seemed like a good time to give in. I see you haven't." He gave a pointed look at her hair.

"I always thought that someday, when I met Adwin, all of my questions would be answered. I thought it would be easier," she admitted.

Eryx took another long drink of water. "Definitely not easier. But better, somehow."

"Better? I'm not sure about that." Their gaze held for a long moment before Tovi looked away, uncomfortable. "I'd better tell Lena you're awake."

Tovi rose to go, but his hand on her wrist stopped her. She looked back.

"Give in, Tovi. Stop trying so hard to do things on your own. I feel so much better." He ended this speech with a deep, hacking cough.

She raised an eyebrow. "You sure sound better."

He laughed, which made him cough harder.

Lena's voice came from the doorway. "You shouldn't over-exert yourself. You've been pretty banged up." She handed him a new coconut of water. She set a plate of cooked fish and chopped fruit beside him. "You need to eat something."

Eryx's eyes lingered on Tovi for another beat before turning toward the newcomer. "You're Lena."

"I am."

"Silas told me."

"Good. Saves me from explaining."

Tovi looked between the two of them, feeling left-out and out-numbered. "What else did Silas say?"

They said nothing. Lena's face was made of stone, and Eryx shifted uneasily. Tovi could hear the surf outside and birds cawing as they soared over the water. Her companions' silence told her everything she needed to know—they were keeping secrets from her.

Tovi stood and threw a towel against the far wall before marching out of the hut. She walked across the soft sand toward the edge of the water and sat down, not caring that the waves washed up to her waist and that her clothes were soaked. Her anger burned hotter than the sun on her shoulders.

She dug a shell from the sand and heaved it as far as she could toward the horizon.

She heard splashing footsteps, but she had no desire to speak to Lena. She kept her face turned toward the sea, wanting to look as uninviting as possible.

He spoke to them, but not to you. After all you've been through . . . He chose to speak to them and not you. And he told them to keep it a secret from you.

The splashes grew closer, and the person sat beside her in the surf. "You wanted to talk," Silas said.

Tovi's face snapped toward him.

Silas matched her stare. "You completely disregarded what I asked of you in Adia. You didn't trust me to bring Tali back in my own timing. You refused to go home when I told you that you were going the wrong way. I gave you water when you asked for it, and you used it to forge your own path. And now, *you're* angry with *me?*"

She threw another shell. She felt childish and foolish, but she was too angry to say so.

"I am confident Lena and Eryx will do what I told them to do, which is all about protecting you. I have instructions for you, too, if you're ready to listen."

Her ears perked. "Yes, I'm ready. I'll do whatever you ask," she said, images of adventure and lofty tasks floating through her mind. Finally, she would join Tali out there, doing something heroic and good.

"Once again, I have three tasks for you. First, don't stray from this cove. You're to stay put and recover your strength. Lena may show you where to find some things in the forest, but don't go any further than where she says. Second, learn from your mistakes. Learn from Lena. Learn from Eryx. They both have quite a bit of wisdom you could benefit from. Third, be still. Let go of this anger. Calm yourself. Wait patiently for me to give you a different task."

"Stay, learn, be still. Those aren't new instructions," Tovi said, so disappointed she wanted to cry.

Silas grinned at her. She did not smile back. "This will be good for you, Tovi. I know it's not what you want, but I won't trust you with something bigger until I know you can do the smaller things. Now," he said, no longer smiling, "we need to talk about the last couple of days."

She cringed, picturing her tantrum in Adia, her stubbornness in the fire tunnel, her attempt to escape through the river, and her near-death in the flood. "Do we have to?"

Silas used his finger to draw three symbols in the sand: a snake, a crown, and flames. They were simpler versions of three of King Damien's marks.

"Which of these lessons made you behave the way you did?"

"Not the crown. I never earned that symbol. Not the snake. I didn't lie. It must have been the flames. It was anger that made me do it."

"Wrong. None of them *made* you do it. It was a trick question."

"That wasn't fair."

"Those marks can't force you to do anything, but the things you learned on the mountain have turned into voices in your mind. These voices and thoughts can tempt you, make you want to do things the wrong way. You're right that you never earned your crown, which proves how flawed Damien's system can be. The crown is all about putting someone first in your life, idolizing them, doing everything you can to serve them and make them happy. You have put Tali in that place in your life. The color of your hair proves it. Damien's symbol didn't register on you because of one great error in his design. No one on the mountain taught you to put him there. You did it on your own. For the purpose of these lessons, let's pretend you had all seven marks. We have to undo the lesson of Adoration in your heart, even if you never earned the crown on your back.

"Let's try this again. When you ran from Adia, which of these lessons was whispering in your ear?"

Tovi considered them again. "I still think it was the flames."

"You are sort of right. It was another trick question."

Tovi grunted in frustration.

"All three played a part. You put Tali in the center of your life, instead of me." Silas touched the crown. "You let your anger consume you." He moved his finger to the flames. "And you tried to control your own circumstances, rather than obey what I said." He touched the snake.

"I thought the snake was about lying."

"It's the symbol for control. People often lie to try to control others. They manipulate them with their words. But there are other aspects to control. Every time you take matters into your own hands, with no regard for what I have told you to do, you sink a little further into Damien's idea of control.

"Damien wants everyone to believe his lessons are neat and tidy, well-defined and easy to understand. The truth is they are messy. They constantly overlap and combine in terrible ways. You can't fully understand prosperity without perfection, or power without control and Damien's version of wisdom.

"Your great task while you are here is working with me and the others to see how the marks are still speaking to you and what happens when you listen."

A wave washed up past Tovi's legs and erased the sandy marks. Tovi wished it could be that easy to get rid of what she had learned on Mount Damien.

CHAPTER 22

BiBi never wanted to leave the enchanting treetops that had so quickly become home. She had never felt as free as when she was climbing and exploring to her heart's content. When she returned to the cottage nestled in the branches, Ganya fussed over her and forced delicious pastries into her hand. Curious villagers popped in to bring gifts and ask how the newcomer was recovering from her frightful escapade. She felt settled and safe and wanted.

All through the months of Damien's game, when the Council of Masters had come to Adia looking for their pawns, BiBi had spent time in these trees, wishing she could stay. She did a lot of watching during that time. She watched fathers teaching sons and daughters how to bake bread. She watched old women gather around a quilt, their needles flying as they gabbed. She watched the owner of the general store slip sweets into children's hands and watched teens climb through the trees in packs, racing, laughing, and discovering their world.

She had wanted so badly to join them, to learn how to be free. And here she was, trapped in Adia, the whole forest hers to explore. She never knew she could be so happy. The flood had been scary and unexpected, but she was thrilled to have an excuse to stay for a while.

After her wet arrival, she stayed up most of the evening talking on the porch with Ganya. She was dry by then, but she kept the blanket around her. They rocked in the rocking chairs, sipping hot tea, while Ganya asked about her growing-up years, her family, and how she had come to be in

Adia. And the strangest and most wonderful part was that she actually seemed to care about BiBi's answers. It had been one day, and she didn't know if she had ever loved anyone as thoroughly as she loved Ganya.

The little bed hadn't been quite what she was used to, but it was comfortable and safe. She woke to the smell of eggs and bacon, and tea during sunrise was just as beautiful as it had been during sunset. She knew she was expected at Silas' house at some point that morning, but no one seemed to be in any hurry.

When she was fully fed and had climbed up to his home, she didn't know how to announce herself. There was no door. Should she knock on the wall? Should she walk in? She settled for calling, "Hello!" into the opening.

"Come in," he replied.

She stepped inside, and as her eyes adjusted, she gasped. "It's just like the throne room. You painted the throne room."

"Yes."

She twirled slowly, the colors and faces overwhelming but beautiful. There were flowers and animals, people and city streets. She saw scenes from both Adia and Mount Damien, along with places she had never been.

He was quiet as she examined the whole room, but she could feel him watching her. She pondered it all, inch by inch, wishing she understood. The sheer beauty of his work made her cry. When she finally turned back to him, she had to wipe the cloudy streaks off her face.

"Tell me about your tears. What's happening in your mind and heart?"

She wasn't sure she could ever find the words for the feeling she had inside. It was yearning mixed with hope, peace mixed with something exhilarating. There were so many opposites racing through her mind that she didn't know how to answer his question. But she was so very happy, there in that studio with him in the trees.

His face was pure kindness, and his eyes were soft. "I'm so glad you're here, BiBi, no matter how you got here. I love you."

She hung her head and cried so hard her shoulders shook. She felt ready to disintegrate and fall to the floor, so overwhelmed that this man could love her. And yesterday, he had said he knew who sent her. What else did he know? Every mistake? Every terrible deed she had done? They paraded through her memory, and she thought she might be sick.

He pulled his stool up close to her and took her hand. He didn't say anything more, and she was glad. She just wanted to be there with him as the feelings flowed out. It was healing and peaceful and exactly what she needed.

She hiccuped and swiped at her face one more time. "So, you know why I'm here?"

"Yes, better than you do."

"You know it's not just Damien? It's Rhaxma and Megara, too."

He half-smiled and raised an amused eyebrow. "All hail the Three Queens."

He knew. Somehow, he knew. "And you still love me."

He squeezed her hands. "More than you could ever know." He let go, reaching for something on a table behind him.

He held up two small jars of paint, one gray and one white. Her blood went cold. All good feelings fled swiftly, leaving only fear and dread.

He looked at the jars, and then he looked back at her. "You have some difficult decisions to make, but you don't have to make them yet. This flood has bought you some precious time. Neither Damien nor Rhaxma and Megara can get to you here. You can sort out what you really want, who you really want to follow, where you want to place your hope and trust. If you choose to stay here, we have much work to do. If you choose to go back . . . Well, I will be heartbroken, but my love for you will not dim. Not even by a little."

His eyes staring back into hers were so green. They made her think of the trees outside. They made her think of peace. And rest. And being alive. "I want to stay forever."

"I know."

He placed the paints on his window ledge. "You know where they are. It is your decision to make. I hope you won't take them, but you know where they are."

CHAPTER 23

"How could you keep this from me?" Rhaxma asked.

From their top-floor terrace, her brother looked out over the city, eating his lunch and not responding.

"Answer me," she said, slamming her fist on the table.

"I was embarrassed."

"Once you knew about the heart searches, you should have said something."

"Why? So you could turn me in?"

She sighed. What a mess. "I wouldn't have, if I had known. But Megara saw it. I had to turn you in once she knew."

She took a long drink and stared into her cup. Her mind mulled over the question she had wanted to ask since she had seen her brother's ungloved hand in the sea of unconscious people.

"Have you ever met him?"

"Who?"

"Adwin."

He stopped mid-bite and wouldn't look at her. His silence told her the answer.

"How long? How often?"

He looked down at the ground. He opened his mouth a few times, starting to say something, but then closed it again. He sat back in his seat and ran his hands through his shaggy orange hair.

"What have you been hiding, Thad? Tell me right now, so we can fix it."

He leaned forward, his forearms on his knees, his hands clasped.

His misery heightened her fears. Not only did he have the heart, but there were more secrets, secrets he didn't want to share even with his sister.

"There's one thing I need you to understand," he said. "I love you. I love Mother and Father and Simeon and Andi. I loved Leeto. My loyalty to Adwin doesn't take away how much I love all of you."

"How long?" she demanded.

"Almost my whole life. I don't see him as often as I'd like. He pops in and out, never stays long."

As she looked at her brother, a memory bubbled up. Arguments between Thad and their father about being seen so often in the Bottom Rung.

"We thought you were visiting the pubs," she said weakly. "All those nights, and all the times Father yelled at you. You weren't at the pubs and brothels, were you?"

He shook his head.

"Where were you?"

"With the resistance."

"The resistance?" she mocked. "The resistance? Resisting *what*? The kingdom that has given us everything?"

"We follow Adwin."

"The one who lost? The one who abandoned us? *Really?*" She stood to refill her glass from a cart in the corner. As she poured, she asked, "Who else is in that club? Do I know anyone? Mother? Father?" She laughed at the thought.

She turned back to Thad. His silence was ominous and chilled her dark humor. She pulled a chair directly in front of him. "Who? Tell me now."

She watched the light in his eyes change. They went from soft and pleading to hard and resolute. He crossed his arms. "Xanthe."

Ice ran through her veins. She never would have guessed Xanthe, the master, the Council Member, the queen-to-be. The fugitive.

"Does this mean you know where Jairus is?"

"He took Xanthe somewhere east of here. I don't know a specific location."

"And the other heirs?"

He fidgeted with his cuff.

"You know more."

He looked pained, but only for a moment. "Our leader, a girl named Meira, took Tali south to the sea. I believe they are still there."

Rhaxma saw the king's map in her mind's eye with the dark sapphire sitting on the caves in the North. Tali had gone the opposite direction. And Jairus' ring belonged in the East. It wasn't much, but it was far more than the king—or Calix—knew.

"You will tell me everything from now on. Understood?"

"Since when does the little sister get to give the orders?"

"You don't know what you're messing with. You've never taken life seriously, and now you're in a position where a wrong move can get you killed or bring dishonor to our entire family. You're not playing your little games with the 'resistance' or getting drunk with Simeon and Andi anymore. You're the commander of the king's forces below the cloud. Has that sunk in yet?"

"Yes, Rhax," he said firmly. "I get it."

"If you fail, our family will pay for it. I understand His Majesty far better than you do, and I know how everything works in that palace. You will tell me everything, and I will tell you what to do. *Everything*. Understood?"

"Understood."

"No more secrets?"

"No more secrets."

She stood, leaving most of her lunch untouched. She kissed Thad's forehead and left the house. She went straight to the Bottom Rung and climbed up to the second floor of the Jolly Barrel. A few of her heart recruits had worked around the clock to turn one of the apartments into their new base of operations. One of them, with bright pink hair and a patched apron, was sweeping the landing when Rhaxma arrived.

Two others were in the upstairs apartment painting on one of the walls. During the heart checks, she had learned that Galen and Lux used to be painters in the palace, specializing in landscapes. A map wasn't exactly a landscape, but they still fit the bill for a very important task.

She had set them to work immediately painting a giant map on the wall. Neither of them had ever left the mountain before, and she had to rely on her own memory of Damien's map, which she sketched for them.

Standing back and looking at their work, she was impressed. It may not be fully accurate, but it would be close enough. And while it didn't really matter, the end result was beautiful. They had painted trees and water, flowers and mountains. It was much more than she had expected.

She grabbed a piece of paper and tore it into four pieces. One of the artists—she couldn't keep their names straight—watched her while the other kept working.

She wrote the names of the heirs, one on each piece of paper, and glanced around the room. "Lyra!" she yelled.

The pink-haired servant popped her head in the door a moment later. "Find me a hammer and some nails."

When she returned with the tools, Rhaxma approached the map.

"I beg your pardon, ma'am," one of the artists said. "But the paint is still wet."

She swung the hammer, anyway, making both Lux and Galen cringe.

When she was done, three of the names were nailed to their most recent location. Tali in the South, Tovi in the West, and Jairus in the East.

She stood back and pondered the map, holding the last name in her hand. Where could Lena be?

CHAPTER 24

Tovi didn't sleep well, struggling to settle her mind that replayed her conversations with Silas. She rose with a heavy feeling in her chest, overwhelmed by the amount of work she had to do to rid herself of the lessons from the mountain and the dark sludge in her veins.

Stay, learn, and be still. It sounded so easy. So why was it so hard? She rolled out of bed, seeking a distraction from the questions that had no easy answers.

Lena looked up when Tovi appeared and squinted in the bright morning light. "Good, you're up. Come help me."

Tovi followed Lena into Eryx's hut.

"Let's get you some fresh air," Lena said to Eryx, who looked embarrassed as they helped him up.

With both girls' shoulders to steady him, he rose shakily to his feet. Tovi glimpsed his back. His marks were gone. She smiled, blinking back sudden tears. She was happy for him, and it reminded her of the mess of marks on Silas' back and the pain he endured for each of them. She shook her head. She didn't know why it worked that way, but she was so thankful the marks were gone.

Lena and Tovi led Eryx outside, and he sat with his back propped against the shaggy wall. He breathed deeply and looked out at the water, looking far more relaxed than Tovi had ever seen him.

Tovi turned back to her companions. "What's for—"

Lena handed a plate of fish to Tovi. She crinkled her nose. It was always the same.

When they were done eating, Lena walked down the beach, a fishing spear in one hand. Tovi watched her go, unsure of what to say to Eryx now that they were alone.

While drying the dishes, Tovi glanced at him. The bruises on his face were turning a nasty purple. He looked up, and their eyes connected. Both looked away quickly.

"I'm sorry," Tovi said, focusing on a plate that she wiped with a towel. It was already dry, but it gave her something to do other than looking at Eryx.

"For what?"

"You know for what."

"For trying to use me, or for nearly killing me?"

She looked up from the plate. He was smiling. He actually had the audacity to joke about it, to make light of all that had happened. She didn't answer his taunt and went back to drying the already-dry plate. She knew her cheeks were burning red, but she wasn't sure if it was fury or humiliation, or both.

"You know this is why, right?" he asked, squinting up at her.

"Why what?"

"Why we have to keep things from you. You're going to have to stop letting everything make you so angry."

"That's nice, coming from a Master of *Power*." She threw down the plate and towel, turning her back to him and looking for a reason to walk away. There was nothing, and she stood awkwardly, having nowhere to go.

"I wasn't a Master of Anger or Temper," he said quietly. "I was Master of Hate, of Wrath. It's different and deeper. It made me want to destroy anyone who came near me. It was a forest fire, out of control and consuming. Your tantrums are different. They explode and burn out quickly, but everything around you is singed. You may not mean to, but you hurt people. You don't destroy them, but you leave them burned. You do this to yourself and everyone around you. And worst of all, you do it to Silas. All the time."

"You think you know me so well," she said, turning back to him, eyes narrowed. She was filled with two warring emotions: anger that he thought he could say things like that to her and shame because she knew they were true.

He shrugged. "I've watched you. I know how you work. Instead of getting mad, you could ask me how to deal with it, how to get rid of it. I know better than most. I want to help you."

Silas' voice from behind her made her jump. "You'd be wise to listen to him. But for now, come with me."

They left Eryx and wandered along the sand. The ocean waves left foam on their feet, and Silas bent down to pick up shells, tossing them into the waves.

"So, what do you need to say to me?" she asked, frustrated by the silence. Frustrated by everything.

"A promise."

Tovi stopped and brushed hair out of her face.

"I don't know why you always expect an angry lecture," Silas said. "I don't have one for you. But my promise is this: the more time we spend together, the less sludge in your body, the less you will explode."

That sounded nice, if she was being honest. To not rage and fall apart all the time, to not defy Silas and go her own way. "The sludge does this to me?"

"That's a complicated question," he said, putting his hands in his pockets. She watched the breeze flutter in his hair. "Let's say it's a partnership. You mostly do this to yourself, but the sludge and the lessons that go with it make it both easier to mess up and harder to get better. When the sludge is gone, you could still fly into a fury, but you probably won't because you'll be thinking more clearly."

He held her hand and wiped away the little bit that was oozing out.

"I'll still get mad sometimes when the sludge is gone?"

He grinned. "I need you to stay feisty. I'm not going to put out the fire in you. I'm going to help you channel it into good."

"Good can come of this?"

"Good can come from anything. Now, show me which symbol you think was at work just now when you got so angry with Eryx."

She used her finger to draw flames in the sand. "Easy."

"I'm not so sure."

"It was anger. You said so yourself when you asked me which symbol was at work when I was *angry* with Eryx. How could it be anything other than the flames?"

Silas traced the flames with his toe. "The mark of power is definitely linked to great, big shows of anger, but it's different at its core. As you yelled at Eryx just now, were you feeling hatred toward him? Did you want to crush him and subdue him so that you could have your way?"

"I didn't *yell* at him."

Silas closed his eyes, his mouth pressed into a straight line as he sighed.

"No, I didn't want to crush him. He just made me so . . . "

"Angry? Yes. So, let's talk about where that came from. What irritated you so much about what he was saying?"

"He thought he knew me."

"And why is that so bad?"

Tovi didn't want to say it.

Silas squeezed her shoulders again. "Come on. Better out than in."

She reached down, picked up a shell, and heaved it as hard as she could into the waves. "I don't like who I have become. And I . . . " She couldn't find the words and stared out into the sea, trying to find a way to say what was burdening her heart.

Silas drew unbalanced scales in the sand. "You're not battling Power. You're battling perfection. Perfection tells you that you have to be, well, perfect. It's that voice in your head that makes you ashamed of all the ways you are imperfect and pushes you to constantly improve or find a way to mask your faults. It calls you a failure and an imposter just for being human and who I made you to be. When these imperfections are discovered by other people, perfection tells you that you have two choices: hide or fight. Your personality leans toward the fight, so you get nasty when your pride has been damaged."

Somehow, when Silas said those things, it all seemed so foolish. He was right. She felt foolish. And stupid. And weak. All because of what the voice said when she wasn't absolutely perfect. And it was so much easier to throw things and stomp away than it was to be still. Why was it so easy to listen to that voice? Why had she fallen so easily for those lies? Sitting with Silas, she saw it all in a different light. So, what would it be like when Silas wasn't right by her side? Could she recognize those thoughts for the poison they were? Or would she fall for them again and again and again?

"You'll fall for them again," Silas said.

"I really hate it when you answer my questions that I never said out loud."

Silas grinned. "I just want to be realistic. You will fall for them again, but not every time. You'll fall for them less and less until one day you realize that more often than not, you recognize the voice for the liar it is and banish those thoughts out of your mind."

"How do I get there?"

"You spend a lot of time with me, and you believe me when I tell you that you are Tovi Tivka, the girl I painted on a stone wall long ago. You are the person I made you to be, and it's not for you to judge if I was right or wrong in my design. My kind of perfect is nothing like what they think it is. It's mine, and I get the last word."

"And those words are?"

"You're strong, smart, and fierce. You're loyal and adventurous."

"Rhaxma focused on the outside. You're focusing on the inside."

Because you are ugly, Tovi. That is why he is focused on the inside. It's because the outside is ugly and of no use. He would have called you beautiful if—

"What is that other voice whispering in your ear right this very second?"

Tears sprang into Tovi's eyes.

"It's going to be difficult, but you have to start recognizing that voice so that you can fight it."

There was pain in her hand, and she looked down to see a steady stream of black sludge dripping onto the sand.

CHAPTER 25

BiBi used to love stretching out in her silk sheets before rising and attending to her business as a master. Now, she stretched beneath a homemade quilt and smiled. Everything about Adia was so cozy and warm. She squinted toward the rays of light that flooded her window and took a deep inhale. It smelled like water and life and peace that she had never known before being swept here.

There was a loud crash in the kitchen that startled her out of her dreamlike waking, and she sat straight up in bed. An excited exclamation from Ganya sounded happy rather than scared, and a deep, male voice answered. She couldn't make out any of the words, but they were chattering excitedly.

The man's voice came nearer, and she heard, "I'll put my things down and tell you the whole story."

"Wait—" Ganya called, but before she could finish the warning, the door to the bedroom swung open and hit the opposite wall.

He was the most incredible creature she had ever seen. Long, navy blue hair was pulled up into a knot on top of his head, and patchy stubble grew on his suntanned face. He was tall and lean, with the wild aura of a man who belonged outdoors. His clothes were dirty and torn in several places. There was a brown stain on his left arm that was probably blood, and there was a cut under one of his startled brown eyes. He looked just how a man from Adia ought to look, she thought.

She knew him right away by those colors. Tovi's brother. Another of His Majesty's heirs.

Ganya squeezed in past dumbfounded Tali, looking between the silent two. "I am so sorry, dear. I tried to stop him, which never works. I'll make some breakfast. You get dressed and come out. I'll make him wait to tell his tales. I'm sure you'll want to hear them, too." Ganya pushed him out of the room and shut the door.

Their voices still carried into her room.

"Who was . . . Why was she . . . What's going on?"

BiBi realized she had been holding her breath. She took in a deep gulp of air and tried to steady her frantic heart. She dressed quickly and dug in a trunk for her padding. She hadn't worn it since her arrival because no one seemed to change their shape in Adia. She held up the hip pads. They would fit beneath the loose cotton dress that once was Tovi's. The chest padding most certainly would not. One without the other would be a strange, unbalanced look, to be sure. She threw them all back in the trunk and slammed it shut. If only she had her gowns and jewels from home.

There was no mirror in the room, and she looked around desperately for something she could use to check her reflection. There was nothing in the window but vines. The knicknacks on her shelves weren't shiny. Then she spotted something promising. Some little, pink flowers smiled from a glass jar. She grabbed at it, momentarily relieved, but her reflection was so warped, it hardly helped. She had to settle for running her fingers through her tangles and pinching her cheeks.

You silly girl. Didn't you get a good look at him? Why would a man like him even look at a girl like you? Save your primping. It won't do any good.

BiBi shook her head to quiet the voice that had plagued her for as long as she could remember. Sometimes, the voice sounded like Damien; sometimes, it sounded more like her brother or father. Occasionally, it even sounded like herself. It always kept her grounded and reminded her that she was a fraud.

As she timidly walked out, Ganya served scrambled eggs onto plates and handed two to Tali. He looked up as BiBi approached, and she suddenly didn't know what to do with her hands. She crossed her arms to keep them from fumbling at her side.

"Come outside with us," Ganya said. "Bring the tea."

Ganya followed Tali out onto the porch, and BiBi carefully carried all three mugs. Standing in front of Tali, she had no hand to accept the plate he offered, and he didn't have a hand free to take his tea. They went through a silent shuffling dance for a moment before Ganya clucked, set her own plate down, and took the tea from BiBi.

"Tell us *everything*," Ganya said.

"Maybe some introductions first?" he replied. He turned his gaze to BiBi, and she wondered if it was possible to melt. "I'm Tali. I live here. Or at least, I usually do."

"I'm BiBi. I'm from Mount Damien."

His fork froze in front of his mouth.

Ganya continued for her. "BiBi was almost swept away in the flood. That's how she came to be staying here. She washed up against the base of Silas' tree."

"But the river flows southeast," Tali said.

"And?" Ganya asked.

"You must have been upriver if you were swept here."

BiBi's insides squirmed. "I left Mount Damien before the flood. I hadn't found a place to settle yet," she said, searching for words. "When I got to Adia, I was too scared to talk to anyone. I kept going. I found a beautiful spot up the river with four trees that grow over it and tangle in each other. I was going to stay there when the water picked me up and took me with it."

"You found the hideaway," Tali said, his muscles untensing just a bit. "I used to go there all the time. Well, I'm glad you're not hurt. What did you do on the mountain?"

"I . . . I was a master."

He stopped eating completely this time, setting his fork on his plate. "And you chose to leave?"

"Clearly, she chose to leave," Ganya said. "Now tell us where you have been and how on earth you got back in the middle of a flood."

He rocked, still eyeing BiBi. She couldn't tell if he was curious or suspicious or both.

"It's a long story, and I can't tell you much. I've been all over the place, have seen all sorts of people. I even got a glimpse of Tovi."

"Tovi?" Ganya repeated hopefully.

Tali nodded as he rocked, his mug hugged between his palms. "Only for a moment. She was in rough shape, but Silas promised she would be fine. I had to run for it. Silas showed me a new way into Adia. We had to circle all the way north into the desert and then west until we came to a narrow land bridge from the desert into the mountains to the north of here. Once we were in the mountains, we climbed into the trees and made our way here, above the flood. It was slow-moving, going limb to limb. Much slower than when we were riding horses on the ground."

BiBi's heart raced. If he was able to get in, she would be able to get out. She had thought she was trapped, but apparently, she was not. The sinking disappointment was almost too much to bear.

"Horses?" Ganya asked.

"You will love them. Big animals that let you ride on their backs. They roam in the wilds east of the mountain, but they liked the desert just fine." He took a drink of his tea. "So, a master. A master of what?"

She had hoped he would drop it. She took a sip of tea, unable to meet his beautiful eyes. "Prosperity."

He raised his eyebrows and grinned. "And you chose to leave, to live in the wilderness? You must not be very good at it."

"At what?"

"Prosperity. You didn't master it. You left it."

"Tali Tivka," Ganya reproached. She smacked him on the shoulder and gathered the dirty plates, taking them inside.

BiBi tingled with uncomfortable awareness that she was alone with Tali. She rocked nervously. "Want to know something that makes it even more ridiculous?" she asked, looking for anything to fill the silence.

Tali nodded.

"I wasn't just *a* Master of Prosperity. I was *the* Master of Prosperity. Damien chose me for the Council of Masters."

Tali's eyes roamed her face. He seemed to be considering something deeply, lost in his own thoughts. Then, more quietly than before, he said, "Council of Masters."

"Yes."

"Then you must be acquainted with my sister."

There was a long, heavy pause. BiBi hated herself more in that moment than she ever had before. She had marked Tovi with the heavy symbol of prosperity, teaching her to fill the emptiness in her life with money and things. "Yes," she whispered.

He nodded. "But you're here now."

She was overwhelmed with a longing to tell him everything, for him to know her soul and her story. She wanted him to know that she wasn't a terrible person, to explain all that had led them here. She opened her mouth, but words wouldn't come.

"Have you learned your way around yet?" he asked.

She shook her head, flustered by the quick change of subject.

"Come on. I'll show you."

She followed Tali through the trees as he pointed out homes and told stories about their neighbors. Each treehouse was so different, and she loved the odd shapes and lack of right angles. Some were lopsided boxes sitting on wide branches. Others encircled entire trunks. Most were one story, but some were two or even three levels high. There was no glass in the windows, but some were covered in curtains. Few of the houses had doors, but several had gates or half doors to keep small children inside. Tali knew every name of every person, and they all called out to him excitedly, welcoming him home.

She heard the sounds of a market coming to life, and moments later, they passed through a curtain of leaves onto what Tali announced to be "Main Street." She had been here before, during Damien's game, but she had stayed hidden. Now she was right in the glorious midst of it all. BiBi wanted to take in every quaint detail. They seemed to have every trade that she could have found on the mountain, just much less refined. A weaver sat at his loom in one store, surrounded by cloth for sale. A general store had a barrel outside with a sign that read "Last Parsnips until the Waters Lower." There were baskets of bread, crates of candles, and sides of meat and sausages hanging from hooks.

She pulled a coin from her pocket. "What can I get for this?" she asked.

"Keep your mountain money." Tali grinned. "It's no good here. We barter."

She blinked at him, confused.

"We trade. And sometimes we just give. Watch this." He led her into the general store and called a greeting to the old storekeeper, who brushed his hands on his apron before shaking Tali's hand with enthusiasm. "Tali! Welcome home. And who's this?"

"This is BiBi, Ganya's newest project." He grinned at her.

"Welcome, Miss BiBi. What are you looking for today?"

Tali scooped up a handful of nails from a box on a shelf. "What do you want for these?"

The storekeeper shook his head. "You know I still owe you for fixing that leak in my roof. Take them."

Tali nodded his thanks and led BiBi back out into the dappled sunshine.

She was dumbfounded. "He let you have them, with no payment?"

"Didn't you hear him? I fixed a leak in his roof about a year ago."

She shook her head in disbelief. "So, what happens if you needed something and hadn't done a favor for him?"

"I'd bring him something of equal value, or I'd offer to help him in some way. Or he'd let me have them, and I'd make up for it in the future when he needed something."

"Doesn't everyone go out of business?"

"No." He laughed. "It'll take you a while to get used to it. The valley is very different from the mountain. We have everything we need right here—and plenty of it. We all do our part and take care of each other."

She sighed and smiled, and she caught him giving her a close look. "What?" she asked.

"You really love it here. You like it better than the mountain."

She nodded.

"Come on. There's more to see."

She followed him out, and they walked along branches and bridges, down Main Street, and up into the canopy beyond, chatting freely like old friends. He was so easy to talk to. Joy and curiosity seemed to shine from him like the sun, and she secretly studied his relaxed saunter and quick-to-laugh reactions to her stories. He seemed to be over his suspicion of her motives, and she inwardly cringed with guilt. If only he knew.

They climbed past all of the established homes and into a vast expanse of untouched leaves and limbs. They crossed a bowed branch that was just like a bridge and climbed up a nearby rope ladder before coming to an opening in the canopy. Perched high in a gigantic cedar tree, a new house was taking shape. A platform wrapped in a semicircle around half of the trunk. Some limbs supported the platform, and others provided a natural roof, and the branches between them had been cut away.

"It's mine," he said. "Silas told me to build here. Wait until you see the view."

She followed him up another rope ladder. When she was close to the top, he reached down and pulled her up by the hand.

Once she was on the platform, she gasped. She had a panoramic view of the valley, with the mountains in the distance and the rest of the canopy rising to just about her waist. There were a few other trees as tall as this one, rising up like weeds out of the forest. But most were shorter, and it made for a spectacular sight.

He gave her a tour of the platform, showing her where walls and railings would go, and pointing out the kitchen, the space for the fireplace, and everything else he had planned. She listened, but she didn't hear much of what he said. As he excitedly chattered about his building project, she had her own private, inner conversation.

Why did her heart beat so loudly in her ears, and why was it so hard to stop looking at his face? She had known many handsome boys on the mountain, and she had little romances here and there. But none of them were like this blood-racing, heart-pounding, I-would-do-anything-just-to-make-you-happy, all-consuming longing to stay close to him.

She hadn't known him long enough to care so much. She barely knew him at all. So, what was it? She studied his profile. He was explaining something about the design of the staircase that he would build.

Maybe it was because he was so different from every other man she had ever known. Everything from his long hair to his cuts and bruises shouted recklessness, adventure, danger, and passion. He belonged in this wild landscape that had so captured her heart.

That must be it. She had fallen in love with Adia the first moment she had stepped foot here. And now she had met the man who embodied Adia in every way.

She loved Adia, not Tali. She wasn't a fool who could fall in love the moment she saw a man, without really knowing him. It was just her love for this place. Surely.

So why did she ache at the thought of leaving him? Silas had offered the paint. And there was a way out through the trees to the north and through the desert. She could accomplish her mission.

She could leave today. She could keep the Three Queens' army from descending and destroying this place.

She looked at the sparkle in his eyes and wanted to cry. How could she leave this place—this wonderful, wild place?

They sat with their legs over the edge of the platform, and the cool breeze was peaceful. "When did you find out that Silas was Adwin?" she asked, surprised by her own boldness and blushing a bit.

He brushed his fingers through his hair, tucking a stray bit back into the bundle, and looked out over the trees. "I think part of me always knew, but he was pretty blunt with me a while back."

"He just told you?"

"He had his reasons. He had a job for me to do, and it was time for me to know."

"What was the job?"

"Can't tell you. Sorry." He looked at her and grinned. "You remind me of my sister when you frown like that."

BiBi laughed. "I liked Tovi. I think we could have been good friends if we had longer together."

They talked for a long time. BiBi pried into his life in Adia and his friendship with Silas, never tiring of his voice and his stories. He asked questions in return, and she was hesitant at first, embarrassed to speak of her life as a master and all the things she had done. His kindness changed all of that. He listened and nodded with warmth rather than judgment.

When the sun beat down on them from directly overhead, Tali walked her back to the house in the willow so they could join Ganya for lunch.

Ganya was sitting on the porch with Silas when they arrived, and she looked between BiBi and Tali with a hint of a smile.

They pulled up two more chairs and talked over their servings of warm bread, cold turkey, and berries. Every time BiBi stole a glance toward Tali, she had to remind herself that she wasn't part of his future. She must leave and fulfill her mission or risk the threat of Rhaxma's army destroying this beautiful place and these wonderful people.

CHAPTER 26

No matter how bored Tovi would get staying in this little cove, she promised herself with new determination that she would do what Silas had commanded. Stay on the beach. Learn to recognize the voices in her head. Be still and slow to anger. Stay. Learn. Be Still.

While cleaning up after their meal, Tovi asked, "What should I do?"

Lena looked up from the knife she was scrubbing. "What do you mean?"

"I don't like sitting around. Put me to work. What can I do?"

Lena looked over Tovi for a moment and said, "All right, come with me." She handed Tovi another knife and led her to the edge of the jungle. "Silas gives us everything we need. We don't need to empty the earth like Damien does with the mines. We don't need to travel far into the unknown to fill our homes with unnecessities. We have fish and shells and so much more in the sea. Everything else can be found here in the trees, and this one"—she slapped her hand against a smooth trunk—"is our best friend." Tovi looked up at the curving trunk that exploded in green, spiky fronds at the top with coconuts clustered beneath.

Lena showed Tovi how to shimmy up the trunk with her knife between her teeth. It wasn't so different from climbing the trees in Adia. It took no time at all for Tovi to get the hang of it. Her body still ached from her battle with the flood, but she relished the feel of stretching her limbs and pushing herself to the limit.

When the girls reached the tops of neighboring trees, Lena showed Tovi how to lock her knees around the trunk, identify a ready coconut, remove the right ones without upsetting the others, and drop them without breaking them. When they were back on the ground, Lena cut one open and handed it to Tovi. "Drink," she said. "You'll love it."

When the coconut water was gone, Lena showed Tovi how to scoop the coconut flesh out of the shell and gave her a taste. She explained that they could eat it or press it into oil for all types of uses. She removed the husk from the outside and showed Tovi how the fibers could be used to make rope or kindling for the fire. Finally, she showed her the empty and smooth shell, which they could use as bowls or carve into other items.

Tovi thought back to her talk with Silas at the strawberry bush. "What happens if you pick a coconut before it's ready?" she asked.

"The green ones are too soft and will break when they hit the ground, and it will be hard to salvage what's left."

Tovi laughed, and Lena gave her a questioning glance.

"It fits."

"What fits?"

"Silas has been trying to teach me that I'm not ready. Like the green coconuts. I need to stay put, so I don't fall and break."

Lena nodded and had just opened her mouth in reply when they heard something crashing through the jungle. The tall undergrowth shook, and a bedraggled girl about Tovi's age stumbled out onto the sand, looking over her shoulder as if she was being chased.

"Oh! Please help me," she cried. Her clothes were tattered; her feet were bare; and there was a nasty cut along her shoulder that oozed black-tinged blood.

Tovi instinctually stepped toward her, but Lena grabbed her arm. "Don't move." Tovi noticed Lena's grip had tightened on the knife.

"Who are you?" Lena called.

The girl stopped, fearfully staring at the blade, her hands up in front of her. There was a heart in her palm. "I don't mean any harm. Please help me. I'm looking for Meira."

"Who sent you?"

"Thad. He told me to show you this, and you would help me," she said, pointing to the brown heart.

Lena's fingers relaxed, and she stepped away from Tovi. "What happened to you?"

"I just got away," she said shakily. "Damien's army is everywhere, trying to round up all of us who got away. Thad told me I would be safe here, but he didn't know I would run into the army on my way. It was terrible. They've been tracking me for days, but I think I have finally lost them." She looked around as if seeing her surroundings for the first time. "Are you Meira?"

Lena nodded. "I am. And this is Lyra," she said, giving Tovi a pointed look.

"I'm Carlyn," the girl said, eyeing Tovi. "I'm so glad I finally found you."

"Come, have a seat in the shade, and I'll get you some water and something to eat. Tell us what is happening on the mountain."

The girl followed them to the huts and gladly took the coconut shell full of rain water. "His Majesty is angry. He and his masters are stuck inside the curtain, but lots of people are disappearing. He knows that it's the heart that gets people out of the city, so he's rounding up all the hearts and putting them to work hunting, farming, mining, serving in the army, or building a giant wall to keep people in. The heart-frees are just stuck in the city. He keeps looking for more people with the heart, but they keep running away. He can't keep them under control, even with soldiers all around the border.

"Now he's offering rewards for rounding up runaways. I was scared to leave, but I knew I couldn't stay any longer. Thad told me to find you, so here I am." She took another drink.

Lena stood. "You're safe with us. Now, you two stay out here. I need to check on Eryx."

"Eryx?" Carlyn asked, a sudden sparkle in her eye. "The fighter?"

When Lena nodded, Carlyn smiled broadly. "Oh, wow. I didn't know someone famous was here." Lena looked at Tovi with amusement in the curve of her mouth and arch of her brow.

Lena disappeared inside the hut.

Tovi and Carlyn's eyes met, and they both grinned shyly. Tovi, having failed her own attempt at running from the mountain, said the only thing that popped into her mind. "This must have been really hard for you. Like Meira said, you're safe here."

Carlyn started to cry. "Thank you, Lyra. That means so much to me." They were quiet for a moment before Carlyn continued. "Thad told me that there would be someone named Tali here. Someone with your colors."

Tovi didn't know what to do or say, but she was saved when Lena stepped back outside. "Thad was wrong. Tali has not been here," she said.

"I'm so sorry," Carlyn said, "I didn't mean to pry."

"Those colors are common," Lena said firmly, ending the conversation. "Carlyn, could you go in and introduce yourself to Eryx?"

She looked confused by this request, but she went into the hut.

As soon as she was gone, Lena whispered in Tovi's ear, "We cannot tell her who we are."

"Why?"

"The more people who know who we are, the more dangerous. Don't you think it is strange that Thad gave her my alias but Tali's real name? She could be a spy, for all we know. Or she could be snatched by the army and tortured for information. No one gets to know who we are until we know it is safe."

"Then why did you give her Eryx's real name?"

"She might have recognized him. I'm sure she's watched him in plenty of fights." Lena paced back and forth. "Do not tell her anything. Do not go anywhere out of my sight."

Tovi bristled at the orders but nodded. "This is silly, Le—I mean, Meira. She seems harmless."

"I don't care what you think about it as long as you do what I say."

CHAPTER 27

BiBi was full of dread, unable to think of anything but Tali's route through the desert. It had been so easy to imagine that she was trapped and there was no way to complete the missions that Damien and the Queens had given her. Now, she knew she could travel through the trees. She would have to find the land bridge, a place she had never been before. If Tali could do it, perhaps she could, too.

She looked out at the darkening willow leaves, listening to the chirping orchestra and watching the fireflies blink in their own secret rhythm. She didn't want to leave Adia, now or ever. But what would happen when the flood lowered? Would Damien come after her? It was only a matter of time before he had an army of hearts that could march through the curtain and do his bidding. And then, there was Rhaxma's threat . . .

She could leave now before she fell any further in love with Tali Tivka. She could leave before Ganya became any more of a mother to her. She could leave before she was too attached to Silas and this beautiful, little village. She leaned her head against the window frame. It was far too late for all of those things.

If she left now, there would be less of a reason for Damien or Rhaxma to send their armies here. She could honestly tell them that Tovi was not there. She would lie if anyone asked about Tali. Then maybe these sweet people would be left alone. She wasn't certain she could lie convincingly, but she was willing to risk it. She had to do whatever she could to keep Damien, Rhaxma, and Megara away.

And if she didn't leave now, she might lose her courage.

Swallowing the lump in her throat, she glanced into the living room. Ganya was busy with some sewing and wouldn't notice she was gone for quite some time. Her heart cracked down the middle. She blew a silent kiss toward the kindest woman she had ever known and climbed through her bedroom window.

She crept along a limb and hoisted herself up onto Silas' porch. The jars of paint sat on the window sill, just where he had left them. She didn't want them, and she gritted her teeth against the sharp pain in her soul. Whether she gave them to Damien or Rhaxma, she knew she couldn't return to the mountain empty-handed. She put the little jars in her pockets and wiped away unwanted tears.

Silas' house was quiet and dark, except for one glowing lantern, and she peered through the window. The studio was empty, and the paintings on the wall beckoned to her in the flickering light. She looked left, then right, and slipped inside, telling herself she would just look at the mural for a moment before she left Adia for good.

She searched the paintings with just as much hunger as when she had first seen them. There were many scenes with people she did not recognize and a few she knew well. She lingered over one in which Tali and Tovi sat in the enclosure of the hideaway while the trees bloomed around them. How lovely it must have been to grow up here in Adia. She touched his painted face and quickly withdrew her hand. How silly to be pining for a near stranger.

On the back wall were scenes from the mountain, and her heart thudded when she spotted images of Leeto, Rhaxma, and all the masters in the throne room. She found herself there in the line. What could it mean? Had Silas intended for them to be masters all along? What good could possibly come from the evil they had done?

She felt the jars, heavy in her pocket. Would Silas come see her after she returned to the mountain? She hoped so. She wanted to ask him why he had allowed them to become masters, why he had allowed them to do such terrible things. Why he had left a way open that would allow her to leave. A tear dripped down her jaw.

She moved further along the wall, and her thudding heart dropped into her stomach. There was an image of Tali—beautiful, rugged Tali—wearing a crown, and there was a light-haired queen beside him. How could she have been so stupid? Her daydream of staying here in Adia with Tali for the rest of their days was nonsense. Silas had something else in mind for him, a different queen designed for him. She cursed her foolish heart.

She took a deep, ragged breath and turned to leave.

"What are you looking for?" Tali asked.

She jumped and crashed backward, nearly upsetting a table covered in paints and brushes. How long had he been there? "Nothing. I mean, Silas . . . Silas said I could have some paint."

"I didn't know you're an artist. Can I see something?"

"Now?"

"Why not?"

"It's late."

"You're the one who chose this hour to come pick out some paint."

"I don't have anything to paint with."

One of Tali's eyebrows arched, and he looked pointedly at a large jar full of brushes.

She blushed and sat at Silas' table. She pulled a piece of paper from a pile and selected a brush. The closest paint to her reach was blue, and that gave her inspiration.

She studied Tali, who was still in the doorway, and brushed her hair out of her eyes. She swept lines of paint onto the surface, trying to mimic the curves of Tali's face. "I prefer drawing with charcoal, but this will have to do for now." She showed him the little portrait when she was done.

"That's really good," he said, still leaning in the doorway.

"After my father died, we moved into the palace. I took lessons with Jairus."

He softly stared at her for a moment, and she wished she understood the look on his face.

He straightened and put his hands in his pockets. He smiled, but it was sad and distant. "Enjoy your painting." He nodded at her with the strangest, pained look and walked out into the night.

"Wait," she called. "What's wrong?"

He paused and turned back. The lines of his face were deep, and his eyes glittered. "I didn't realize you grew up with my family. It's a lot to think about."

There was so much she wanted to say. *I'm so sorry you grew up without your family. It's not fair that I had time with them and you didn't. What can I do to take the hurt away? I would do anything. You know that, right?*

"I didn't mean to upset you," she whispered.

"You didn't. Don't worry about me."

Don't worry about him? The precise reason she was there in Silas' house crashed back into her mind. She had come to get paint so that she could return to the mountain and keep the armies away. Away from Adia. Away from Ganya. Away from him. The jars of paint felt heavy in her pockets.

"Come on. Let's get out of here," he said, some of his usual cheerfulness returning.

BiBi followed him, studying his body language. He had been so sad just moments ago, but now he walked with a bounce in his step as he led her into the trees. "You don't like talking about sad things."

He didn't stop or turn around. "Who does?"

"Where are we going?"

"I don't know. That's the fun of it," he said over his shoulder.

Before long, they were walking side-by-side down Main Street. The shops were closed for the night, but a few candles glowed in upstairs windows. They passed only a few people, but each one hugged Tali or thumped him on the back, welcoming him home.

They sat down at a small table outside of the tea shop. It was breezy enough for glimpses of the moon to escape through the waving leaves, and BiBi thought it was absolutely magical.

"Why'd you really come here?" he asked.

She didn't respond at first. She appreciated the straightforward question, and she wished she could give him the same kind of answer. "There was a lot going on. I had to leave, and this is the only other place I know."

"You'd been here before?"

"Yes, on an assignment from King Damien. It was a game he played with the Council of Masters. It's why Tovi ended up on the mountain. Calix and Leeto were playing the game."

"And you didn't play?"

"I did. Just not very well. I came here and sat in the trees and wished I never had to leave."

"And now you don't. You're one of us now."

Her heart ached. "Tell me a story," she said, hoping for distraction.

"What kind?"

"Tell me about when you and Tovi were kids."

"We were always up to something. Avi and Ganya let us roam pretty wild. I spent some time with the other kids, but Tovi didn't. She always felt out of sorts around a lot of people. She preferred adventures with just me—and maybe Avi, Ganya, and Gil. Silas came sometimes. But mostly, it was just Tovi and me.

"We always thought we would discover other cities and villages if we just went far enough. Now that I've seen more of the world, I realize we never traveled nearly far enough to find the other people out there. We stayed pretty much in the valley between here and Mount Damien."

"Have you met those other people now?"

"Some of them. I've been all the way around the mountain. Most of the tribes and towns are further out, but I've come across a few."

"What's the most dangerous thing you've ever done?"

"Teased Tovi when she was already mad."

BiBi laughed and yawned.

"That is our sign that we need to get back," Tali said.

He led her back to the willow, squeezed her shoulder, and said goodnight with one last brilliant smile.

When she finally went to her room, she pulled the jars of paint from her pockets and opened the trunk at the foot of her bed. There was a soft blanket folded on top of Tovi's other belongings, and BiBi tucked the jars into the folds. She should have left Adia, but she was glad that she hadn't, at least for tonight.

CHAPTER 28

Tovi ran on the beach under the pale pinks of sunrise. The wet sand shifted a bit under her feet, and she liked the gritty feel. The salt air played in her hair, and she felt free.

The curve of the shore allowed her to run while staying in Lena's view. She was grateful for the time alone, even though she was under her sister's protective eye. To run again, to feel her breath expand her lungs while her legs pumped, was bliss.

She was just turning around when a scream cut the peaceful morning in half. It was coming from near the huts. Tovi raced back, sand flinging behind her. Her mind swirled with images of Damien's army following after Carlyn, finding their little cove.

When she was close enough to see what had happened, she slowed down and sighed with relief. Carlyn, surrounded by noisy, white birds, swung the frying pan with all her might. The birds retreated for a second before inching closer to her again.

"You shouldn't have fed them," Lena laughed.

"I was just trying to be nice!" she wailed, swinging the pan again. "I have none left for you. Go away!"

Tovi, Eryx, and Lena helped shoo them away, and they finally departed. The four sat on the sand, Carlyn looking rattled but calming enough to poke fun at herself. "Well, good morning, everyone. Nothing like a little humiliation to start the day."

Lena cooked some new breakfast for them since the birds had enjoyed all that Carlyn had prepared. The fire crackled, and the ocean breeze washed over them.

"Tell us more about you," Tovi said. "Where did you live on the mountain?"

"Just above the Bottom Rung, but we spent a lot of time below the cloud. My father was a farmer on the eastern slopes before the curtain appeared. We had a house on the mountain, but during sowing and harvest time, we lived in the camp near the fields and helped."

"I didn't know anyone from the mountain lived below the cloud," Tovi said.

"Not many do. But there are little camps all over. It doesn't make sense for the farmers to travel up and down the mountain every day. Same with the fishermen and hunters."

Carlyn paused and locked her eyes on something in the distance. Tovi followed her gaze and saw Silas approaching along the beach.

"Who's that?"

"Silas. He's a friend," Lena responded.

When he reached them, he looked straight at Carlyn. "Good morning, Carlyn," he said. "Come walk with me."

The plate in her hand shook. "I think I know who you are."

"Good. That saves us some time." He helped her up.

Tovi watched them go. "How do you think she knew?"

"Not everyone is as stubborn as you," Eryx said.

"You're one to talk about stubbornness," Lena jabbed.

Tovi couldn't hear Silas and Carlyn, but she could see the way Carlyn trembled and stayed a good distance from him.

"I'm worried," Lena said.

Tovi made brief eye contact with Eryx before hurriedly turning to Lena. "Worried about what?"

"I just can't shake this weird feeling. Why did Thad use Tali's real name and not mine?"

Eryx frowned. "You think it's some kind of message from him?"

"I don't know," she said, poking at the fire. "I just don't feel right about it. I'll talk to Silas about it later, I guess."

"She seems so sweet," Tovi said. "And she has the heart in her hand."

"The heart doesn't mean much."

"Doesn't mean much?" Tovi sputtered. "How could you say that? It means we belong to Silas."

Lena cocked an eyebrow. "And who created it? Damien, not Silas. He and Silas were once very close, and Silas made him a partner in creation. He showed him how to make things, to use his imagination and a paintbrush to change the world. The heart was one of his first designs. And he got it all wrong. The heart doesn't prove your devotion to Silas. I don't know exactly what Damien was thinking when he designed it, but it seems to stay on a person's hand until they have completely given up on Silas."

Eryx nodded. "I had the heart all of my life, and I wasn't devoted to Silas until, well, now."

"It makes no sense," Tovi said. "Why would Damien design it that way?"

"Why does he do anything that he does?" Lena replied. "Everything he does is backward, illogical, unreasonable. I'm sure he thought he was doing a good thing. He said he was marking people with a symbol that showed they had not turned their backs on Silas, a symbol to be proud of and wear for all the world to see. Deep down, he was always obsessed with deciphering someone's loyalties so that he could use them for his own gain. And when he took control of the mountain, it all backfired. There were so many hearts, so many who had not turned away from Silas, that gloves became a necessity to hide what was there.

"But I misspoke when I said the heart doesn't mean much. What I mean is that out here, when someone could be dangerous, we can't judge a person just by the heart in their palm. Up on the mountain, the hearts were the sole purpose for the HH and everything we did. We tried to gather as many as we could. While they don't prove that a person is devoted to Silas, they do mean that a person is at least open to him. So, up there, we looked for them and tried to teach people about him and the better way of life that he offers when he is our king and guide. So yes, they do mean a lot. But not here. Not until we know more about her."

They were all quiet for several minutes. Tovi mulled over the idea of Damien creating the hearts out of a sinister desire to use a person's loyalties against them. Her mind turned to Carlyn. What did her heart mean? Was she good? Was she one of the hearts that could easily have become a member of the HH, working for Silas and the good of the mountain? Was she like Xanthe, having a heart and desperately searching for Adwin, despite her life of depravity as a master? Tovi shook her head. What a mess.

When Silas and Carlyn returned, she looked shaken. She walked to the edge of the water and sat alone. Silas told the others to give her some space for a while. She needed time to think.

"Your turn, Tovi," he said, reaching out to help her stand. They walked along the warming sand, letting the water lap at their feet.

"What's going on with Carlyn?"

"That's between her and me." His tone was kind but firm. "She's had a difficult journey reaching here. But I think the sea and all of you could be good for her."

"Can we trust her?"

Silas took a while to answer. "I will rarely tell you to start with mistrust. What you should start with is wisdom. Real wisdom. Not the kind of wisdom that Damien teaches. What do you know about the person? Do they follow me? With that in mind, what do you know about Carlyn?"

Tovi mulled it over. "She has lived her whole life on the mountain, but she has the heart and recognized you when you came."

"And what may be true about her if she has lived her whole life on the mountain?"

"All sorts of things could be true. She could be ruined by the lessons of the mountain. Or she could be like Thad and Eryx and all those people in the HH who follow you. I don't really have a way of knowing."

"Very wise, Tovi. You don't know someone's heart. Only I do."

"So, what do I do? Do I trust her or not?"

"That's the wrong question. The question is should you love her and be kind? And the answer to that is always yes."

"But . . . but that's not what I'm asking." Her frustration was growing.

"I know. And you think you are focusing on the right thing, but you're not. Be kind. Do your best to care for her. And until you know more about her, just be cautious. We'll see what this salt air, time with you three, and time with me can do for her."

"But what if she is here for some sinister reason?"

"She might be, and she might not. That is not your concern."

Tovi stopped and stared. "Not my concern?"

"What have I told you to do?"

"Stay. Learn. Be still."

"Exactly. Do those things. That is your concern."

"I can't believe you are choosing now to be so cryptic. Why won't you tell us what is going on?"

"Let me tell you a story. Remember your friend BiBi?"

"Yes."

"Right now, she is in Adia for a 'sinister reason,' sent by Damien. But time with Ganya and others in Adia is turning something bad into something good. I'm not worried about Ganya being influenced by BiBi. Ganya will keep doing what I say, and BiBi will have a chance to learn more about me and grow closer to me. She'll have a chance to become more of whom I made her to be."

"Was Carlyn sent by Damien?"

"You've missed the point, but no, she was not sent by Damien."

The fear that had been growing in Tovi calmed.

"And again, that is not your concern. Do what I say. Stay and learn. Take deep breaths, and try to be still. Be kind and caring to Carlyn. You don't have to trust Carlyn, but you should trust me."

"You are frustrating me today," Tovi said, scowling at him.

"I can tell." He laughed and put his arm around her shoulder.

CHAPTER 29

Tali scooped the last bite of gooseberry pie into his mouth while Ganya bustled around the kitchen. He stood, wiped his hands on his pants—making Ganya scowl—and gave her a quick squeeze before heading out the door. The afternoon stretched ahead of him with no plans except building the railing for his new house.

Motion near Silas' tree caught his eye, and he looked up in time to see BiBi hurrying away, tears streaming from red, swollen eyes.

Twenty years of brothering Tovi Tivka had made him wary of crying women. When Tovi cried, a firestorm of anger and irrational ranting was sure to follow. He did his best to avoid those episodes, and everything in him wanted to rush the opposite direction from wherever BiBi was running.

But something held him back. He and BiBi had formed a friendship over the last several days. She had been shy at first, but she had warmed up to him over dinners at Ganya's house and walks along the branches. He still held a bit of suspicion—she had been one of Damien's most prized weapons, after all—but that distrust was evaporating. She seemed so innocent, and it was hard to imagine she was capable of the things he was sure she had done on the mountain.

They could talk for hours, their companionship so comfortable and easy that it felt like he had known her for years. She always wanted to hear stories of his adventures, and she readily answered his questions about her life. They discussed Silas, his paintings, and the way he made them feel; and he opened up to her far more than he usually did. It was almost like he was talking to Tovi, whom he missed more than he liked to admit.

But what was he supposed to do now that she was crying? He liked her when she was smiling and laughing, or even when she asked a million questions about him. But this was new territory. He watched her disappear through some leaves and reminded himself that she wasn't like Tovi. She was sweet and kind and clearly in distress. She probably wouldn't yell like Tovi. She might need a friend. He leaned his head back, sighed into the sky, and grudgingly took off after her.

She headed west, and she dropped lower in the canopy as she went. Tali noticed the branches he walked were slick with the spray from the raging river below. This was no place to be rushing around, especially for someone who didn't quite have her tree legs yet.

Sure enough, just as he thought those words, BiBi slipped. She caught herself and stood with her arms out, balancing on the limb, stiff and frightened.

"Be careful," Tali called, passing through the leaves that had hidden him from view.

BiBi jumped, shrieked, and lost her balance, tumbling off the limb and landing in the crevice between two larger branches further below. She hugged one of the limbs, her cheek against the wet bark, while her legs were battered by the angry flood.

Tali groaned and looked for a way to climb down. By the time he reached her, she had pulled herself completely onto the larger of the two limbs and out of the water. She lay her head back against the branch and breathed deeply while he stood over her. "You frightened me," she said.

"And the river didn't?"

She stood up quickly and nearly lost her balance again. He took hold of her arms to steady her. "I'm fine," she said, walking more carefully toward the trunk of the tree and climbing up to the next branch. She sat with her back to the trunk and combed wet hair out of her face.

He pulled himself up onto another branch and sat facing her. "What's wrong?" he asked, hating the hesitance that he heard in his own voice.

She stared at him, and he noticed her lip tremble. He searched her face for clues, but found none. Then with a loud sputter, she buried her face in her hands and wept.

Dread and pity filled his whole body to overflowing, and he felt clumsy and unprepared. *Silas, you better come take her off my hands. I have no idea what to do.*

He looked around, but there was no sign of a savior. He was trapped. In all of the dangers he had faced, he had rarely felt so nervous as he did sitting with crying BiBi.

She lowered her hands and met his eye. "I'm sorry. I bet you wish you hadn't followed me."

"Pretty much," he said without thinking.

She blinked twice, and a small laugh made her snort.

Good, a smile. He could handle that.

"Your honesty is refreshing," she said. She took a deep breath and leaned back against the tree. "I'll be fine. You don't have to stay."

An internal battle kept him rooted to the spot. He so badly wanted to accept her offer and flee, but she was upset. Didn't that mean he should stay? He thought about Silas and how he would handle just such a situation. He always knew what to do and how to make someone feel better.

"I'll listen," he said. "I don't know if it will help, but you can talk to me."

She looked down and played nervously with her fingers. "I just came from a talk with Silas," she said, not meeting his eye. "I don't think I can do what he's asking of me."

He nodded, and she went on. "He wants to take my marks and keep me here in Adia forever."

"What's so bad about that?"

She still wouldn't look at him, and a tear trickled down her cheek. "You don't understand. If he takes my marks, I can't go back."

"Isn't that a good thing?"

She shook her head. "If I don't go back, he'll send someone after me."

Tali's heart pounded, and his suspicions roared back. "Damien? Why would he send someone after you? Does he know you're here?"

She blinked several times and looked everywhere but at Tali. Finally, after a painfully long silence, she choked out, "Yes, he knows I'm here. He sent me."

"You've been lying to us."

"No!" she cried, finally meeting his eye. "I didn't lie. I've just left some things out. And Silas has known the whole time."

"And he wants you to stay?"

She nodded again.

"So, stay. Let Silas take your marks and stay."

"But Damien—and the army."

Tali shrugged. "Silas will know what to do."

"It sounds so simple when you say it like that."

"It *is* simple. Trust him. Do what he says."

"You really think I should stay?"

He nodded.

She played with the hem of her dress. There was an awkward silence, and he didn't know how to fill it.

After what felt like several miserable minutes, BiBi changed the subject. "What was it like when you found out you're Damien's grandson?"

His mind traveled back to the day he had met Lena. He could still picture her as she came into the cave, so fierce and somehow so familiar. "We had just lost Avi, and Tovi had run away. Leeto had captured me, and I was tied up in a cave."

"Leeto? But he's so small. How did he capture *you*?" Her cheeks turned red.

"He knocked me out while I was sleeping. Let's be clear that it wasn't a fair fight."

"Understood," she said, and he could tell she was holding back a laugh.

"Then my sister came to me. Lena. I had never seen her before, but she looked so much like Tovi. She's the one who told me everything. She said Silas had sent her to free me and that I was supposed to travel with her. She told me that she was my sister, and that we had a brother. She took me to see our mother." He smiled at the memory of meeting Thomae for the first time. "It was a lot to take in."

"So, you don't mind then? Being Damien's grandson? An heir of the mountain?"

Tali took a deep breath and exhaled slowly. "I guess not. I try not to think about it too much."

"But you *have* to think about it. You have a future, a destiny. You have to go to the mountain and defeat him."

He shrugged, unsure of what she expected him to say. "I'll do whatever Silas asks of me. And when he doesn't have something for me to do, I'll build. I'll explore. I'll get into trouble. He'll get me out of it."

He shrugged his shoulders and grinned before standing and offering a hand to help her up. "I think we should get further up, away from the river. I'm soaked."

They talked about their families all the way back to the willow. He was glad she was happy and not crying anymore, but her deception still weighed on his mind. She had told him the truth, and that had to be worth something. But she had been sent by Damien. His grandfather. Were there other things she was lying about? She seemed so innocent, so sincere. Was that an act?

While BiBi was back in his old room changing clothes, Tali sat on the porch with Ganya.

"You be careful," she said, peering at him over her steaming mug.

"What?" he asked, brow furrowed.

"You be careful with that sweet girl. She looks at you like you make the sun rise. Next time you leave, she'll be heartbroken. Be careful."

His stomach did a strange flip. "That's not how it is."

"Oh, it's not?" Ganya smirked. "Noticing a woman's heart is such a strength of yours."

He cringed. "And I'm not so sure you should call her 'sweet.' She's here on Damien's orders."

"Of course, she is."

He stared at Ganya. "You knew?"

"Of course, she is," she repeated softly. "I didn't know for sure, but I could guess. The poor thing is a wreck. Her heart is in the right place, but the mountain has done quite a bit of damage. I just hope we can keep her here."

CHAPTER 30

Life was good at the sea, and Tovi slowly relaxed and let go of some of her usual moodiness as the days passed. She loved the salt air and the sand between her toes. The rhythm of the waves and the crackles of their nightly fires soothed her soul.

The most unexpected turn for Tovi was the camaraderie with this strange collection of people. She, Eryx, Lena, and Carlyn spent nearly every moment together. There was a lot of talking and a lot of laughter, two things that weren't always natural to Tovi. And she liked it.

Eryx had been up and about for several days. He had lost some weight, but his strength was returning. He had also lost his embarrassment and awkwardness around Tovi. She guessed that his new colors had something to do with that. Or simply not sharing her colors anymore. She enjoyed the new Eryx. He was still gruff at times, but he enjoyed talking with the girls. He even joined their laughter occasionally, and it made him look much younger than Tovi had guessed him to be.

Carlyn had proven helpful and hard-working. She always offered to stay up late to clean up dinner, and she was the first one up each morning, gathering fruit and fish and laying the fire before anyone else stirred. She was soft-spoken and timid, with a sweetness that balanced Lena's command and Tovi's temper.

Time here at the sea had a strange quality of making every day stretch longer than usual. She felt like she had been with this little family for years.

She often thought about Ganya, and the rocking chairs on the porch, and the peace of the canopy. She thought about the just-started treehouse taking shape next door. Would others finish it while Eryx was away, or would it be waiting for him to continue the work when he returned?

She dug her toes further into the sand, pangs of homesickness rolling over her with a bittersweet rhythm. She loved it here, and she missed there.

She heard someone coming along the beach and turned to see Eryx approaching with two plates. "Good morning," she said as he handed breakfast to her.

"Good morning," he said, taking a seat beside her and digging in.

"What are we going to do today?" Tovi asked wryly.

"Oh, you know," Eryx said between bites. "Something new like walking up and down the beach and doing some fishing."

She grinned. "What do you think is up there?" she asked, nodding her head to a tall cliff wall and what looked to be a dark entrance to a cave.

Eryx followed her gaze and shrugged. "I don't know. Rocks."

Tovi kept looking. Her eyes had been drawn to this spot many times. She longed to go explore it, but she knew she shouldn't. She was supposed to stay right there on the beach, a frustratingly restrictive expectation. "You could take me," she suggested. "Then I wouldn't be alone."

"Absolutely not."

"Why?" she asked, flinging down her fork.

"Stay on the beach until Silas tells you otherwise."

"You could ask Lena if it's okay."

"Don't use her name."

"Don't tell me what to do."

They stared at one another, brown eyes with a purple star meeting yellow-green speckles. Eryx laughed.

"What's so funny?"

"You."

"Oh, really?"

"Yeah," he said, elbowing her in the side and smiling so big, his white teeth sparkled in his suntanned face. "You get so mad over the dumbest things."

She elbowed him back and looked out at the ocean, trying to ignore the sudden tightness in her belly and thumping of her heart. His hair had grown in brown and just a little curly, and he was smiling so much more these days. His scars were mostly hidden by his patched clothes and his mop of hair. But when she saw them on his arms, neck, and face, her heart squeezed; and she wanted to take them away.

"Hey, look," Eryx said, elbowing her again. He pointed down the beach. Silas was coming.

They watched Silas approach Carlyn. They couldn't hear their words, but Carlyn shook as she always did when she saw him. She dropped the plate she was holding.

"You'd think she'd be happier to see him," Eryx said with a nod in their direction.

"Oh, I don't know," Tovi said. "It can be overwhelming."

While Silas walked and talked with Carlyn, Eryx and Tovi cleaned the breakfast dishes, and Lena climbed coconut trees with her knife between her teeth. When it was Lena's turn with Silas, the other three took their long, wooden spears into the shallows to fish. Carlyn was even quieter than usual, and Tovi made a mental note to check on her later.

Then it was Tovi's turn.

Silas took her into the jungle instead of along the shore.

"Where are we going?" she asked, excited for the change in scenery.

"You'll see."

They wound up a steep path, coming out into the sunshine on a granite outcropping. The cave's gaping archway was in front of them, and Tovi could see their little huts on the beach far below.

"You asked. I wanted to show you," Silas said.

It took a moment for Tovi's eyes to adjust to the darkness after being in the bright sunshine. Colors emerged all around her. Every inch of the cave was covered in paintings, and she recognized the style right away. This was Silas' work. Just like in his treehouse in Adia. Just like in the palace on the mountain.

One wall was a large picture of the sea—the beach, the trees, the blue-green water. The other wall was covered in scenes she did not recognize.

"Look closer," Silas instructed.

She moved around the cave, investigating the paintings and looking for familiar faces. She saw Silas everywhere. Then, there were several scenes of the palace with a young king and queen and a little prince. Her father.

She took in the scenes of their family life, unsure how to reconcile them with the monsters she knew her grandfather and father to be. She followed the pictures deeper into the cave and stopped in front of four towering figures, painted larger than life-size, their heads brushing the ceiling.

A woman with wild, lemon-yellow hair and violet eyes was first. The aqua stripe in her hair matched the ocean waves behind her. She held a spear in her hand and wore a golden circlet around her head.

She looked even fiercer than the real-life Lena. Above her head were the words "Queen of Meiradin."

Next came "King of Sansea." Tovi recognized Jairus' face, but his colors were different. His hair was split perfectly down the middle, with dark brown on one side, maroon on the other, and a crown resting on top. The crown was thin and did not have the pointy peaks and gems like Damien's. Instead, it was adorned with a diamond-shaped pattern etched into the band. He looked much tougher than the prince she had met on the mountain. He wore clothing more suited to the desert than a palace. Behind him were sand-colored bricks and palm branches, and he held a wooden shield.

Tovi stared at the next figure, her twin painted on the stone. The King of Adia—with his messy, navy blue hair and purple star in his eye—had a hint of a grin on his face. His stance showed strength. The trees were behind him, and there was a bow leaning against his leg. The tops of arrows poked out of a quiver at his back. He did not wear a crown.

She then looked into her own face, and somehow, she was the fiercest of the four. Her eyes were piercing blue, and the gold streaks in her hair radiated light. Her tiara of bent metal was in a floral pattern, and an indigo flower with orange pollen was tucked behind her ear. Strawberry vines wound around one of her legs with alternating pink flowers and red berries. She held a sword that crossed her body near her heart. Above her were the words "Queen of the Wild Range."

"You must have many questions," Silas said, stepping next to her and looking over the paintings.

Tovi nodded. "I don't know where to start."

"This is who each of you will become, but you're not there yet."

"Where is the Wild Range?"

"To the east."

A stone dropped in Tovi's stomach. "And Adia is in the West."

"Yes."

"I will not be with my brother."

"No."

She swallowed hard.

She continued to scour the paintings in silence. Silas put a comforting arm around her shoulders. "I know it's a lot to take in. This is what I have intended for you since long before you were born. I painted this before even your parents were born. I have great plans for you and your people, but I won't send you until you are ready."

"What if I just want to be a normal person, living in my treehouse in Adia? I could help Tali there."

"Your love for your brother is a beautiful thing, but your destiny is much greater than being his helper."

"What if I don't want this?" she asked, waving her hand at her image.

"In time, you will understand, and you will want what I want. And what I want is for you to lead the people of the Wild Range."

"Are there many people there?"

"Yes."

Tovi stood silently for a long time, taking in her daunting future.

CHAPTER 31

It was late in the evening when Rhaxma answered the king's summons to hear an update from Thad, who had returned from his scouting mission much too soon. Listening to his report, she was flabbergasted and, admittedly, a bit proud. Foolish, drunk, lazy Thad. Suddenly, he was running errands for His Majesty. And now, in the throne room, he sounded firm and in charge, confident like someone with experience. She had missed so much over the last few years. Missed so many signs. But no matter. Now she knew her brother's secrets. And most shocking of all, he was living up to the Pyralis name.

"No sign of the missing regiment," he said. "They could be on the other side of the flood, for all we know. No sign of Tali either. We are still searching the caves and will bring a report when we know more. I just thought you should hear about the flood as soon as possible. I don't think you'll hear from BiBi until it lowers."

"Thank you, Thaddeus. Very helpful," the king said from his throne. "Did you leave your lieutenant below the cloud, or is he here with you?"

"He returned with me, Your Majesty. I didn't want to leave him there alone."

"Good, good. You both will breakfast with me tomorrow, and we'll make some new plans."

Rhaxma and Thad left and crossed the courtyard to go home. "Don't get comfortable," Rhaxma said. "You're coming with me tonight."

"Where?"

"It's time for you to see something. It's time for you to know the future of this family."

His brow was scrunched. "I've been sleeping on the ground. All I want is a real bed. Can't this wait?"

"He'll send you out again soon. Probably after he meets with you in the morning. We're going now."

She left him standing there and climbed up the stairs to change her clothes and get her own things. At the top landing, she looked down at his unmoving form. "Go change. We'll be gone all night." He stared up at her but didn't move. "Now," she commanded.

She changed from her gown into clothes more suitable for a long journey. She braided her hair into one long tail, and she stuffed a few supplies into a pack that had been used frequently in the last few days. She wrapped herself in her traveling cloak and dropped a small, silver dagger into the pocket on the inside. She checked herself in the mirror.

She hardly recognized herself these days. Her usual love of color was gone, replaced with a darkness that she could see in the circles under her eyes and feel in the coldness of her heart. She would ruin him. She was sure her happiness would return when Calix had paid for all he had done.

Thad was waiting for her downstairs. They didn't say a word to one another. On their way through the parlor, Rhaxma leaned down to kiss the glass coffin that held their brother. She pressed her hand against the cold surface. "It's all for you, Leeto. It's all for you. Everything."

Once outside, she stuck to the shadows, motioning for Thad to do the same. They zig-zagged through worsening neighborhoods. In the quiet stillness of midnight on a deserted street in the Bottom Rung, Rhaxma eyed the shimmering waves of light. Her nerves were alive and jumpy, and she kept the hood up. She knew they must not be seen, especially by the guard sitting just a few feet away.

He was half-asleep as he sat on a stool, his shoulders slumped and his head bobbing. He was tall and skinny, except for one pudgy roll around his middle on which he rested his crossed arms. He was starting to bald. Rhaxma had seen him before; he was stationed in the dungeon, where the king kept his most dim-witted servants, until recently when he was needed along the border. She had chosen this spot for two reasons. This post couldn't be seen by any other guards, and this man was the dimmest of them all. She put her hand inside her cloak and wrapped her fingers around the hilt of her knife. The guard's head fell forward and stayed there. She heard a snore.

It was time. She motioned for Thad to stay still.

The guard didn't hear her approach or see the flash of silver before the blade sank deep into his neck. His eyes opened momentarily with a look that seemed to shout, "What happened?" Then, he fell off his stool and landed in a heap with a thump.

She yanked out the blade, wiped it on the guard's tunic, and placed it back in her pocket.

"What was that for?" Thad hissed, looking from Rhaxma to the man on the ground.

She smiled. "You'll see."

She raised her left hand and touched the waves of light. They were warm, almost like sunlight. Nothing was stopping her. She walked confidently through the curtain.

Thad followed her, looking stunned. "How . . . ?"

She stripped the gloves off her hands and stuffed them in a pocket. She wouldn't be needing them for a while. She glanced at the brown heart that marred her left palm. After years of shameful hiding, it had turned out to be useful after all.

"Rhax, I didn't . . . I had no idea . . . "

"I didn't know about yours either."

"Does this mean you follow Adwin?"

Thad had stopped and was eyeing his sister. She couldn't tell if he was happy, confused, or angry. "Of course not," she said with a laugh. "I just never figured out how to get rid of it. Come on."

She led Thad down the south face of the mountain, on a new path that was already worn from thousands of feet in just the last few days. After just less than an hour, firelight became visible, dancing through the trees. Thad was very quiet, and Rhaxma relished his shock. He might have his own secrets, but she was glad hers were rendering him speechless.

A few more minutes of hiking brought them to the edge of a vast camp of tents.

"My army," Rhaxma announced.

"How? How did you do it? Where did they come from?" Thad asked, and she could tell he was trying to tally the number of tents.

"Through the census in the Bottom Rung. For every one heart sent to Calix, ten were sent to Megara or me. We gave them papers saying they were heart-free and smuggled most of them off the mountain. Their first jobs were to build the camp and gather food and provisions. Now, they are training."

"For what?"

"To fight. To do what I tell them. To fulfill Leeto's dreams, bring glory to our family, and demolish Calix."

"Don't you mean Damien?"

"No. I said what I mean. I no longer care about Damien. I want to make Calix suffer the way he has made our family suffer. I want to be the person who makes him so miserable that he begs for mercy. And I have a plan."

CHAPTER 32

Megara stared into her wine glass, watching the reflection of the stars twinkle on the surface. She alone was stuck in the city. This was the only part of the plan that Megara hated.

BiBi was in Adia. By now, Rhaxma should be showing Thad their secret little army in the forest to the south. And here she was, on the terrace of her home, with nothing to do but wait for their return.

Three Queens, indeed. She took a sip of wine and swirled the rest in her glass. Rhaxma had promised glory and victory if the three women banded together, combined their efforts, and thwarted the men. "Three Queens" had been her rallying cry. But it sure seemed like one pathetic girl trapped by a flood, one pathetic girl waiting on the balcony, and *one* queen out with her army. So much for Three Queens.

The night was balmy, and the courtyard was quiet as she looked over it.

A whisper broke the silence. "Are you up there, Meg?"

She rose and leaned against the railing to get a look at him. This was certainly unexpected.

Calix's face was turned up toward her. A few minutes later, they were both on her balcony, and he was pouring himself a drink from a cart as she watched from her velvet sofa. He refilled her glass and sat beside her, leaning back into the corner of the sofa and crossing one leg over the other.

"What are you after, Calix?"

"What am I after?" he asked, one eyebrow cocked. His smile showed his straight white teeth. "Can't I spend an evening with a . . . friend?"

She couldn't help smiling back at the devil. Goodness, he was handsome. She wanted to believe he was there just to be with her, but she knew better. He had never come to her—alone—so late in the evening.

But tonight, he had. An uncomfortable hope purred. She tried to swallow it back.

"You should just tell me now what brings you here."

He laughed. "You're not going to let me play with you first?"

"No."

"All right, I'll get right to it. I've been thinking about the future, Meg. I want you in it."

She cursed her thumping heart.

He sat up, putting his glass down on a small table. He moved in very close to her face, and his hands found her waist. She could feel his breath on her cheek. "You have everything I need, Meg. You are wise and in control. You are beautiful and fearsome. I want you beside me."

She clung to every last bit of willpower, all too aware that she was near the end of it.

His face was so close that she could see nothing else. His voice was soft but confident. "His Majesty has all but promised this kingdom to me. I want to do this work together."

"We already work together."

"I want more than that," he whispered. He kissed her cheek, letting his lips linger. "These weeks of running the census together slowly opened my eyes." He pulled slightly away to look at her. "But what you did at the party? Incredible. Unfathomable. I must have you as my queen."

Her pulse raced, and she felt dizzy. Not Three Queens. *The* Queen. By *his* side. The most coveted man on the mountain who had given his attention to all but her. Until tonight. He had finally seen her. Finally wanted her. Of all the women on the mountain, he could see her as the queen.

The years of being overlooked came rushing into her memory, and she laughed at them. Now was her time. Her pining and sadness and being alone had been worth it if she came out of all of it on the throne beside King Calix.

He leaned his forehead against hers. "I wish you could see what you look like when something makes you happy."

"It happens so rarely."

He kissed her lips, and she returned it, letting go of any remaining doubt. They passed the darkest hours this way, holding each other, whispering plans for their kingdom.

When the first gray light changed the air around them, they were still on the velvet sofa, her legs across his lap. His elbow was propped on the back of the cushions, and his face rested against his fist. "I can't believe it took us this long to know how right this is," he said.

"Worth the wait," she said.

"We're both going to be exhausted today."

She nodded. "Worth that, too."

"Maybe we should just forget about our tasks for a day." He wiggled his eyebrows.

She hit him softly on the shoulder, grinning. "That is so unlike you. Wouldn't that displease His Majesty?"

"You're right," he said. "No matter how deeply I fall in love with you, I don't know if I could bring myself to disobey His Majesty."

Megara blinked, her smile vanishing. Every nerve in her body sparked ominously.

His face fell, too. "I'm sorry, Meg. I don't mean to hurt you. You can be second place in my life, but you'll never be number one, as long as he is living. You understand that, don't you?"

"It's not that part," she said, wishing her voice didn't tremble. She put one hand on each side of his face. "You said love."

His head fell a bit to the side. "Oh, Meg." He laughed and pulled her just a bit closer. "I meant it. You are my future." He kissed her again, and she willed herself to relax and believe that all of this was happening.

Calix's head snapped up. "What have they been up to?" he whispered.

Megara followed his gaze. Rhaxma and Thad crossed the courtyard, seemingly unaware that they were being watched.

"You don't seem particularly surprised or curious. Do you know where they've been?" Calix asked. Megara turned to him. His face was very close, and there was a sharpness in his tone that hadn't been there before.

She crossed her arms and looked back at him, her eyes narrowed. "You love me?"

"Yes." His face softened.

"We'll be married?"

"Yes." Now he smiled.

"I'll be queen?"

"Yes." He leaned in and kissed the corner of her mouth.

"You'll put me second, before everyone but His Majesty?"

"I promise."

"Then I have a few things to tell you."

CHAPTER 33

Eryx peered into Tovi's face, his brow scrunched in concern. "Are you all right?" he asked.

Tovi nodded and said nothing as she sat in the shade between the huts.

She had been lost in thought since returning from the painted cave the previous day. The glimpse into her future was both frightening and intimidating, and she had fretted all night. She was nowhere close to being ready to be a queen. She could hardly control herself, let alone lead other people in a vast wilderness. Yet she looked young in the painting. This wasn't a far-off future. Silas was preparing her for what was to come in the next few years, not decades. She was disheartened. How could she ever prepare? How could she ever be ready? And must she do it alone?

"Tovi needs some time to think," Silas said, returning with Carlyn. He smiled at her, and it helped. "Your turn, Eryx." He clapped him on the back, and they walked toward the water. Eryx looked over his shoulder, catching Tovi's eye, but followed Silas.

Tovi watched them without really seeing them. A queen. And in a land far from Tali. She wouldn't even have Lena or Jairus. What was the point of the four finding one another if they would all be split off into their own kingdoms? She was so torn. She wanted so badly to be used by Silas. She wanted him to give her lofty tasks. But not this. Not by herself. Not so far away. She never dreamed he would ask for this.

A roar came from the edge of the water, and Tovi sat up straight, her eyes focusing on Silas and Eryx. While her mind had wandered over her future, Silas had pulled out his knife and was slowly opening one of Eryx's scars across his chest. Eryx sat on the sand, turned so Tovi could see his profile. Even at this distance, Tovi saw the pain in Eryx's creased face and the tension in his body. He roared again, lurching forward onto his hands, his head lowered like a charging bull.

Silas, done with the knife, kept one hand on Eryx's shoulder while he used the other to scoop away the black tar that was oozing out. He dropped it by handfuls into the ocean, where it was swept away on the waves.

Eryx breathed heavily. He pushed back into a seated position, and Tovi could see dark sweat on his brow. Then his voice boomed across the sand. "More."

She couldn't hear Silas, but she saw his mouth moving.

"Now," Eryx demanded, wiping his forehead with the back of his arm.

They spoke a while longer, the words too quiet to carry over the breeze.

Tovi thought back to the moment when Silas had taken that first drop of her own darkness and how much that had hurt. Eryx had just been drained of so much more and was clearly in pain, but he was begging to continue. Tovi watched in horror and fascination.

Eryx cried out again as Silas took his knife to another scar, this one on Eryx's back. His roar shook the beach, and several birds took flight nearby. Silas continued to speak to Eryx, who gritted his teeth and spasmed. Tovi couldn't believe the tar, coming out in waves and pulses, that could have filled at least a dozen of Ganya's jam jars.

Tovi stood and shielded her eyes with her hand. She knew that Silas was not torturing Eryx. She knew it was good for him. She knew the pent-up darkness of years on the mountain was leaving him, which could only be a good thing. But why did it have to be so awful and painful?

"I don't think I can take much more of this," Carlyn said weakly. "Can we go on a little walk?"

Tovi glanced at Carlyn, whose face looked a bit green. "Sure. Come on," she said, turning her back on the scene by the shore.

They took their usual path among the berry bushes. They could no longer hear or see Eryx, and Tovi took a deep breath.

"Why do you think it has to be like that?" Carlyn asked, voicing Tovi's thoughts.

"I've been wondering the same thing," Tovi said. "It seems like there should be an easier way. When Silas took the marks from my back, it just happened. I didn't even notice they were gone. I don't understand why he doesn't do the same with the sludge."

They walked on, both in deep thought. Carlyn veered deeper into the jungle.

Tovi stopped. "We need to go back. I'm not supposed to leave the beach unless I'm with Silas or Meira. We shouldn't be here." Guilt bubbled up in her.

"There are orange trees just through here. Let's go get a few, and then we'll go right back," Carlyn prodded.

Tovi hesitated.

"It's just a few more feet. We've already come this far."

"Fine," Tovi said, following Carlyn to the orange tree grove and plucking a ripe one from the nearest tree.

Carlyn looked closely at Tovi. "I think I know what's going on."

"What do you mean?" She pulled another orange off with a snap.

"I've been suspicious for a while," Carlyn said sheepishly. "Your hair, your eyes . . . I don't think your name is Lyra."

Tovi stood very still while her mind raced.

"It's okay," Carlyn said, placing a reassuring hand on Tovi's arm. "Thad told me some different scenarios to expect. I thought I would find Tali here with Meira, but it's not that shocking that it is you instead. Tovi, Tali's sister, His Majesty's granddaughter who came to the mountain but escaped."

Tovi's chaotic mind went horribly blank.

"It's you, isn't it?" Carlyn continued. "I understand why Meira doesn't want you to trust me. I wouldn't either. You didn't know me when I arrived, but I hope you know me now. I want to help. I want tasks from Silas, too."

Tovi let out the breath she hadn't realized she was holding. "I was constantly afraid we'd slip and use our real names."

"Our?"

Tovi's skin prickled, and her heart filled with dread again.

"Who else has a different name?" Carlyn prodded.

"Just me," Tovi faltered.

"Eryx is famous. I know that's his name. So, who is Meira?"

"We need to go back." Tovi walked quickly back toward the beach, pushing branches out of her way as she went.

Carlyn chased after her but didn't ask any more questions.

When they came out on the sand, Lena was standing on the beach, a spear in her hand, fury on her face.

"Where have you been?" she asked with quiet fire in her voice.

"We went on a walk. It was too awful to watch Eryx."

They stood eye to eye, Tovi flinching a bit under Lena's imposing stare.

"How dare you?" she asked through gritted teeth. "Don't you understand what is at stake?"

Carlyn piped up. "It's my fault. I asked for the walk," she said.

Lena did not look away from Tovi. "This doesn't concern you, Carlyn."

Tovi felt her anger simmering but willed it down. She had left the beach, which meant she had disobeyed Silas. It was her fault. "I'm sorry; it won't happen again," she said, though it was painful to keep calm.

Lena pursed her lips and exhaled forcefully through her nose. "It better not."

Tovi didn't dare tell Lena that Carlyn knew too much.

CHAPTER 34

BiBi jumped and spilled her tea as a loud bell clanged from Main Street, interrupting their peaceful porch breakfast. Ganya squealed in delight, dropped her plate and fork onto the table with a clatter, rose to her feet, cupped her hands around her mouth, and cried, "Low Tidings!"

Faces appeared from windows, doors, and even roofs all around the village, and a chorus of unruly, "Low Tidings!" came from each direction. Children jumped up and down, begging their mothers for ribbons, and BiBi soon knew why. By midmorning, the village was festooned in colorful banners, ribbons, and garlands. The smell of baking pies filled the air, and no one went about their normal chores. Instead, they gathered on porches, eating, drinking, and telling tales.

Ganya explained that the festival of Low Tidings meant one thing: the flood waters had lowered. BiBi's heart sank. She had put off leaving this place that she loved so dearly, but now with the water receding, she would have to leave as soon as possible. Maybe even tonight. She knew in her bones that the armies would come as soon as the flood dried up. She couldn't let that happen. She couldn't let them destroy this place. She couldn't let them come and find Tali.

Tali appeared moments later, and Granny Leora joined them, too, bringing a basket full of goodies and wrapped packages. Ganya pulled three bundles tied with string from beneath a quilt. She handed the first to Leora, who unwrapped an embroidered apron. She burst out laughing and tossed a parcel to Ganya. Another apron, this one made by Leora for Ganya. "Low Tidings," she giggled. "We think too much alike."

BiBi's heart sank, and she bit the inside of her cheek. She would have purchased gifts if she had known.

Next, Ganya handed a perfectly-wrapped present to BiBi.

"For me?" she asked, near tears. She wanted to hide beneath the quilt on her bed, rather than receive a gift and have none to give in return. She pulled at the strings, letting the cloth fall away from her present. She held the beautiful dress in her hands, taking in the detailed stitches that made a colorful floral pattern across the front.

"I thought it was time you had your own, dear. No more wearing Tovi's old ones."

"When did you ever have the time?" she asked, not taking her fingers from the embroidery.

"Oh, here and there while you were out with Silas or Tali."

"I love it, and I . . . I wish I had something for you."

Ganya patted her hand. "Don't be silly, sweetheart. You didn't even know about Low Tidings."

"Still, I can't . . . It's just so beautiful."

"Nonsense," Granny Leora said with a big smile. "Your gift to us is your sweet company."

Tali had carved a new set of bowls for Ganya's kitchen and a cutting board for Leora. Leora added an apron for BiBi. Leora and Ganya had worked together on a new set of everyday clothes for Tali to "replace those rags you insist on wearing." Then, Tali pulled out one last parcel and handed it to BiBi.

It was long and thin, wrapped in a clean cloth, and tied with twine. She unrolled it to find a set of beautiful paint brushes. The handles were carved from red wood, and she ran her fingers across the soft, navy blue bristles. She looked up and met his twinkling eyes. "And where did this hair come from?"

He ran his fingers through his mane, showing her the spot in the back that was shorter than the rest. They all had a good laugh, and Ganya threatened a full sheering soon.

"They are perfect. Thank you." She had trouble making eye contact with him after such a personal and sweet gift. Her mind whirled with urgent warnings that she should leave immediately. But how could she? It was a holiday. She could leave tomorrow.

After clearing the mess they had made, they wandered through the crowds toward the center of town. On the platform near the general store, some young actors bowed to loud applause from the audience. An old woman, bent over and so wrinkly that her eyes were mostly hidden, walked to the stage, leaning against a cane. A man pulled a rocking chair onto the platform, and she sat down. At once, the whole crowd took their seats on limbs, crates, doorsteps, and railings.

Her voice was surprisingly strong, like a general or schoolmaster. "Do you know who sends the floods?"

"Adwin!" the crowd cried.

"And do you know who gives us all that we need, even when the flood rages?"

"Adwin!"

"And who lowers the waters and puts them back within their banks?"

"Adwin!"

"Who brings the earth back to life, making all things new and green?"

"Adwin!"

"Let me tell you the story of our Adwin."

BiBi half-listened to the familiar story. She sneaked a glance from the corner of her eye at Tali. Silas stood next to him, and they made quite the pair. Both tall and trim and handsome. Tali's wild, dark blue hair contrasted against Silas' green. She liked looking at them both, but her gaze lingered on Tali the longest.

" . . . and great darkness spread over the city. Many hearts turned away from Adwin. The lure of gold and fame and power was too great, and they . . . "

Tali had one arm draped across Ganya's shoulder, and he seemed so completely at ease. He laughed and gasped at all the right places in the story, a twinkle never leaving his eye. Ganya looked so content next to her boy. It was so sweet, and it made her long for the other arm to be around her own shoulder.

" . . . braved the trek through the cloud and down the mountain, following Adwin no matter the peril . . . "

As the story reached its zenith, she quietly slipped away, her heart so heavy and her throat so tight, she could hardly breathe. Back in her room, she held the jars of paint, thankful for a quiet moment alone to think.

She didn't know how long it would be until the flood fully receded and the ground was dry again. But it was coming. If she wanted to protect Tali—Adia—she should go now while she had plenty of time to find the way through the desert and back to the mountain—and before Rhaxma could make good on her promise.

Silas' voice from the first day of the flood came back to her. "You have some difficult decisions to make, but you don't have to make them yet." Now, her time was up. She had to decide. "If you choose to stay here, we have much work to do. If you choose to go back . . . Well, I will be heartbroken, but my love for you will not dim. Not even by a little."

She took a deep breath. He had given her the choice, and he had even set the jars of paint out for her to take. Her mind moved from Silas to Tali. Damien's grandson. An heir of Mount Damien. The armies would come, likely looking for Tovi. But they would find him instead. She couldn't let that happen.

She gathered up a few of her belongings and packed them into a bag that she could strap across her back. She rewrapped the jars of paint in the small baby blanket from the trunk and put the bundle at the top of her bag. She didn't dare write much, but she left a farewell for Ganya and Tali on the kitchen table.

She used both hands to gather her hair so that she could braid it over her shoulder, and what she saw made her freeze in terror. Her hair was not black. It was dark blue. She held it before her eyes. It had been black that morning. When had it changed? She knew a little of how colors worked. Why today? Why had her hair registered her love for Tali today? Just now?

She felt the heat rise in her cheeks as she pondered her circumstances. She had chosen Tali's safety over what Silas wanted for her. "Well, that'll do it," she said darkly under her breath.

If she had any doubts before, they were gone. There was no way she would let Tali see this proof of her love for him—proof of her failed loyalty to Silas.

While the rest of Adia celebrated, she moved north through the trees.

CHAPTER 35

While Tovi's mind danced from sludge to Eryx's pain to Lena's fury to the painting showing her destiny, the evening campfire at the sea was subdued. No one spoke much except to politely ask for more fish or to pass the bowl of fruit. Eryx was exhausted and didn't have many words for anyone. He kept his eyes averted, quietly eating his dinner before turning in.

Tovi pondered how far she had come in her time at the sea. Her daily walks with Silas had brought her peace, and she was learning to control her temper and impulsive desires—most of the time. So, why had it been so easy to take that walk with Carlyn when she knew she shouldn't have? And what would happen if Lena learned that Carlyn knew the truth about Tovi?

Lena ate quietly, refusing to look at Tovi over the fire. It wasn't long before the girls went into their darkened hut and prepared for bed without speaking.

Tovi lay awake, overwhelmed by the future Silas had shown her coupled with her failure at such a simple task as staying on the beach within Lena's sight. She was not up to the challenge to be a queen. She hadn't even been able to keep her identity a secret or obey the basic rules put forth by Silas and Lena.

Sniffles and a rustling sound from Carlyn's bed broke Tovi out of her thoughts. Her heart sank. Sweet Carlyn had tried to take the blame, and now she was suffering through unnecessary guilt. It was Tovi's own fault, and she knew it.

She heard Carlyn move from her bed, and there was a deeper darkness in the hut as Carlyn blocked the moonlight that usually spilled in through the doorway. Tovi argued with herself for a few moments before getting up to follow her. She hoped she could convince Carlyn that it wasn't her fault and there was no need to feel so bad.

Out in the moon and starlight, Tovi looked all around. There was no movement besides the waves coming ashore and the trees swaying. Moonbeams lit a white path on the water that mesmerized her, and she walked toward the sea. She noticed a dark form by the edge, much too big to be Carlyn.

Eryx looked up briefly as she approached before turning back toward the water. She sat beside him and joined his quiet vigil. The sound of the waves was soothing after such an intense day. She hugged her knees into her chest, resting her cheek on top and looking at his profile.

The angles of his nose told the story of many breaks. His scars were shiny in the moonlight, and she could see the one from the fight that she had watched on her first day on the mountain. It seemed like a lifetime had passed since then.

"What was it like?" Tovi asked, her voice almost drowned out by a wave.

He didn't seem to need any explanation. He swallowed and then answered, not turning to look at her as he spoke. "Hardest thing I've ever done. Awful. But needed."

"Did he tell you why it has to be this way? Why it has to be so painful?"

"It's the undoing of everything I've learned. Everything I've done. The emptying and undoing and unlearning are painful."

"But couldn't he—"

"Don't blame Silas. This is my fault," he interrupted, his voice harsh. Tovi felt like he had slapped her face, and she didn't ask any more questions.

Eryx was quiet for a few seconds before cursing under his breath. "I'm sorry. I didn't mean to take it out on you." He glanced at her and held her gaze. She saw pain and confusion where there had been so much sparkle in the last few days.

"I—I guess I thought you would feel better after some of it was out," she said.

Eryx turned back to the water. "I thought so, too. And maybe it will feel better once it's all out. Right now, all I can think about is how much more we have to go. All the things I have done. The person I have been. The hate and rage I have lived. It's . . . it's a lot to relive and think about in one day. He told me I had two choices. A little bit at a time for as long as it takes, which could be years. Or getting it done quicker. He said it would be harder, but well worth it when it's over. I guess we'll see about that."

He had been so brave to take the harder option, the option that would empty him quicker, make him healthy and vibrant in less time but with so much pain. She didn't know if she could ever have the courage to do that.

"Do you want to talk about it?"

"No." Gruff, harsh, and so like the old Eryx. She had thought they were becoming friends, and his cold tone stung.

"I'll leave you alone to think." She stood and brushed sand from her legs.

He looked up. "Could you stay?"

She was surprised and taken aback, and she stood frozen, trying to understand.

"I don't want to talk, but it's nice to have . . . to be with . . . I like having you here."

"Oh," was the only sound she could find. She sat again, leaving more space between them than before.

He surprised her by hanging his head and laughing quietly.

"What?"

He looked up, a grin barely turning up his mouth. "We're both really bad at this."

"At what?"

"Letting people in. Having a friend."

"You have Silas," Tovi said, remembering Eryx's back that was blank, without its marks from Damien.

"Yes, I trust Silas. Most of the time."

She glanced at him, but he was looking out at the waves. She studied his profile again, and she wondered what had happened to turn him into this closed-off fighter. It occurred to her for the first time how similar they were, and this wave of recognition tugged at a deep place in her heart. She knew her own pain, and she wished it on no one else.

They were quiet for some time, looking out on the dark waves. The roar and rhythm were soothing, and Tovi breathed deeply, glancing occasionally at Eryx. His face was relaxed, and his eyes reflected the moonlight. She couldn't name the strange, off-kilter feeling that swirled in her mind when she looked at him. It wasn't like the warmth that came over her when she was with her brother, Silas, or Ganya. It was nothing like the once all-consuming pull to be near Calix. She grimaced as she pictured him.

This was different, a growing tension between staying and running. She wanted to know everything about him. She wanted to hear the story of what made him so much like her. In the same breath, she feared he might recognize it in her, too. He might see the loss and the pain in her and know, without words, the things she had only shared with her chosen few.

While the two halves of her heart clashed, she searched for a question she could ask, something safe that would take her mind to a more welcome place. Before she could find one, he stood, said goodnight, and walked back to his hut.

CHAPTER 36

Alone in his library, King Damien listened to the clock tick toward the next hour and ran his hands over the drawing of the wall that was slowly taking shape around his city. He stared at the empty, cold fireplace, but he didn't really see it. His mind was on a day long, long ago.

***

He was a young man, and the mountain was still green. His friend and mentor, King Adwin, decided that it was finally the day. After years of teaching and tutoring and molding, King Adwin was ready to share a secret with young Damien.

King Adwin's pale yellow hair fluttered in the breeze as they sat on a hillside looking out on a bare expanse. It was just a dusty field for as far as the eye could see, and they had traveled together for several days to reach this spot. Their journey had been full of fun, adventure, and a little danger. Damien had never felt so close to another person in all of his twenty years. And for it to be the king himself . . . Well, there were no words for the pride he felt at being King Adwin's chosen friend.

"Do you have this sight etched in your mind? Will you always remember it?" Adwin asked.

"Yes, we have been staring at it for hours."

"Good. Come with me."

There was a large, flat outcropping of granite. Adwin ran his hand along the surface of the granite and nodded. He put his pack on the ground and

211

pulled out paints, brushes, and a palette. He mixed blue and green to make turquoise, and he painted directly onto the rock. With a different brush, he used white to add details. Then, he leaned close to his painting and breathed onto it. It was like an exhale but with the sound of the wind.

A great roar broke out in the distance, and Damien turned toward it in fear. The loud sound was from the horizon, where a wall of water rushed over the barren field. The water was the exact color of the paint. As it settled, waves rhythmically washed across the edge of the field, and the froth on each wave was the white Adwin had used in the painting.

Awed and speechless, he watched Adwin create trees and flowers and shells and birds. He made fish; sandy shores; and funny, little, red animals that scurried away from the waves. As the sun set, Adwin used orange, pink, and purple to set the heavens aflame. He designed all of it on the rock wall and breathed it into reality, right before Damien's eyes.

They climbed down to the new beach and spent the night on the warm sand. Damien had a hard time sleeping as each crashing wave reminded him of their incredible day. His mind turned and turned with the wonders of new creation.

In the morning, Adwin cooked fish over a fire. When the bones were licked clean, Adwin handed Damien a paintbrush. "Your turn," he said.

Damien stared at it, holding it tenderly before him. "You mean it?"

"Yes, I mean it. It's your turn to create and make this world better. My lessons these last several years have been preparation. I want you to be my partner."

Damien wrapped his hand around the paintbrush handle. He turned it this way and that. "I will be able to paint something and make it real?"

"Not at first. You will create, and I will fix it and make it real." Damien's brow wrinkled, which made Adwin laugh again. "This is going to take a lot of practice, and you must be willing to take my correction. When you are ready, I will give you the power to make your creations real on your own."

They spent several weeks on that rocky hill overlooking the beach. When they ran out of room on the granite, Adwin enclosed their painting in a new cave that looked like it had been there forever. They moved on to the next bit of rock that would work as a canvas.

Damien struggled at first. He was clumsy with the brush and couldn't get the shapes to form just right. Adwin worked with him on his technique, and he always had several questions about the purpose and intent of each creation.

At night, they sat on the beach next to a warm fire, talking about each idea and the impact it would have on the world. Adwin always pushed him to look for creative ways to bring joy to the people on the mountain, and he also made him explore potential, unintended consequences.

Those weeks by the sea were the happiest of Damien's life. His heart sank when Adwin told him it was time to pack up and leave. But they did not go back to the mountain. They circled around and moved toward the hills in the north.

"We placed a sea to the south. What should we place to the north?" he asked Damien as they walked. It took several days for Damien to answer.

At first, he wanted to try his hand at another ocean, but he didn't think he could rival the one Adwin created. A forest? Too common, unless he made it a forest of something other than trees. But he couldn't think of what else would make a forest.

Frustrated and wanting to give Adwin a good answer, he thought long and hard about the dusty field becoming a glorious ocean. His favorite part was the warmth of the sand on the beach and the way he could dig his toes in it or use a stick to draw designs. And then it hit him. He would make a sea of sand.

Damien and Adwin discussed the plan for the sandy sea, and they named it desert. Many nights were spent debating the benefits and consequences of a vast expanse of sand. They spoke of wind and rain and plants and heat. Adwin was particularly delighted by the idea of an oasis, a sign of hope in the middle of what seemed barren. And when they reached the northern hills, which looked over the northern dusty expanse of nothingness, Damien found a large boulder and painted his vision. When it was complete, Adwin smiled.

Adwin took up his own brush and painted Damien, his mouth puckered in a strong exhale. From his mouth came waves of wind and color. Adwin breathed on the painting, and Damien felt the wind wrap around him, whipping his hair—shaggy from their journey—and almost knocking him down. It filled his lungs until he thought they would burst. When the wind calmed, he opened his eyes.

Adwin motioned toward his desert painting, and Damien knew what to do. He had watched Adwin do it, and now it was his turn. He breathed deeply onto the paint and stone, and he heard a distant rumble. The field shook, and the earth quaked. When it settled, there were waves of sand for as far as he could see. Far in the distance, he could just make out a spot of green—the oasis of beauty and bounty in the middle of the desert.

"I'm pleased that you are now my partner in creation," Adwin said, sitting with Damien and watching the way the sun sparkled on the sand. "There are a few things you need to know before we return to the mountain. First, this magic only works when using my paint, which is made from my blood. Using anything else will be a waste of time. Second, there is nothing that can undo creation. It is permanent. If you make something that you come to regret, you cannot reverse it. All you can do is create something new to try to work around it. Third, I trust you, and you are permitted to use this gift how you see fit. But remember that it is wise to ask me for direction and to include me in your plans. Fourth, you are brilliant, imaginative, and good-hearted. Use this power to make lives better all around you. I can't wait to see what you do."

***

It was only a few years later when Adwin had taken away the paints, angry over some of Damien's inventions, like the marks on backs and the voices in the dungeon.

Now, many decades later, he could still see the flames from those camp fires on the beach. Damien gazed at the fire in his library and wondered if BiBi was making any progress in securing a few jars of paint.

Adwin couldn't reverse his own magic. As his old friend once said, there was nothing that could undo creation. All Damien needed was some of Adwin's paint, for the wind of creation still stirred in his lungs.

CHAPTER 37

"Where have you been?" Tovi asked Carlyn. Carlyn hadn't returned by the time Tovi fell asleep, and she wasn't there when Tovi woke either. It was early afternoon, and she had finally turned up, appearing with a basket over her arm.

"I got up early. I wanted to find something different to eat," she said. "I had to get far enough inland to find these. They're my favorite." She showed off the basket of strawberries. Tovi hadn't seen one since sitting with Silas back in Adia.

Lena eyed her closely. "Lyra says you were up in the middle of the night, too. Where did you go then?"

Carlyn looked surprised and turned to Tovi. "I'm sorry I woke you. When I can't sleep, I like to go on walks."

"It's dangerous," Lena said. "Don't leave the beach."

"Oh, yes, all right," she stammered. Tovi noticed dark circles under her eyes. "Have I missed Silas?"

"He's with Eryx, further up the beach," Tovi answered.

Carlyn nodded and set the basket down. Lena grabbed a spear and walked toward the water. As soon as Lena was out of earshot, Carlyn turned to Tovi and grasped her arm. "I found something, something that you *have* to see."

"What is it?" Tovi asked.

"I went to that cave up there," she said, pointing to the archway in the granite above their beach. "It's incredible. You're painted inside."

"I know. Silas showed me."

Carlyn's face fell. "Oh. I didn't realize you had seen it already. I really want to go back. Will you walk up there with me? Will you tell me everything Silas said about it?"

"I can't. Didn't you hear her? We're supposed to stay on the beach."

Carlyn looked up at the cave. "Please? Is it really leaving the beach if you can still see the beach from there? It's not far."

"No."

Carlyn continued, "If Silas took you there, it can't be wrong to go back, right?"

Tovi hesitated.

"Please, Lyra. I mean, Tovi. I felt so close to Silas when I was looking at those paintings. I really want to go back. It's been hard on me these last few days. He's asked me to give up so much, everything I know. Somehow, it feels easier when I'm looking at what he made."

Tovi's mind battled. She was supposed to stay on the beach, but it *did* seem unlikely she would be forbidden to go somewhere Silas had taken her before. And she was supposed to be kind and caring toward Carlyn. Her heart was touched by Carlyn's desperation to know more about Silas' paintings. She knew how it felt and pictured her moments in the throne room on the mountain when everything had suddenly become clear.

Then, her mind sorted out all the messy pieces. "I know that feeling, Carlyn. You'll feel that close again. Silas will be done with Eryx soon, and then I'm sure he'd take you up to the cave himself. That will be better than going with me, anyway."

Carlyn frowned. "I want to go now. He might take all day with Eryx. I guess I'll just go alone." She trudged into the trees.

Tovi sighed and went back to weaving coconut husks into rope. This must be how just about everyone felt about her when she was impulsive and moody. She laughed at herself and twisted the fibers.

She looked down the beach. She couldn't see Eryx or Silas. Lena was far away, knee-deep in the waves and looking tiny in the distance. It was a moment of quiet, a rare bit of alone time. She stretched her fingers and looked out on the sparkling water, breathing in the peace and rest.

"Help!" Carlyn's scream startled her, and Tovi stood quickly, spinning toward the sound. "Help me, Tovi!"

She took a step toward the jungle before stopping. She turned back toward the beach and cupped her hands around her mouth. "Meira!" she yelled as loud as she could. "Meira!"

Lena didn't look up. She was too far away, and the waves and the wind must have drowned out Tovi's cries.

"Help, Tovi! Please!" Carlyn's voice was desperate.

Tovi grabbed a knife and started toward the woods, but she halted at the tree line. What was she to do? Could she disobey Silas to help a friend? Wasn't she supposed to be kind and loving?

"What's wrong?" Tovi yelled back.

"I-I think I broke my leg."

Tovi's heart calmed. She could handle a broken bone, and it didn't sound like Carlyn was too far inside the trees. "I'll be right there," she called. She ran into her hut, exchanging the knife for some rags that she could use to bind Carlyn's injury.

She stepped into the trees. "Say something, Carlyn. I don't see you."

"Over here," she cried. She sounded further away. Tovi moved toward Carlyn's voice, but still, she did not see her.

"Over here," Carlyn wailed again.

Tovi parted the thick underbrush and stepped into the same orange grove they had visited before. Light trickled through the trees, giving the grove an eerie green light.

Carlyn stood on both legs, very still, staring at her.

"I'm so sorry, Tovi. I promise I didn't want to."

Tovi's heart pounded. "What do you—"

There was a rustling behind her, and Tovi spun around. Four armed men blocked her escape. Her eyes locked on the only familiar face.

"Thad," she gasped.

"Don't make a scene. This will be easier for all of us if you come willingly," he said, his voice flat.

"How does she know your name, sir?" one of them asked.

"She was acquainted with my brother and sister during her short stay with Calix," he explained, looking at her with no emotion or affection. "Who has the ropes?"

"Don't do this. Please," Tovi begged. But it was no use. She was weaponless and defenseless. There was no escape when it was four to one. The soldiers tied her hands behind her back and pushed her through the trees, away from the sea.

Please, Silas, she thought. *Save me. Where are you?*

A rustling in the trees made hope bloom within her, but it was Lena, not Silas, who burst through the leaves. "I told you . . . " Her scolding stopped when her eyes took in the scene in front of her. She turned to run, but it was too late. One man grabbed her spear while two others subdued her and tied her hands. Her eyes shot fire toward Tovi before turning to Thad. What passed between them left Tovi cold. It was a look of utter betrayal. Thad looked away.

The sun had already set as Tovi and Lena were half-pulled, half-pushed through the south arch of the mines. One of the men lit a torch, and they walked in its glowing globe. Thad hoisted Tovi and Lena into a metal cart. Carlyn climbed in after them but kept her gaze down. She hadn't spoken or even looked at Tovi or Lena since the orange grove.

The cart lurched and started its climb. With her hands still tied, Tovi overbalanced and fell, hitting her chin and lip hard on the metal side. "Oh!" Carlyn cried. It echoed several times through the mines. She helped Tovi up. Tovi could taste blood, and her mouth throbbed.

They were met by even more armed men at the top of the mine.

Then came the next surprise. They were not taken to the palace.

With the four new guards in front, Carlyn by her side, and the four who had captured her holding Lena behind her, they marched up a quiet street in the Bottom Rung. A building with a swinging green sign and sagging iron balconies came into view, and she felt relief for the first time in hours.

That hope was dashed when she wasn't taken into the HH headquarters. Instead, she was unceremoniously pushed inside the neighboring tavern. After a flight of stairs, she was met with a vision that sent chills down her spine.

Three makeshift thrones had been made of dining chairs placed on large crates in the middle of the room. They were draped with old curtains. Sitting on the right was the sickly Megara. In the middle was the fierce, terrifying, yellow-eyed Rhaxma. The third chair was empty. A beautiful, painted map covered the wall behind them. She saw her name nailed to the green portion in the west.

Rhaxma's orange hair was braided into a crown; her eyelids were dramatically lined with black makeup; and her lips—usually bright and bold—were bare. "Tsk tsk tsk." Rhaxma stood and took hold of Tovi's face, turning it this way and that. "You weren't supposed to harm her. Lyra, get her something to wash the blood off."

Tovi's eyes swiveled around the room, finding the bright pink hair of the real Lyra.

"Yes, ma'am—I mean, Your Majesty," she said, bustling from the room.

Rhaxma's fingers tightened, and Tovi looked into her face.

"Oh, and Lyra?" she called. Lyra paused in the hallway. "Get the children."

Carlyn stifled a cry, her knees buckling. She sagged against the wall.

Rhaxma let go of Tovi and went back to her throne. A moment later, Lyra returned, a small girl at her feet and a baby in her arms. Carlyn openly wept as the little girl cried, "Mama" and ran to her.

Carlyn kissed her all over her curly head. "Are you all right? My darling, Mama missed you." She took the baby from Lyra, cradling the small bundle, her cheek on the little forehead. She looked up at Tovi and Lena. "I'm so sorry. I hope someday you will understand."

"You've done well, Carlyn," Rhaxma said. "Now, go, and remember the price if you tell anyone what you have seen or heard. One of my soldiers will escort you back below the cloud to the camp."

With one more glance at Tovi, Carlyn took the girl by her plump, little hand and hurried from the room. A soldier followed her out.

Lyra wiped Tovi's chin with a wet cloth. Her bottom lip stung, and she knew it was split open. She looked up at Rhaxma.

Rhaxma glared back. Gone was the playfulness Tovi had seen upon her first arrival on the mountain. So much had changed.

"Who is this?" she asked, turning her attention to Lena.

"My name is Meira."

"Liar."

"Then you must know who I am."

"Ah, she doesn't play games, this one." Rhaxma's smile was catlike. "Your colors match Xanthe and Jairus, and they match a little girl in the portraits in the palace."

Lena remained quiet, staring fiercely at Rhaxma, as if they were on equal ground.

"How did you survive? You're supposed to be dead."

Lena smirked. "Am I?"

Rhaxma's smile chilled. "I suppose there is time to learn your secrets later." She rose and approached the map painted on the wall. Rhaxma ripped Tovi's name from Adia, placed it over the very center of the mountain, picked up a hammer leaning against the wall, and smacked a nail through it. She did the same with Lena's. She gestured to the other names nailed to the map. "Where are the others?"

"I don't know," Tovi said.

Rhaxma considered her for a moment, and then her face gentled. She pulled Tali's name from the map. "Will someone please bring Tovi a chair? Bring one for Lena, too. There is something I need to tell them. Some bad news I must share."

Thad brought forward two chairs that matched Rhaxma's throne. It was awkward to sit with her hands still tied behind her, but Tovi was grateful for the rest.

"Much has happened since you left the mountain, Tovi," Rhaxma began. "Your brother came here on a mission for Adwin."

Tovi's heart thudded uncomfortably.

"He was caught here in the Bottom Rung, and he was taken to the palace. He didn't cooperate, and he was tortured. He refused to tell

Damien what he was up to, what Adwin was up to. Damien was tired of playing games, so . . . " She ripped Tali's paper into several pieces.

Tovi's knees shook, and she braced for the words she feared above all others.

"Tali is dead."

Tovi roared like a wounded lion and fell forward out of her seat, her face to the floor. "No," she moaned. "No."

Through tear-filled eyes, she saw the blurred image of Rhaxma descending from her throne and pouncing on her. Rhaxma's pointed fingernails clawed into her as she turned Tovi onto her back. Rhaxma held her there, one hand on each shoulder, staring at Tovi, madness in her face. "That's how it feels," she said. "That's how it feels!" There was black sweat across her brow, and it dripped onto Tovi. "That's how it feels to know your brother—your favorite person—is dead. Gone. Forever. You will *never* see him again."

Tovi wailed, her mind blank, except for the misery.

Rhaxma stood up, brushed off her dress, and looked down upon Tovi. "Lyra, take them upstairs. Find someplace for them to sleep, and guard their door. We'll take them to Damien in the morning."

CHAPTER 38

Eryx rested against the curve of a palm tree, far north of where he wanted to be. Every muscle and joint ached. He didn't know if he would ever get used to being jostled by a horse's gallop, no matter how thankful he was for the quick getaway provided by Silas.

As he approached the palm trees and growing city around the oasis, three riders on horses, just like his, trotted out to meet him, kicking up sand behind them.

Eryx's horse pranced nervously while they approached. As they grew closer, Eryx could tell it was a man and two women. They drew up close to Eryx, and he recognized the younger woman and man immediately.

Jairus and Xanthe. A totally changed, fearsome Xanthe. A strong, full-of-life Jairus. Eryx looked between them, unable to find words. All three were wild and regal. Xanthe's brown hair was braided over her shoulder, but there were wisps dancing all around her face. The other woman had white hair piled on top of her head and looked older. Jairus was shirtless, and he carried a spear that was much larger than what they had used to catch fish at the sea. All of them were suntanned, muscular, and radiating power and light.

"You made it," Xanthe said, tugging on her reins to still her horse. "Silas told us to expect you."

"You're different."

"Yes," she said. "So are you."

The white-haired woman smiled. "My name is Thomae. I am Jairus' mother."

"And Tovi's," Eryx added.

She smiled. "Yes, and Tovi's. And Lena's and Tali's."

"They've been captured. Tovi and Lena."

The mood turned somber, and Jairus nodded. "We knew that was a possibility. Please, come with us. We'll feed you and give you a place to rest, and you can tell us the whole story."

The city's lodgings were mostly tents, but a few yellow brick buildings were taking shape. Eryx was offered space in Jairus and Xanthe's large, multi-room tent.

Eryx took a swim in the large, natural spring at the very center of the city to clean off some of the grime from his journey. When he was done, dinner was set out on a blanket in the center of the enormous tent. They reclined around the food, and Eryx was thankful for his first meal in a long time that didn't consist of fish and fruit. They ate bread covered in honey and a thick meat and vegetable stew. "Where does all of this come from?"

"You'd be surprised how much can grow here near the springs and how many animals come to get a drink. And we'll be eating through the provisions from the Jolly Barrel for months. Silas has provided everything we need," Jairus said.

A woman barged into the tent. "Jairus, Xanthe, you should come. Illias stopped a woman from crossing the land bridge. He is bringing her now."

They all rose to their feet just as a man dragged a petite woman into the tent. She was kicking and clawing at her captor, and Eryx's heart nearly stopped. Navy blue hair on a tiny, little frame.

"Tovi," he said, taking long strides to reach her, to save her. "How did you—"

His question caught in his throat when she threw her head back, her hair flying away from her face. It wasn't Tovi.

"BiBi," Xanthe said, rushing to her. "Illias, let go. She is a friend."

For that one short moment, Eryx thought Tovi was safe and that she had found her way to them somehow. He hated the sinking feeling of hope lost. Where was she? What had happened to her? Was she safe?

"What has happened?" Xanthe asked, embracing BiBi and escorting her to their dinner. "Your hair . . . You have different colors."

"I could say the same about all of you," BiBi said.

"We'll start with you," Jairus said. "Your tale seems more important right now."

"Sweetheart, let her eat. She looks famished," Xanthe reproached.

As BiBi ate a piece of bread dipped in stew, Xanthe retold the story that Eryx had just heard about her healing in the cave, the sudden appearance of Tali and Thomae, their journey to the desert, and their instructions from Silas to help refugees escape the mountain.

"Your turn," Jairus said with a smile.

BiBi put down her plate and glanced around at all of them, her eyes tired and her brow strained. "I'm on a mission, and I can't tell you anything except that I have to get back to the mountain."

Eryx eyed BiBi's colors. "Does it have something to do with Tali?"

BiBi seemed to melt under the intense gaze from Thomae. She looked at the picnic blanket and picked at the stitches along the edge. "Yes. My mission is to protect Tali."

"Is he in danger?" Thomae asked, one hand pressed to her heart.

"No, but he will be if I don't go."

"If you *do* go, *you* will be in danger. Every eye will be on those colors," Eryx said.

BiBi looked around at them, and tears welled in her eyes. "I have to. You don't understand."

Eryx knew the fear in her voice and recognized the desperation in her words. "Did Silas send you on this mission?" Eryx asked, filled with suspicion that the answer was no.

BiBi looked him in the eye, cringed, and said, "Yes."

Later in the evening, as most of the tent city hushed for the night, Eryx rested against the palm tree and rolled his shoulders, trying to work the soreness out of them one at a time. He shoved Tovi's face out of his mind as hard as he could, but it was no use. She kept coming back.

A flash of her colors appeared between two tents. Had it been his imagination, or was BiBi making a run for it?

He jumped to his feet and took off for the edge of the encampment. He moved as quickly as he could through the rocky sand, cursing his aching body and urging it to move faster. When he cleared the tents and came to the open expanse that opened to the south, BiBi rounded a different corner and froze, staring at him with wide eyes that reflected the moon.

"Where are you going?" he asked, his voice meaner than he had intended.

She breathed hard and continued to stare, but she said nothing.

"You aren't on a mission for Silas, are you?"

More silence.

"Don't do this, BiBi. Stay here and wait for Silas."

"I can't." Her voice trembled when she finally spoke.

"Why?" He gritted his teeth and willed himself to sound less harsh. "Why can't you stay?"

Her eyes filled with tears again. "I'm on a mission for Rhaxma and Damien, not Silas. They'll attack Adia if I don't finish my task."

"Silas can handle it. Wait for his instructions."

"But I chose them over him."

"Haven't we all? He won't hold that against you. Choose Silas this time."

"Let me pass," she whispered.

"No. Stay here."

"What if I promise not to return to the mountain? What if I go somewhere else . . . and just hide for the rest of my life?"

"What good will that do?"

"I can't face them."

"Who?"

"Silas and Tali." She lifted a lock of her hair. "Do you know how humiliating this is?"

"I do know," he growled.

"Oh, Eryx! I'm so sorry. Of course, you do."

"Learn from my story," he commanded, trying hard to be gentle but failing. "Stay and wait for Silas. It's so much better this way."

She hesitated and looked at the stars while dark tears rolled down her cheeks. Finally, she nodded and followed him back to Jairus and Xanthe's tent.

When Eryx woke in the morning, BiBi was gone.

CHAPTER 39

Tovi leaned against Lyra on the way to a bedroom on a higher floor. Her mind searched for understanding, but the haze of shock and grief was too thick.

"It's not true, Tovi," Lyra assured her as she tucked her into a lumpy bed. "Your brother—it's not true."

Tovi blinked. The words pulled her out of her stupor.

Lyra nodded and combed Tovi's hair with gentle fingers. "She's just trying to punish you. I heard her just this morning, angry because her spies haven't found him yet. Don't despair, sweetheart."

The tension Tovi had held all day rushed out of her, replaced with uncontrollable shaking and weeping. Lyra held her hand and whispered comfort until she calmed.

Lyra turned and embraced Lena. "Oh, Meira, dear. It is so good to see you."

Lena hugged her back. "Let's let Tovi rest. Is there somewhere we can talk? I want an update."

Tovi drifted into an uneasy rest.

She was shaken awake, a hand over her mouth. In the moonlight, she could just make out an unfamiliar face.

The man put a finger to his lips and pointed to the heart in his palm. The pounding in her ears subsided, and her pulse calmed.

She nodded, and he dropped his hand. She looked around. There were several others in the room with him. "Where's Lena?" she whispered.

The man bounced his finger on his lips again and shook his head.

Tovi followed the men quietly through the old pub and out a door in the kitchen. A guard lay ominously still on the floor.

When she stepped outside, she turned toward the curtain and the mines beyond that would lead her to freedom.

"We aren't going that way." He wrapped a thick arm around her waist, and she yelped in surprise. A hand covered her mouth again as she was pulled against a solid body. "No, miss, don't be screaming. We have orders to take you to our master."

Images of the palace's dungeon filled Tovi's mind. She saw a knife push into her hand and the dark webs that took over the king as he stormed and raged. She could not go back there. She kicked and jerked, trying to get away. The man held her tighter. One of his buddies was beside him, looking cheerful.

Four men came out another door, dragging a kicking and biting Lena between them.

They marched them up through the cleaner streets of Mount Damien, past the Halo, and into the courtyard. The palace glowed with candlclight, even in the middle of the night.

They didn't take them to the palace.

"Hello, my love," Calix said as he came down from his room. He wore a silk robe, and his hair wasn't quite perfect. But he was wide awake and looked positively gleeful at the sight of Tovi. Megara, in a similar robe, was a few steps behind him.

He ran a thumb over Tovi's lip where it had split on the ride up through the mines. She flinched, and he laughed.

"Has someone been sent to wake His Majesty?" he asked, his eyes still on Tovi.

"Yes, sir. Just now."

"Good."

Oh, Silas, how many times will I have to beg for your help? Just this one more time, Silas. I promise I'll do what you say in the future. I've learned my lesson. Please come get me.

She expected him to burst through the door, but he didn't.

"Now, who do we have here?" Calix's eyes sparkled with intrigue. He combed his fingers through Lena's hair. "This is certainly a surprise, if you are who I suspect you might be." He looked to the guards. "What did you tell His Majesty? One or two?"

"Just the one, sir. Just Tovi."

"Excellent," he said, patting Lena's cheek. "This will be a most wonderful surprise for him."

Lena did not speak, and she did not meet Tovi's eye.

Ten minutes later, they were forcefully ushered into the throne room. Tovi looked around, taking in the mural, wondering how she had found herself back in this place so soon. She had hoped to never see it again.

Damien entered, flanked by his guards. He had taken the time to dress, or he hadn't yet been to bed.

"Tovi!" he cried. His grin was broad and grandfatherly as he approached her, but his dark eyes were cold and piercing. He took her hands and held them against his heart. "What a delight. I have been so worried about you, my dear."

She didn't answer. Every muscle was tensed, ready to fight.

He patted her hands. "You have been through a lot today. Let's get you cleaned up and comfortable. Perhaps we can catch up tomorrow after you have rested. Guards, take the princess and her friend to the chambers that are being prepared."

Tovi was flummoxed by the kind treatment.

As the king was turning to go, Lena spoke, her voice quiet but deadly. "Don't you recognize me, Grandpapa?"

He froze and took several stilted breaths. He turned back slowly, his eyes roving over Lena for the first time since they had entered. He trembled and reached out for the supporting forearm of one of his guards. Tovi had never seen such weakness in him.

"Lena?" he choked. "My darling, Lena?" He took a shaky step toward her, and a tear slipped down his cheek. "Everyone, out. Except Lena. Leave us. Now."

No one said a word as the guards led Tovi up two flights of stairs into the living quarters of the palace. The servants were silent as they bathed her and slipped a soft nightdress over her head.

One of the girls looked familiar. She smiled sadly as she tucked the covers around Tovi and blew out the candle. The servants left the room, but Tovi was sure there were still guards stationed on the other side of the door.

Tovi couldn't sleep. Her mind swirled. Hadn't it been the right thing? To help someone she thought was in need? Now, somehow, she was back on the mountain, back in the palace, back with her grandfather. King Damien. And Lena was here, too, and it was all her fault.

She had no idea how to get out of this mess.

The moon was full and bright, and she could see intricately-patterned wallpaper, ornate wooden furniture, and a large mirror in the gray light. There was a vase in the corner that was probably taller than Tali, and there were crystal droplets on a chandelier. The luxury only reminded her that she should not be here. She longed for Adia, or even her seaside hut. "Silas," she whispered. "I swear I'll do everything you ask of me for the rest of my life. I will never disobey again. Just please get me out of here."

Her mind went to her brother. That moment when she thought he was dead had been the worst of her life. Worse than Avi's death. Worse than Damien carving her hand with a knife. It felt like she had been hit by a fierce wave, knocking her breath out of her lungs. She was drowning, with no idea which way was up.

And then to find out so quickly that it wasn't true . . . Her mind had spun, but she hadn't felt any relief. The pain of those moments still echoed in her, and she didn't feel safe believing he was all right quite yet. The blow was too fresh. She wanted to see him for herself and know that all was okay. He was out there somewhere, somewhere he wasn't intended to be. All because she had disobeyed and left Adia.

She tried to get comfortable in the bed, but it was no use. It wasn't the mattress or bedding. Those were the finest she had ever known, but her body and mind couldn't relax.

So much had changed in just one day, and it was all her fault.

She lay still, and tears trickled out of the corners of her eyes and down onto her pillow. The rules had been so simple, and she had let Silas down. She had let everyone down.

She wondered where Eryx was. Had Silas warned him to flee just in time? Where did he go? Would she ever see him again?

CHAPTER 40

"Calix, my boy. What a day this has been," Damien chuckled, filling two glasses. Calix reclined in the chair near the fire. "Tell me how you did it."

Calix's smile faltered, and Damien detected a few nerves poking through his triumph.

"Your Majesty, I have been . . . suspicious of the other masters for some time. I believed they were working against you, but I had no evidence until recently. I learned they were close to having an heir in their hands, but I didn't know which one. I just knew that the three girls—Rhaxma, Megara, and BiBi—were in league against you."

Damien's vision darkened. How had he missed this betrayal? "How did you come by this knowledge?"

"Megara thinks we are engaged."

"And she told you they had Tovi and Lena?"

"She told me they were amassing an army below the cloud, had convinced BiBi to send Adian paint to them instead of you, and had search parties who had spotted an heir."

Damien took a sip of his wine. "Well, this is good news."

"Excuse me, sir?"

"If she was willing to tell you all of this, their little alliance could not be very strong." He considered the boy, and Calix shifted uncomfortably in his seat as the silence went on. Good. "And why am I just now hearing of all this?"

"I wanted to be sure before I came to you. I have no way to go through the curtain to see this supposed army for myself. We haven't heard from BiBi since she left, and they could have been bluffing about knowing the location of an heir. But tonight, Megara came to me saying they had captured Tovi and someone with Jairus' colors. I made a plan right away and brought them to you the moment they were in my hands."

"That was just this evening? They had been on the mountain for mere hours?"

"Yes, Your Majesty."

His anger evaporated. "Good job, my boy. Good job. And now, we must consider our next steps. We may have Tovi and Lena, but if there is an army growing below the cloud and if your sister betrays me, we have much more work to do."

"Can't we enjoy our victory for just a little bit?" Calix asked, raising his glass in salute.

"No. No rest. Our power depends on us concentrating on the next move." He took a sip of his wine and looked over his weapon, this young man who had proven himself in glorious fashion. Pride swelled within his heart, and he realized he had more hope in Calix than in his own son and grandchildren.

He thought back to the day when Princess Thomae had begged him to allow the nanny and her two children to move into the palace. They had been a ragtag bunch, hardly removed from the Bottom Rung. They would have been just fine in the servants' quarters, but Thomae had insisted on spoiling the little family, treating them like royalty. BiBi and Calix grew up taking music and art lessons, wearing fashionable clothes, and learning the keys of Damien's success, the seven lessons that turned them into masters.

He never would have dreamed that the skinny, little urchin would become the hope of his kingdom.

"Believe it or not, I won't live forever," Damien said. "And I want to know my kingdom is in capable hands when my time comes."

"Don't speak of this, Your Maj—"

"It is not pleasant to think of, but we must be wise and have a plan."

"Isn't Prince Ajax the plan?"

"He doesn't have to be," Damien said, giving Calix a pointed look. "It could be you instead."

Calix sat up in his chair and set down his drink.

Damien held his silence for a few more beats, enjoying the hopeful tension in his young mentee. "You will marry Tovi."

Calix raised an eyebrow. "You think she'll allow that?"

Damien cackled. "Don't let me catch you thinking like that again. We won't give her the chance to *allow* anything. She'll marry you, and she'll give you heirs who carry my blood."

"Why not Lena? She is the eldest."

"I have different plans for Lena." He would never tell Calix—or anyone—the truth. The girl was his weakness. Her happiness was paramount to him. He couldn't force her into an arranged marriage, not after all she had been through. He would let his precious Helena chart her future. And if she provided heirs for him, all the better. At least, he would have Tovi and Calix's children as spares.

Calix's eyes took on a distant look, and he was quiet as the fire crackled. Damien let him dream for a bit before bringing him back to the moment. "As the future king, you will continue to build our defenses and military. We must have regiments with hearts and without. Those with hearts can be deployed to the mines to quarry stone as quickly as possible. It is more important than ever that we complete our protective wall. We will send other regiments to defeat their so-called army. Still others will search for Tali and Jairus and dispose of them. The heart-frees will defend the kingdom from inside the curtain."

"And what of Megara, Rhaxma, and BiBi? Will you arrest them? Execute them?"

"Excellent question." Damien brought his fingers together in front of his face and tapped them together. "Do you think you can pull any more information from Megara before we show our hand? Do you think she'd tell you more about this army?"

"Yes, I think so."

"Then I will pretend ignorance for now. I don't see any danger. They are hardly a threat. See what you can learn, and then we'll decide what to do with them. It seems my Council of Masters is down to only you. As the potential future king, we must surround you with weapons that both you and I can trust. Expand your search for their replacements, but keep quiet about it. Let's not startle the girls. We need them to think they are yet unknown to me."

There was a tap on the door, and a butler entered holding a small package. "Your Majesty, this was just delivered by one of the border guards. He claims a woman insisted it be brought to you immediately."

Damien stood and took the parcel. He untied the twine and let the small jar of gray paint drop heavily into his hand. His heart pounded in his ears and he felt faint.

A note was wrapped around the jar.

Your Majesty,

A great flood has kept me from sending news from Adia until now. There are no heirs there, but there is much talk of them gathering and hiding in the wilderness to the east. I found a way out, and I am traveling there now to see what and whom I can find. I will bring you a report in person when I know more. Enclosed is the paint you asked me to retrieve from Silas.

Yours, Bibianna Leonidas

Damien handed the note to Calix and lifted the jar to eye height, turning it this way and that. Could it be true?

Calix put the note down. "This makes no sense," he said. "She was in league with Rhaxma and Megara."

Damien smiled. "And she chose me. Be careful, my boy. It almost sounds like you are upset that she obeyed me."

"Of course not," Calix said defensively.

Damien moved to his map in the center of the room. The locket and brooch rested on top of the mountain. He slid the sapphire and ring to the east.

"I have Tovi and Lena, and I have Adwin's paint," he said dreamily, overcome by the victories of the day. He looked up and met Calix's eye. "Do not tell Megara or Rhaxma that I know about their betrayal. Do not tell them that I have the paint or that we've heard from BiBi. Do not speak of your marriage to Tovi."

"I promise, Your Majesty."

"You will trust me and not interfere with my plans."

Calix winced and looked a bit wounded. "Of course, sir."

"Now, off with you. Go get some rest. The taming of Tovi Tivka starts tomorrow."

CHAPTER 41

Rhaxma marched across the courtyard in the reddish gray light of dawn. Calix was eating breakfast on his terrace, and they made eye contact as she approached. He raised his glass to her.

She banged on the door and bullied her way past the butler. Calix would not get away with this. She felt for her knife in its sheath, safely tucked in the folds of her dress.

He didn't turn to greet her when she passed through the doors onto his terrace, so she circled him and stood near the railing, arms crossed, staring at him. "How did you do it?"

"Do what?" he drawled.

"You know exactly what I'm talking about."

"Why would I give you my secrets?"

She approached him, towering over him as he sat. She did not touch him. She breathed heavily, shakily. "I will ruin you, Calix."

He stood, forcing her to back up a few steps. Now, he looked down at her. "You're not doing a very good job."

"I found Tovi and Lena."

"And I delivered them to His Majesty."

"I will discover your spy, and I will rip his heart out. Do you want to watch?" she snarled.

He laughed. "Come now, Rhax. You should play nicely. Then maybe I'll let you live when I am king."

She matched his laugh. "You'll never be king. His Majesty uses you. You've never been his blood, no matter where you grew up or how close you think you are. You are a pawn, and that is all."

His smile vanished, and the veins in his neck throbbed. He grabbed her shoulders and shook her, digging his fingers into her flesh. She willed herself to show no pain.

She reached for her knife and swung it up so the point just grazed the bottom of his chin. He froze, looking down at the silver. He gripped harder, and she moved the blade down to the center of his throat. "Your cheap victory will be short-lived. There is much you don't know," she said.

With his right hand, he grabbed hold of her left wrist and put one finger down the neck of her short gloves. She tugged her arm away, and he used the momentum to strip the glove from her hand and knock the knife from the other.

Rhaxma made a fist with her left hand, and she scrambled after the knife. Calix grabbed her around the waist and threw her to the other side of the terrace. She crashed against the railing. He picked up the knife.

She stood shakily, nostrils flaring.

"Show me your hand, Rhax," he said, studying the blade.

"How long have you known?" she asked through gritted teeth.

"Come on, show it to me." He sauntered toward her.

"Why haven't you told His Majesty?"

"Maybe I have. Or maybe I'm saving it."

She circled him, moving toward his door.

"Oh, Rhax, don't go. We haven't even talked about your little army yet or your plans for the paint BiBi is stealing from Adia."

She squared her shoulders toward him, glaring with all the hatred that had burned for years. "You have always underestimated me, and someday, when my *little* army destroys you, you'll regret it."

She left with a slamming of the door, and he did not follow. As she stepped onto the cobblestone below, her knife crashed and clattered in front of her. She refused to look up at him. She stooped to pick it up and marched home with her head held high with more pride than she really felt.

Her whole army knew of her heart. She had shown it to them below the cloud. But few knew about Tovi and Lena. And only two knew about the paint. She had been betrayed by Megara or Thad.

And it was only a matter of time before King Damien found out about her heart and what she had been up to below the cloud. Perhaps he already knew.

She should leave. She should collect the other heirs and stay safely below the cloud until she was ready to return and conquer the world.

But it would mean leaving her parents and brothers. It would mean leaving Leeto. She walked into the parlor and sat beside him. He looked so perfect. So handsome. She leaned her head down onto the glass, resting her forehead, black tears dripping onto the coffin. "I'm so sorry," she whispered. "I'm so sorry to leave you. I'm so sorry that we aren't doing this together, taking control together. I'm doing this for us. Our family will sit on the real throne someday, and I'll write your legacy down for all the generations to know your name and revere it. Soon, Leeto, my dear brother. My hero. Soon."

She would leave, but not yet. First she must find out who had betrayed her.

She stormed down the streets, letting her cloak and hair billow behind her. She didn't care who saw her. A rage like she had never known coursed through every vein and made her feel invincible.

She threw open the door to the old pub and marched up the stairs, ignoring the terrified faces of their servants.

"Was it you?" she bellowed.

Megara, sitting at a desk in their makeshift throne room, looked bored and unaffected. "What do you—"

"You betrayed me."

"I don't know wh—"

"You told Calix everything."

"I've told Calix nothing," Megara snapped.

"Don't lie to me," Rhaxma hissed. "It was you or my brother. Thad wouldn't do this to me. It had to be you."

"Tell me what you think I've done," Megara said, leaning back and crossing her arms.

"Calix knows about my heart."

"You were a fool to show it to our army. Anyone could have come back through the curtain and told him."

"He knew about Tovi and Lena within hours of their arrival."

"Then question the search party."

"He knew about the paint."

Megara laughed. "His sister probably told him."

Rhaxma matched her laugh. "You think BiBi would tell her brother, the most disgustingly pathetic pawn of His Majesty, that she was plotting with us against the king?"

Megara took off her glasses. "I don't know what to tell you."

"I do," Rhaxma said, sweeping her arm across the desk. Inkwells and paper crashed to the floor. "Get out."

"You're paranoid. I've done nothing to betray you. Think about it. Thad has the heart. He's been fooling your whole family for years.

Who is more likely to have betrayed you, him or me? Have I ever been anything but fully myself around you? Have I ever been anything but mean, bitter, and honest about it?"

Rhaxma breathed heavily, glaring at Megara. "Three Queens," she said quietly. "So much for Three Queens. You're on your own. Get out."

Megara gathered a few papers and walked calmly from the room, her back straight and a much-too-light spring in her step.

Rhaxma sat on the edge of the desk and stared at the map on the wall. She needed a next move.

There was a tap at the door, and a servant entered and cleaned up the mess of ink and papers from Rhaxma's temper.

"Ma'am?" she said. "I mean, Your Majesty. Is this for you?" She picked up a small parcel wrapped in cloth and handed it to Rhaxma. It was round and fit in the palm of her hand. It was heavier than it looked.

Rhaxma untied the twine and unrolled the cloth. A note and a small jar of white paint fell into her lap.

No heirs in Adia. I am going in search, following several clues they are in the eastern wilderness. Will return when I know more.—B

She put the paint in her pocket along with her small dagger. Megara may have betrayed her, but BiBi had proven herself. Strange. She would have guessed the other way around.

She took a few calming breaths. She should leave soon, but she must first learn the significance of the paint. There was no point having it if she didn't know why the king wanted it so badly.

She went home and packed so that she could be ready to leave at the next hint of trouble.

CHAPTER 42

Tovi fretted, tossed, and turned until a soft yellow light crept through the window. "Silas, where are you?" she whispered.

"Right here," he whispered back.

She jumped nearly out of her skin and sat straight up. He was sitting in the armchair near the window. And he had the audacity to be smiling.

She flung herself at him, hugging his neck and whispering over and over again, "I'm so sorry. I've made such a mess of things."

When she was calmed and sitting across from him, he whispered, "Yes, you've made a huge mess. And I'm here to tell you what you're going to do about it."

She nodded. "Please, I'll do anything. Just get me out of here."

"You're going to stay."

"But—"

He raised a hand to silence her. "You told me you'd do anything. This is what I'm telling you to do. You've struggled to obey me, so maybe it will help that you are under lock and key here. I have three tasks for you."

Tovi's cheeks grew warm. "I have a feeling I've heard them before."

Silas nodded. "Stay, learn, be still. I want you to stay right here, in the palace, until I tell you it is time to go. Spend time in the throne room, studying the mural, learning about me and looking for the patterns in my story. I also want you to learn about your grandfather and look for ways to thwart his efforts, but you will need to be sneaky.

Behave yourself, and be compliant with him. He can't know that you are working against him. Finally, be still. Trust me. Spend time thinking about the ways I have always taken care of you, and let that knowledge bring you peace. Still those urges that tell you to run or rage or go your own way. Stay. Learn. Be still. Repeat that back to me."

"Stay. Learn. Be still."

"You got it."

"How long will I be here?"

"I'm not telling you."

"Why?" she cried in frustration, and Silas shushed her, pointing at the door.

"This time will be good for you. I'll be with you, even when you can't see me. And when the time comes to leave, I'll tell you. Now, don't look at me like that. You've wanted a mission. This is a big one."

"How is Tali? And Ganya?"

"Tali is fine. I won't tell you any more, just in case they try to get it out of you. Ganya is worried sick about you, but I have assured her that I am watching over you."

"And Eryx?"

"He's not all right, but he will be."

Tovi's heart skipped a terrified beat. "What's wrong?"

"Nothing permanent. He got away just fine. He blames himself for not keeping a better eye on you."

"That's ridiculous. He couldn't have stopped me."

"Oh, I know." Silas laughed. "And I've tried to tell him that, but he is beating himself up. And he is worried about you."

"And if I had never left Adia, we—Tali, Eryx, and I—would all be together there right now."

Silas nodded.

Tovi leaned her head into her hands. "Fix it, Silas. Can't you just fix it?"

When he didn't answer, she looked up. There were tears in his eyes. "I hate that you are in pain, Tovi. I hate that you are sad. I hate that you are separated from the people you love. I also must remind you that you did this to yourself, and sometimes, you have to be brave and face the consequences. I'm here with you in them, and you will never be alone. But you still must face the mess you have created. I'm not going to magically transport you back to Adia. You will learn and grow while you are here. And when it is time, I want you to go east, not west."

"Queen of the Wild Range," she said, remembering the painting in the cave.

"Yes, Queen of the Wild Range. When it is time, I will send you east."

"I don't want any of this. Can I refuse?"

"Remember the fire tunnel?"

She nodded miserably.

"You can always refuse. But look at where that has brought us. I can't promise what will happen to you or anyone else if you turn away from what I have planned for you. But want to know a secret?"

She nodded.

He smiled, leaned closer, and whispered, "You will be a great queen."

She took a deep breath and looked at her hands in her lap. "Can you at least give me some ideas of what I'm supposed to do while I'm here? How I'm supposed to thwart Damien? Staying and learning is fine, but I need some specifics."

"Sure," Silas said, annoyingly chipper.

Tovi looked up long enough to frown at him.

"Learn to paint."

"Paint? How does that fight against Damien?"

"He'll be thrilled with the idea for his own purposes, believe me. And someday, your skills will come back to haunt him."

"Fine. I'll learn to paint."

"Stay. Learn. Be still."

"I heard you."

Silas stood, kissed her on the forehead, and said, "See you soon." He disappeared.

The door opened, and she jumped.

"I thought I heard you up, Your Majesty," a servant said sweetly. "Let's get you dressed. King Damien wants to see you as soon as you're ready."

"Please, don't call me, 'Your Majesty.' You can call me Tovi."

The girl hesitated as she pulled Tovi's nightgown over her head. "I don't think His Majesty would like that very much. We have been told to serve you with the same reverence that we are to serve him."

"I've just never been called that before. I'd rather not start."

Tovi froze when she saw herself reflected in the three full-length mirrors that surrounded her. Bright blue eyes. Long, light brown hair with golden streaks. She touched the locks and blinked back tears. It was strange. She hadn't felt the change and wondered when it happened.

The girl looked at the ground. "Please don't make me call you by your first name. I don't know what he'll do to me."

"Of course," Tovi said, touching the servant's arm with a gloved hand. "I don't want him to be angry with you. Call me whatever you must."

The girl paused, buttoning Tovi's gown. "I'm so sorry. They're your family. I should be more careful with what I say."

"Don't worry. I hardly know them. And I don't like what I do know."

Once Tovi was dressed and made up, the servant curtsied and left.

When Tovi stepped through the door, Thad was there with another guard. She glared at her betrayer. He had betrayed her, betrayed Silas. He had chosen Damien. She had hoped to never have to speak to him again, but here he was, lurking outside her room.

She walked past without saying a word. She could hear him following her down the stairs, but he didn't try to speak to her.

"My darling girl, good morning!" Damien said, looking up from his quiche and fruit.

She smiled with everything but her heart. "Good morning, Grandfather."

Damien tilted his head and raised an eyebrow. "I see you have decided to behave."

"I . . . I will try."

He chortled into his teacup. "Some honesty. I can appreciate that. Why the change of heart?"

She hadn't expected the question and cursed herself and Silas for not being more prepared. She decided being mostly honest would have to be the way to go.

"I thought about it all night. Since I have to be here, I might as well be pleasant. You offered a beautiful room rather than the dungeon, and I suppose I am taking that as a peace offering. I give you my kindness in return."

"Very good. Very, very good."

The door opened again, and a guard led in Lena. She had been cleaned and dressed in a similar fashion to Tovi.

They ate their breakfast under Damien's watchful eye, Lena hardly saying a word. When they were done, he asked, "What would you like to do today?"

"I thought you'd have lessons for me, like the last time I was here," Tovi said.

"There is plenty of time for that. I want you to have some fun, to enjoy the things I can give you here in my kingdom."

"I would like to learn to paint, if that is all right with you, Grandfather."

He cocked his head and studied her with a hint of a smile. "Really? Of all pastimes, why that one?"

She cursed Silas again in her mind. Another question she was not prepared for.

"It's just the first thing that popped into my head," she said. "Maybe it's being surrounded by your collection. I want to learn to create beauty like that."

The king beamed. "Splendid. Absolutely brilliant." He summoned his butler. "Find a suitable instructor. By this afternoon." He looked back at Tovi. "To learn this art, you must study the masters. Spend your morning exploring the works on the walls of the palace. I suggest the second floor of the south wing to get started. You'll find some brilliant pieces there."

He turned to Lena. "And you, my darling? How do you wish to spend your day?"

She didn't hesitate. "I have missed this place, Grandpapa. Would you take me walking and show me all that has changed since I was a little girl?"

He seemed positively delighted.

Tovi did as she was told and wandered the halls, two guards staying several paces behind her as she studied the paintings on the walls. After getting thoroughly lost in the maze of corridors and elegant sitting rooms, she turned a corner and found herself facing the entrance to the throne room. She glanced at the guards before opening the doors and stepping inside. They didn't stop her.

She spent the rest of the morning taking in the mural and soaking up the colors and stories. The guards stayed by the door, and she felt almost free in the vast space.

She had seen these scenes before, but now, her heart took in more than her eyes. She breathed in Silas' compassion, his kindness, and his protection preserved in each color and stroke. She soaked up his teaching and stories. And the more she looked upon these images, the more they swirled inside her, shaking things up and making her see the world, her life, and herself differently. And as she took it all in, a steady stream of black oozed from her palm. She wrapped her hand with a handkerchief so that it wouldn't drip on the floor.

As much as she wanted to get home to Adia, she didn't ever want to leave the paintings. Then she remembered the walls of his treehouse and the cave by the sea. No matter where she went, she was sure she could find his creations.

There was a red curtain hiding part of the mural, and she eyed it curiously. She remembered how the HH had so desperately wanted to get behind it, to see the secrets and the reasons for King Damien's obsession.

She approached it. Damien had said she could go wherever she wanted, and the guards hadn't blocked her entrance to the throne room. Would Damien be angry if she went behind the red curtain?

She pulled it aside. Where there should have been a short expanse of wall, she found the opening to a corridor, and she stepped inside before the guards could stop her. As the curtain swished back into place, she listened for their footsteps. All was quiet.

The mural was darker in parts, with terrible scenes of mobs and hate. Other scenes were bright and green, reminding her of home. And then she saw herself. Not once, but many times. Her hair was navy in some of the scenes, light brown in others. Her story was on this wall.

It was obvious which scene had caused the king such worry. There she was with her siblings, their eyes on the mountain. There was a mass of people behind them. And in the next scene, there was nothing but a flat expanse with some rocks and a blue sky. But what did that mean? It looked as if Silas had run out of time to paint what was supposed to be there. It was clearly the end of this story. But what was the last chapter? She could not tell.

That's when she noticed a circlet on Lena's head and a tiara on her own. There was a crown on Jairus, but Tali's head was bare. It matched the painting in the cave.

It was not time for this scene to come to be yet. She would be the Queen of the Wild Range first. She gulped, terrified of the future but glad it was not imminent.

She returned to the throne room, and she didn't go back into the corridor after that. She just couldn't look at it, not knowing what happened next—not knowing how to become a queen, how to do as Silas commanded, how to come back to finish the story.

Instead, she spent the rest of the morning with the brighter colors and many faces of the throne room walls, wiping black sludge on the petticoats beneath her gown after her handkerchief was soaked through, until she was called to her next meal and the reality of her new life.

She could feel herself growing stronger, even after just one morning with the paintings. Not just physically, but also in her heart, mind, and soul. She felt braver, more sure of herself and her actions. More sure of what she was supposed to do and who she was supposed to be.

After lunch, a dressmaker came to take her measurements and help with fabric selections. "Your grandfather said to use this as an inspiration," she said, pulling out a velvet box. Inside was the opal necklace Tovi had purchased with BiBi in what seemed like another lifetime. The dressmaker draped it around Tovi's neck. "Yes, yes, yes. This gives me all sorts of ideas." She held up different shades of silver and gray.

"Not gray. Her dresses should be black."

Tovi hadn't noticed Damien enter.

"Black is the color for royalty."

"Yes, Your Majesty. I'm so sorry. How foolish of me." The dressmaker looked scared to death.

"It's all right," he said. "It will take some getting used to, having princesses back in the palace. She will only wear these gray frocks until you are able to complete her new wardrobe. Have the first one ready in three days. Lena will need one, too." He left soon after, the dressmaker gaping at him. Tovi felt sorry for her, knowing she likely would not sleep for three days as she raced to meet the king's deadline.

When the fabrics were chosen and the necklace was back in its box, Tovi went to the garden for her first painting lesson. Her teacher was an aging woman with agile hands, despite their wrinkles and knobby knuckles. Tovi wanted to jump straight to floral designs, but her teacher insisted she slow down and learn colors and strokes and shapes and shading.

"You will regret it if you rush," her instructor said. "You want precision and perfection to make your dreams come alive on the canvas.

And to reach that level of expertise, you must embrace starting from the beginning. You are not ready."

Tovi's eyes burned with their need to roll, but she controlled the instinct. Another lesson about not being ready. She suspected Silas had whispered those words into her instructor's ear.

She watched the woman and followed her examples. Her frustration at the slow pace was balanced by the thrill of success. Each new step came easily to her, and her teacher never had to explain anything twice.

Mixing colors was her favorite part. As Tovi dabbed white into a drop of blue, she realized it was almost a perfect match for Silas' eyes, and she wondered if she would ever be good enough to paint a portrait of him.

When her instructor packed her things and said goodbye until tomorrow, Tovi realized she was completely alone for the first time since arriving on the mountain. She entered the palace through the back garden doors and peeked down the hallway. Yes, very alone. No guards. No grandfather.

She took off her high heels and walked quietly across the carpeted floors, holding up her dress so it wouldn't swish on the floor. She had one destination in mind and Silas' voice in her head. This was a prime opportunity to learn about her grandfather and look for a way to thwart him.

When she reached Damien's library, it was empty. She ran her hand across the spines of some of the books. They had a few books in Adia, but nothing like this collection. There was a map on a large table in the middle of the room with random bits of jewelry and tokens scattered on top. A brooch with green and pale blue stones in the shape of a flower was centered on the mountain. A locket's gold chain surrounded it.

She looked around her, checking to be sure she was alone and the doors were closed. She sat down at her grandfather's desk. Most of the papers made little sense to her, numbers and names and plans for running a city. There was a ledger of some sort, and several lists of names. One sheet was in a different handwriting and listed types of food with various numbers next to them. She opened the little drawers and found quills and paper. Another drawer was full of keys. Then she came to a little drawer that was locked. She tried each of the keys from the previous drawer, but none of them fit. She turned to the last drawer, which was wider than the others. Inside was a stack of drawings. On top was a sketch of the wall that surrounded the city. She was just about to look at the rest of the pages when she heard footsteps in the hall.

She closed the drawer and stood, turning her back so that she faced the wall of books behind the desk.

"What are you doing in here, my dear?" Damien asked.

She turned. He didn't look angry, but he was watching her closely.

"I wanted a book to read." She was ashamed how easily the lie came out.

"Ah, a wonderful pastime. However, you are looking at my accounting ledgers." His smile was less than warm.

She forced a laugh, trying her best to sound natural. "No wonder I didn't understand the titles."

"Why don't you try this wall over here? These may be more interesting. May I suggest this one?" He pulled a volume from the shelf.

It was called *The Lies of Adwin.*

CHAPTER 43

"I'll miss you, sweetheart." Ganya hugged Tali and rested her cheek on his chest. "Be safe. Do as Silas tells you."

"Of course," he said, squeezing her in return.

Ganya could see the light of adventure shining from his eyes. She loved that he was happy, but she was miserable watching him go.

He strapped his bag across his back and kissed her forehead. He jostled the bag a bit and frowned at her. "Why is this heavier than it was a few minutes ago?"

She put her hands on her hips. "Tali Tivka, you are never prepared enough when you go. You hardly had any food."

"I've told you, we'll be there by nightfall. I don't need much."

"You never know what will happen."

He smiled, giving in. "You're right about that."

"Watch out for BiBi. Maybe you'll see her and can send her back," she said hopefully.

"I'll keep my eyes open." He hugged her again.

She watched him meet up with Gil outside of Silas' house. They waved and climbed out of sight, moving north to where Gil would drop him off at the land bridge. Others would be there to usher him to his next destination. He hadn't been pleased that he couldn't go alone, but Ganya was glad.

She looked up at Silas' house. "You better get down here," she called. "I know you're watching."

Silas came to the door, wiping his hands on a towel and smiling. "Let's have some tea. I'll be right down."

He was sitting in a rocker by the time the tea had steeped.

"I can't take much more of this, Silas. I love these young ones like they are my own, and I am worn out with worry. Tovi, Tali, Eryx, BiBi. I love them all. I want them back here, safe and sound. Do you hear me?"

He rocked back and forth and sipped his tea. "I hear you."

"Hmmph," she replied, not knowing what else to say. She stopped rocking and hung her head. "My greatest fear is I'll never see my babies again."

"Ganya," he said softly, taking her hands in his. She did not look up. "We have traveled this road a long time together, haven't we?"

Her nod was her only answer.

"You have made many requests, prayed many prayers—some from the very bottom of your heart. When have I said no?"

"Plenty of times," she wailed.

"Yes. Exactly. And what happened every time I said no?"

It was a painful question. She thought about her young desperation, trying to convince Silas to stay on the mountain and take his throne back from Damien. She thought about the many conversations—hand-in-hand with Avi—when they had begged for children of their own. The nights spent praying that Leora's son would come to find her so that her pain could be over. The pleas to keep Avi alive, to keep Tali out of trouble, and to keep Tovi safely at home.

Silas squeezed her hand. "What happened every time?"

She rocked back and forth. "You stayed by my side. You cried with me. You let me yell. You gave me peace. You . . . you helped me understand the no."

"If I say no this time, all of that will still be true. I will stay by your side. I will hold you and listen. I will give you peace, and I will help you understand the no."

She nodded, and the tears came. "I'm going to keep asking until I know the answer."

"Good."

CHAPTER 44

Tovi watched in the mirror as her servant dressed her in black satin. It was so gloomy, yet elegant, and her blue eyes stood out against the darkness.

It was late afternoon, and Tovi mentally prepared for another lavish dinner with her father and grandfather after another long day of wandering the palace, learning to paint, and looking for ways to fight back against Damien. She was growing more comfortable in the palace each day, learning the names of the servants and getting lost less often. But she longed for home, and she repeated Silas' commands to herself over and over again. Stay. Learn. Be still. It kept her hope alive and renewed her purpose. Stay. Learn. Be still.

"Now that you're dressed, Your Majesty, there is someone who wants to see you."

"Who?"

"His Majesty, Prince Ajax."

She clenched her teeth. Her father. He had never tried to speak to her privately before. He had hardly looked at her.

The servant left, and a moment later, there was a soft knock. Tovi stood awkwardly in the middle of the room.

He entered and closed the door behind him. He turned to look at Tovi, but he stayed near the door. She met his eye, and his face softened. His brow relaxed a bit, and he blinked several times. "There is so much I want to explain," he said. "There's so much I need to say."

He took a step forward, and Tovi instinctively stepped back.

He looked down at the floor. "I understand if you hate me. I would, too, if I didn't know the whole story." He took another step forward.

Tovi took another step back.

He stopped and sighed. "May I tell you what happened?"

"I don't know if I can believe you, no matter what you tell me," she replied.

Ajax nodded, an apology written on his forlorn face. "That makes sense. I understand. But maybe this would help?"

He pulled his glove off by the fingertips, and Tovi already knew what she would see when he turned his palm to her. The brown heart.

He quickly re-gloved.

"I've already been fooled by too many hearts. And your hair and eyes," Tovi said. "They match Damien's."

A small smile turned up the corner of his mouth, and she was strongly reminded of Tali. "A gift from Silas. He has made my hair and eyes black, and he has left the images on my back so that I could stay here without raising questions. The symbols on my back are not real. And the black of my hair and eyes are not my true colors, nor do they mean I am devoted to my father. I doubt you will believe me, but it is the truth."

"I don't understand. Why would you pretend? And why would Silas want you to?"

"May I tell you the whole story?"

Tovi nodded. Somewhere deep inside, hope stirred.

"I've known Adwin—Silas—most of my life. I don't remember a time before our friendship. I hated my father for the way he treated Adwin, for the way he turned the people against Adwin and into a machine to build his power and prosperity. Adwin introduced me to my sweet

Thomae, your mother. He told us he had great plans for our children, that they would lead their own kingdoms in his name someday.

"Father didn't know what Adwin had told us, but he had seen the mural and was terrified by the prophecy. He noticed that Lena and Jairus looked like the first two conquerors in the mural. But I knew better. I knew the plans Adwin had for Lena and Jairus and the next two who would come.

"Adwin spent a lot of time with Thomae and me as we prepared for your arrival. We made a plan. I would stay here in the palace with Lena and Jairus. Adwin would take Thomae and you twins into hiding. We were devastated that we would be separated, but it would be worth it to keep you safe. And Adwin said it would not be forever. We cried so much in the days and weeks leading up to your birth. She mourned her little Lena and Jairus and worried about me. I grieved that I was losing her and that I would not watch you and Tali grow up.

"The night came. As soon as Father realized you were twins, we had to put the plan into action. We hadn't accounted for one thing: Lena's curiosity. We had told her to stay in her bedroom, but she wanted to see the new baby. She sneaked in and saw there were two of you. Father's decision to have her executed proves how scared he was. He doted on her, loved her above everyone other than himself. We cried out to Adwin, and he gave us swift new instructions. I stayed, but only with Jairus. Thomae took Lena. And Adwin took you babies, we knew not where."

He swallowed and closed his eyes. When he spoke again, he sounded like he was choking. "It was the darkest night of my life."

Tovi wanted so desperately to believe him.

He continued with his eyes closed and his face creased against terrible memories. "When you turned up all those weeks ago, and there was talk of Tali, I can't tell you how much hope filled me. I have had Jairus all these years, but I had no word of your mother, Lena, or you twins. Adwin told me it was better that way, in case Father discovered the truth and tortured me. I had no information to offer.

"But then, there you were, and I could see that you were more than all right. You were feisty and beautiful and smart and strong. I could not have been prouder, but I couldn't let on. It would put everyone in danger if Father knew anything. So, I had to stay silent, and I had to stay away from you. Oh, Tovi, it was almost as hard to stay away as it had been to let you go."

The hope in Tovi's heart moved up into her throat. She noticed wet streaks down her face. She hadn't realized she was crying.

"Then you escaped, and Jairus disappeared. Suddenly, I was alone. I almost packed and left to go searching for Thomae and all of you kids, but Adwin came to visit me. He said he needed me to stay. He said that there was a chance any one of you four may end up back here. And if that ever happened, I needed to be ready to protect you, to keep you safe, to guide you where you need to go. And then you showed up with Lena. I should be sad that you found yourself in this danger and predicament. Selfishly, I could not be happier than I am in this moment."

Tovi closed the gap between them, and they reached their arms for the other at the same time, holding the other tightly in an embrace that tried to recapture so many lost years. He cried loudly. She cried silently. Neither said a word for a long time.

When they finally pulled apart, they sat down in the two armchairs near the window. "I'll tell you what little I know," Tovi said. "When I was in the dungeon, I was across the aisle from Xanthe's cell. Jairus came. He spoke of getting her out and taking her away. I think they are somewhere in the East. Mother and Tali were by the sea, to the south of here. When I arrived, they had to run for it. I think they went to find Jairus."

"Why did they have to run?" he asked.

Tovi hesitated.

"Something went wrong," he provided for her.

She nodded. "Yes. I was supposed to stay in Adia. Everything fell to pieces when I didn't."

Ajax cringed. "That tends to happen. So, you think they are all in the East now?"

"I don't know. We think Mother and Tali went to find Jairus, but we could be wrong. And even if they did find Jairus, they could have moved on by now, gone somewhere different."

Ajax nodded. "It is a relief to—"

The door to Tovi's room swung open and thudded against the wall. Calix stood framed in the doorway. "I came to escort Tovi to dinner." He wore a strange, cold smile, his eyes on Ajax.

Tovi looked between the two and wondered how she and Ajax could explain their meeting without causing trouble. Nothing came to mind, so she stayed silent.

Wishing she could sit somewhere alone to ponder all she had just heard, she instead took Calix's arm and tried not to cringe at his touch.

CHAPTER 45

Damien sat on his throne, his son on one side of him and his granddaughters—in their jewels and new black gowns—on the other. His mind whirled, but he kept his face stony. He couldn't let his audience know the chaos within.

He had sent most of the dinner guests home with his apologies for the short evening. He couldn't let them witness what was about to happen. Tonight would be the second worst night of his life.

Rhaxma, Calix, Megara, and Thad stood in a semicircle in front of him. The energy between them matched his agitation.

A full contingent of his finest guards were spaced around the perimeter of the room and blocked every exit.

"We are gathered tonight to set our loyalties straight," Damien began. He looked at each of the masters and Commander Thaddeus. They returned his gaze but with varying degrees of pale, clammy faces. Calix alone looked proud instead of nervous.

Damien stood, walked to them, and considered them slowly. Each one tensed as he came near. Just what he wanted. They should respect him. Love him. Fear him. But tonight wasn't about them.

With as much grand drama as he could muster, he turned on his heel, facing the royal thrones. He took his time staring at his son and granddaughters. Tovi squirmed under his scrutiny. Ajax remained still.

"Guards, please take hold of my son."

The two closest to Ajax did as they were told, holding him by the shoulders and elbows. He looked back at Damien, confusion and terror written on his face.

"What . . . what's happening?" Tovi stammered. "What did he do?"

"My darling girl, he betrayed our family. He sided with the enemy. Didn't you, my son?"

Ajax said nothing. His eyes moved from Tovi to Lena, back and forth.

"But, Tovi dear, you already know this," Damien said, icy and unforgiving. "He told you everything. You knew before I did."

Guards moved toward her.

"No, do not touch her," Damien commanded. "Just block the doors. Make sure she watches." Damien glanced toward Lena. Her face was blank, void of any weak emotions. Good girl. She had what it took to be queen one day.

Damien squared his shoulders toward his only son. Images flashed through his mind of a bundle in the arms of his mother on the day he was born. A little boy learning to walk. A young man whom he loved, despite his lack of ambition. Ajax had been the single biggest disappointment of his life, but he was still his son. And now, he would be a lesson for all those who might betray him.

The pictures in his memory changed. The day Ajax married Thomae. Ajax carrying a little baby girl out to meet her grandpapa. Ajax's quiet desperation for twenty years as he missed his family and tried to do his best with Jairus.

If he let his mind go much longer, he wouldn't be able to do it. But he was resolute.

Damien turned back toward the masters and Thad, pacing slowly with his hands clasped behind his back. "You are about to witness something few on this mountain have seen. When I execute my son, he will disappear. Does anyone know why?" He looked around.

No one responded, so he continued. "It's because he has the heart in his hand. It's because he has betrayed me and stayed loyal to Adwin. What happens when a loyal follower of Adwin dies? They disappear. They cease to be. There won't even be a body to bury. That is what all of you are about to witness: a man becoming *nothing*."

He asked the closest guard for one of his swords. He held it before him and examined the blade. Then, he turned to Thad. "Prove your loyalty to me." He handed him the sword.

"No!" Tovi cried, launching herself toward Thad. Calix blocked Tovi's path and grabbed her by the arm. "Thad, don't do this!" Tovi wailed as she fought and writhed. There was a hint of a smile on Calix's face.

Thad held the sword, looking down its shiny length. Damien watched him closely.

"Tovi, Lena," Ajax said with urgency. "I love you. Tell the others I love them. Tell them how much I miss them."

"This is so sweet," Calix said nastily. "Anything else?"

Tears rolled down Ajax's face, and his hands were not free to wipe them away. "I wanted more time. I wanted longer with you."

"Papa," Tovi wept. She couldn't get any other words out, but it seemed to be enough. Ajax smiled, the saddest smile Damien had ever seen. He looked away and deadened his heart so that it would not break there in front of his subjects.

Thad took a few steps forward, lifting his eyes to Ajax.

"Please, don't," Tovi moaned. She looked at Lena, hoping to see something there. But all she found in Lena's face was frozen detachment.

"Wait," Damien said coldly. Thad looked to him, pale and uncertain. "I think I'd like Ajax to know what is going to happen to his daughters. His last thoughts will be of the future I have planned for them.

"Tovi, dear, you were doing so well, fitting in so nicely. Imagine my hurt and surprise to learn that you were not being honest with me. So now, here we are, and we must decide what to do. You escaped my dungeon, so that is not an option. So, I have asked Calix to make sure you behave. You will marry him and give him children. Then my blood will be in the veins of the future kings."

The feel in the room changed, and Damien looked around. Tovi went very still. Calix, still holding her tightly, grinned victoriously. Lena watched closely, but there was no emotion on her face. Megara breathed hard, her chest heaving up and down and her mouth pressed into a firm line. Rhaxma watched Megara with shrewd eyes.

"Or there is another option," Damien said. "All those many years ago, on the night you were born, I sent you to die. Perhaps it is the only way forward, the only way to subdue you. Perhaps I will execute both you and your father tonight."

"My choices are to marry Calix or die?" she asked through gritted teeth.

"It appears so."

Calix loosened his grip but kept one hand on her arm. "Come now, darling. It won't be so bad."

"I believed you," Megara hissed.

Calix turned to her. "You couldn't have really thought—"

"He said he would marry me," Megara said, turning to Damien. "He said he loved me. That I would be his queen."

Rhaxma let out a terrifying cackle. "Love? You thought this wretched man *loved* you? And you gave up all that we had planned? For *him*?"

It was just what Damien had been waiting for. "And what exactly did you have planned, Rhaxma?" he asked.

Rhaxma froze, her cheeks draining of color.

"Take off your glove."

Rhaxma recovered and laughed again, harder this time. Black sweat rose on her forehead and lip. She took several steps toward Megara. "Look what this got you, Meg. You're alone. You don't have Calix, and you don't have me. You're on your own and trapped here with no escape." She leaned so close to her that their noses almost touched. "When I am finished destroying Calix, you will be next. Three Queens, Megara. So much for Three Queens." She burst out laughing again, and Damien was sure Rhaxma had lost her mind. He motioned for one of the guards to step closer to her.

Thad approached and put an arm around Rhaxma. "Go home. You're not yourself."

"No!" she cried, pulling a knife from somewhere in her dress. "I am fully myself. I am more myself than ever before."

Thad backed away. Rhaxma pointed the knife at Calix and swung it around to point toward Megara. Back and forth, she pointed the knife at the two while stepping backwards toward the door. A guard closed in from behind.

"You will all regret this someday. When I am queen of this mountain, you will regret it. I have a larger army of hearts than you could dream of building. They are on the other side of the curtain, where you can't get to them. But they can come get to you."

The guard was right behind her. Damien gave him a nod.

In one fluid movement, Rhaxma turned, sank her knife into the guard's throat, and ran from the room before anyone could react.

"Go after her," Damien said. "Bring her back, dead or alive." Several of the guards ran after her. Thad started to move toward the door. "Not you, Thaddeus. We have some business to take care of here." He turned to Megara. "What shall we do with you?"

She did not speak.

"Megara, I'm trying to decide whether or not to forgive you. I know the betrayal wasn't your plan to begin with, and in the end, I have Tovi because of the information you gave to Calix. Yes, I just may forgive you. You'll spend the night in the dungeon with a guard posted directly outside your cell. Use this time to think of all the ways you will make this up to me. I'll send for you when I'm ready to hear what you have to say."

She nodded and looked at the floor.

Damien surveyed the room once more. "There's just one thing left to do. Thaddeus, please proceed."

Damien watched him closely as he approached Ajax with the sword. He was sweating, and his hand shook. The tip of the sword touched Ajax's chest and stopped.

Several tense seconds ticked by.

The coward couldn't do it.

Damien grabbed the sword out of Thad's grip and did the job himself, sinking the sword into his son's stomach. Ajax cried out and held his wound with trembling hands.

The door to the throne room crashed open, and Damien turned toward the intrusion just in time to watch an arrow lodge in his shoulder.

CHAPTER 46

Chaos erupted all around Tovi as hooded archers swarmed the throne room. Damien slumped against the foot of his throne, clutching the arrow protruding from his shoulder and breathing heavily. The remaining guards and their swords were no match for the flying arrows that rained down on them. One by one, their bodies fell. Some were still, and others writhed in pain.

Tovi knelt by her father, pressing his wound. There was so much blood, and it was everywhere. Kneeling there by the thrones, she was completely defenseless, and her only hope was that this army wasn't after her. She looked around. An archer pushed Lena through a doorway. She didn't see Thad.

Calix pulled Damien behind the thrones to shield him from further arrows. Megara scooped up the sword that Damien had dropped. She looked around, like she was searching for something. When her eyes found Calix, she walked toward him resolutely, holding the sword with both hands. His back was to her, and she approached from behind. Just as she raised the sword, an arrow pierced her temple. She fell into a heap of silk and blood.

All of the guards were down. About a dozen hooded archers surveyed the room. One notched an arrow and pointed it at Calix. He tried to run, but the arrow pierced his knee and sent him to the ground.

"We have to be quick," Thad said in Tovi's ear, pulling her away from Ajax.

"Let me go." She fought against him and reached for her father.

"Get out of the way," he growled.

"No!"

Thad grabbed her around the waist and tugged her away. She kicked at his shins and tried to elbow him. He held her tighter.

Two of the hooded men picked Ajax up by the armpits and feet.

"Where are they taking him?" she cried.

"Behave yourself and come with us," Thad barked.

The men carried Ajax out of the throne room, through the dining room, and into the back hallways used by the servants. Four men and Lena were waiting in the kitchen with a makeshift stretcher made of canvas and poles. The archers put Ajax on the stretcher and pulled off their hoods.

"Hesper," Tovi stammered as the four men took over the carrying. She looked from Thad to Hesper and the other men whom she recognized as part of the HH. "You all knew and let it happen."

"Yes," Hesper said.

"How could y—"

Thad, red-faced and straight-mouthed, motioned for the men and Lena to get going, and he turned to Tovi. His yellow eyes pierced hers, and there was intense anger in the set of his jaw. "Sometimes, when Silas' plan gets messed up, other people have to pick up the pieces. I have been picking up your pieces for weeks. You have no idea all that Silas asked of me. And I did it. It was terrible, but I did it because I wanted to make Silas proud and I wanted to do what he said was best and because I believe him when he says that what he asks is the best way forward. So, I did it," he yelled. He took a deep breath and continued a little softer. "Everything I've done has been on Silas' orders. Obeying my sister, being honest about what I knew, working for Damien, even capturing you. It was the hardest thing I've ever done, *but I did it.* Then, when we knew Lena might end up here, Silas told me to be ready. He had a plan, but we didn't know how Damien would react. So, we had the stretcher ready in case. And aren't you glad we did? We're getting Ajax out alive. So quit it, okay? I can't take your questioning or your insistence that another way would have been better. Just trust us and come on. Damien and Calix are wounded but alive, and it's probably only a matter of time before they are well enough to send more guards after us."

"But what if Father dies?"

"Then he goes on to his adventure with Silas, which would be way easier and way better than what his recovery is going to be here," Thad said, clasping a hand on her shoulder. "Now, come on. We don't have a lot of time."

Tovi nodded and followed him into a large pantry. There was a stone staircase at the far end, and Hesper and the other men were carefully carrying Ajax down to the floor below. Lena pressed a hand to Ajax's wound.

Thad and Tovi followed. They were in a chilly, damp cellar. A small stream flowed through it, and there was food, packed in crates, submerged in the water.

They splashed through the shallow stream and went through an arched door. It was very dark, and Tovi could just barely see the stone walls and floor of a long hallway. They took many turns and passed several staircases that led back up into the palace.

They turned a few more times. Ajax moaned, and his eyes fluttered shut. Blood had seeped through the canvas and dripped on the floor. "I'll mop up after you," Thad said. "You hurry ahead. We can't leave a trail."

After what felt like miles, they stopped at the end of the hallway. A set of wooden stairs led up. Behind it was a rock wall. There was nowhere left to go. Tovi started moving toward the stairs, but Hesper halted her. "We aren't going up."

Hesper cleared away a pile of straw underneath the stairs. He pulled a thin metal rod from his boot and pushed it into a tiny hole in the stone that Tovi wouldn't have noticed otherwise. She heard a distant click, and a square of the stone floor popped up an inch. Hesper pried it all the way open. It looked heavy.

Lowering Ajax through the hole would have been nearly impossible on their own, but down below were several sets of hands waiting to help. More of the HH. As soon as Ajax was safely below, Hesper climbed down a ladder. Tovi and the rest followed. Thad shut the trap door as soon as they were all inside.

The other HH members took over the carrying. Tovi looked at her father, her concern doubling as she took in his graying face. But he was still there. He had not disappeared. There was still hope.

They walked quickly through a dirt tunnel that wasn't quite tall enough for some of them to stand straight. They moved as fast as they could, hunched slightly so their heads wouldn't brush the ceiling. The path was on a steady decline, and they descended lower and lower into the earth. When they had walked this way for about twenty minutes, they stopped.

Hesper pulled the same metal rod from his boot and pushed it through another tiny hole, this time in the rock wall. A door swung open. Tovi took in the giant, open expanse before her. They were in the mines, near the top. The doorway led them to a small ledge overlooking at least a thousand-foot drop. Her stomach lurched.

A metal basket was waiting with Lyra inside. She embraced Hesper for just a second, kissing him quickly on the cheek before helping them lift Ajax. There was just enough room for Lena and Tovi to join them. Hesper stayed behind. Somewhere in the distance, someone operated the basket pulleys.

The basket lowered quickly, dizzyingly. She could see that there were more people waiting below. Several of the faces were turned up toward her, and when they came into focus, her heart nearly stopped. Eryx, Tali, and Jairus stood beside one another, waiting for her to reach them.

Lena wailed and threw herself at Jairus. Eryx and Tali each grabbed one of Tovi's arms and lifted her from the basket. She looked between the two and wondered if she had fallen into a dream.

Tali crushed her in a bear hug, kissing her forehead and swinging her around. She squeezed her brother, resting her face against his shirt and breathing in his smell. He tugged at Tovi's light brown hair. "I almost didn't recognize you," he said with a grin.

She put both hands on his cheeks, savoring his closeness and looking at the face she adored so much. Her brother. Here. With her right now. She didn't have to miss him anymore. She cried and buried her face in his shoulder.

When she finally let go of Tali, Tovi looked up at Eryx, who was watching her with a soft smile. She returned it.

"I'm glad you're all right," he said.

She nodded, awkwardly playing with her fingers and feeling her cheeks redden. "I'm glad you got away when you did."

Tali's eyebrows climbed halfway up his forehead. He looked between the two. "Is there something—"

Before he could finish, Eryx said, "Looks like they need help."

The three joined several people who lifted Ajax's stretcher from the basket. Thomae was there, already taking over his care and putting pressure on his wound, whispering love and encouragement to her long-lost beloved. Tovi wanted so badly to go to her, to embrace her. But she knew her father needed her mother more right now, so she settled on watching her every move and waiting for the right moment.

Another basket was lowering, filled with more archers who had removed their hoods. All members of the HH.

Tovi took a moment to look around, and despite the chaos, the world seemed to still. Her whole family was right there, together. Her mother, her father, her sister, her brothers. She let her eyes linger longest on Tali, her twin, whom she had missed beyond words, and her mother who was too beautiful and graceful to be real. They were together at last. She smiled, filled with anticipation for the life that lay ahead of them.

"What happens next?" Tovi asked.

Eryx swallowed and looked away. Tali's smile faded.

She looked between the two, her joy turning muddy with fear over what their faces could mean.

And then Silas' commands came back to her. Stay. Learn. Be still.

She bit her lip as her eyes welled. "I . . . I have to stay." Her voice shook as she said it.

Tali nodded, rare tears in his eyes matching her own. "We came for Lena, not you."

"I have to stay," she repeated, a wobble in her voice.

Her mother left her father's side and approached Tovi, placing bloody hands on each side of Tovi's face. "My darling girl. Be brave. Do what Silas says. I will ask him every day to bring you back to us." Tovi sobbed into her mother's chest, trying to memorize the arms that wrapped around her.

Long before she was ready, the embrace loosened. Ajax was ready for the journey into the desert. Tali hugged her one more time, and Eryx squeezed her shoulder without meeting her eye. At the last moment before turning from her, Lena looked up at Tovi. She smiled and called out, "You can do this. You're ready."

Tovi watched them go, until only she and Thad were left behind.

"When we return, we'll have to pretend that I caught you trying to flee," he said.

"No," Tovi said, suddenly seeing things clearly and understanding all that Silas was asking of her. "No, he won't trust me if he thinks I ran. Say you rescued me. Say that the archers had taken me, and you were able to free me from them."

Thad looked at her with new appreciation in his gaze. "All right, I like that story. Are you ready to go?"

She took a deep breath, Silas' words spilling into her mind. How much time had he spent telling her she was not ready? How often did he have to remind her that she was still a work in progress? She pictured the queen on the wall of the cave. It was time to become that woman. It was time to be what Silas had intended for her all along. The Queen of the Wild Range. But first, she would have to be the Princess of Mount Damien, a princess betrothed to a man she hated, in the palace of an evil king who happened to be her grandfather. A terrifying world awaited her, but she did not go alone. She had Thad. And most importantly, she had Silas.

She took another breath, lifted her bloody chin, and said, "I'm ready."

For more information about
Maggie Platt
&
Queen of the Wild Range
please visit:

www.maggieplatt.com
www.facebook.com/AuthorMaggiePlatt
@_maggie_platt_
www.instagram.com/_maggie_platt_

For more information about
AMBASSADOR INTERNATIONAL
please visit:

www.ambassador-international.com
@AmbassadorIntl
www.facebook.com/AmbassadorIntl

*If you enjoyed this book, please consider leaving us a review on
Amazon, Goodreads, or our website.*

More from Ambassador International

When Ari finds herself with a job offer to work undercover and find her purpose again, she can't resist. But as her undercover case deepens, she discovers that the voices in her head aren't as imaginary as she thought.

The adventures of The Seraph and his growing band of super heroes continue as Gideon seeks the truth about the origins of his powers. Jeremiah Ashcroft has other plans as he perfects his serum and prepares to make an army of super-powered villains. Gideon and his team must thwart Ashcroft's schemes and stop Ashcroft to save the world . . . and their families.

Rune has grown up all of her life in the mountains of Kansanai. When everything she thought she knew is turned upside down, will she be able to let go of the life she thought she deserved for something far greater than what she could have ever imagined? Rolf goes through the motions of everyday life yet, his routine is disrupted when a voice claiming to be the one true God speaks to him. While listening to his heart, he is thrown temptation after temptation on his journey. Will Rolf be able to resist the temptations?

www.ingramcontent.com/pod-product-compliance
Lightning Source LLC
Chambersburg PA
CBHW051537260626
47170CB00003B/978